I0461031

SAFETY
NATION

Published by BrikHaus Press
http://www.brikhauspress.com
Copyright © 2017 by Jeffrey Brichta
Cover artwork copyright © 2017 by David Huxtable-Reid
All rights reserved.

This book or any portion thereof may not be reproduced or used in any manner whatsoever without the express written permission of the copyright holder except for the use of brief quotations in a book review.

This is a work of fiction. All names, characters, places, businesses, and events are fictitious. Any similarity to actual events, real persons, living or dead, places, or businesses is purely coincidental.

United States of America
ISBN 978-0-692-80674-6

FOR MY PARENTS.

SAFETY NATION

JEFFREY BRICHTA

1

Sex Detail.

I hated this job. Of all the possible assignments, this was the most disgusting. We spy on people having sex. Not the glamorous movie version of sex where two attractive people make well-choreographed love. It was usually two sweaty slobs clumsily slapping their bodies together. After several years away from this assignment, I was back, and not by choice.

The van was hot, and the stagnant air choked me. I tore at my tie and jerked the collar of my shirt down. That didn't help. The stifling air was made worse by the body heat of the man next to me. Huxley sat with a pair of binoculars stuck to his face like they were an appendage. He sported a perverted grin.

Huxley was getting into it now. A rivulet of drool trickled from his mouth. I caught a glimpse of a substantial bulge in his pants, and quickly wished I hadn't. He was a man who loved his job.

"Huxley, let's get going," I said.

". . . not yet."

"We confirmed the safety violation. What are we waiting for?"

". . . it's not . . . the right time."

"Let's get this over with."

"I'll say . . . when it's time."

I let out an exasperated sigh. I was trying to play by Huxley's rules, but I didn't know how much longer I could hold out. If this continued, I would have to put a stop to it.

I picked up my binoculars and peered at the house. The blinds were drawn. I turned on the infrared sensor, and two red shapes appeared. They were on the couch, the woman on her back, the man on top, practically smothering her. Her legs were wrapped around him as he thrust his pelvis rhythmically but out of sync with his partner. Like every couple I'd seen on Sex Detail, they were as ungraceful and bumbling as the next. I put my binoculars away.

"Huxley, can we get a move on, already?"

". . . almost. Another . . . minute."

Huxley was in charge, but I'm not sure why that compelled me to listen to him. I used to be in charge, but now, with the demotion, I had to answer to him. They could have put me anywhere, but they purposely sent me back to Sex Detail. Everyone knew I hated Huxley, and making me his subordinate was another way for the higher-ups to twist the knife in a little deeper.

I had showed up for my shift at seven o'clock p.m. All departments worked around the clock, but Sex Detail worked primarily at night. The heaviest number of violations occurred when people were home from work, relaxing, perhaps having a few drinks, and making poor choices. Some said the department was useless since ninety percent of violations went unnoticed. Nevertheless, the government kept the operation running.

As soon as I arrived, I went to Supply to get my equipment.

"Name and serial number," the guy behind the bullet-proof glass said, disinterested.

"Smith. Number 1872124482."

The disinterested guy clattered at his computer terminal. I knew he recognized me; we had both worked here for decades. But he had to go through this rigmarole every day because it was procedure. If he didn't follow procedure, he'd violate safety regulations.

The terminal clicked and whirred. Eventually, he got the information he needed. "Welcome back, Inspector Smith. You've been approved. You can pick up your equipment at the Retrieval Station. Do you need directions?"

"No thanks."

Of course I didn't need directions. There was only one way I could go. I turned right and walked down a long, blazingly bright corridor. The ceiling was comprised almost entirely of fluorescent lights.

At the end of the hall was an automated box, like an old-fashioned package drop-box. The metal door was dented in several places. It greeted me with a robotic female voice.

"Please state your name and serial number."

"Smith. Number 1872124482."

"Processing . . ."

I could sense the line of agents behind me growing. As we drudged through the hallway, we were often delayed by this infernal machine.

"Error. Please state your name and serial number," the robot voice said.

I leaned close and shouted, *"Smith! Number 1872124482!"*

"Processing . . ."

The person behind me murmured. The other agents were growing impatient. For the safety of the nation, one would think the government would pay for more efficient equipment, but I guess it wasn't in the budget.

"Approved. Welcome back, Inspector. Please collect your equipment and proceed to the Unlocking Station. Do you require directions?"

"No."

I threw the metal door open, and pulled out a small box. It was made of thick, clear, bullet-proof plastic, and, of course, it was locked. It contained all my equipment: badge, weapon, handcuffs, binoculars, and multi-tool. I would have preferred to smash it open and bypass the next station, but that was impossible. Burgess had shown me that.

Burgess had been an agent, too. One day, he brought his equipment box to Unlocking, but it malfunctioned and they couldn't open it. This was the fourth time it had happened that week. That's when Burgess snapped. He flung the box down and pulled out a real gun, the kind that shot real bullets. He blasted the box at point-blank range. The bullets ricocheted, and one of them hit another agent in the chest, killing him. When the gun was empty, Burgess was hauled away. Nobody heard from him in the two years since. He was probably in the asylum now.

So, I carried my bullet-proof box down another impossibly long, impossibly bright corridor until I reached the next window. Another guy sat behind another pane of impenetrable glass. "Name and serial number," he said.

"Smith. Number 1872124482."

He was a little friendlier than the first guy, but not much. He punched my information into his terminal and waited. We were always waiting. A study once showed that slowness led to fewer accidents, which was safer than the alternative. And so, we waited.

"Hello, Inspector Smith," the slightly friendlier guy said. "Pass your equipment box through the slot to your right. If your serial number matches the one on the box, I'll unlock it."

I did as instructed and returned to waiting. I was great at waiting. After a solid four minutes, the guy said, "Please take your equipment."

I reached into the slot and removed my equipment. I attached everything to my belt except my badge, which was secured to the inner breast pocket of my suit jacket. The equipment was small enough that it wasn't noticeable, and it didn't impede my movements. I turned right again, and circled back to where I had started.

After I had my equipment, I went into the Central Office. It was a huge room with a million lights shining down on a thousand desks. The walls were drab and devoid of color or artwork. There were no partitions of any kinds. Partitions obstructed things from view, and that wasn't safe. Black signs with white block text hung over areas where the different departments were located: Transit,

Healthcare, Hair Care, Construction, Maritime, Education, Sewage, the list went on and on. I waded through the vast sea of desks until I reached the middle of the great room.

Huxley was there, leaning against a desk, his black hair tussled, his clothes smeared with ancient stains. When he saw me, he bared his mossy teeth in a sinister sneer. I had only seen him for a second and I was already annoyed.

"Look who's back," he said.

"We're working together again?"

"Just like old times."

"Wonderful," I groaned.

"And you thought you were done with Sex Detail."

"I was."

"Nobody ever really leaves. We all love it too much."

"You're the only one. You're too perverted to work anywhere else."

"That's no way to talk to a superior," he said in a mocking voice. "I'm gonna pretend I didn't hear that. I'll let ya off easy this time."

"You're a saint."

We stared at each other while Huxley's brain tried to process my sarcasm. Breaking the silence, I said, "Where are we heading tonight?"

Huxley slapped his arm around the back of my shoulders and squeezed. He was strong, and the pressure quickly started to hurt. With an undercurrent of venom, he said, "Smith, my man, a lot has changed since you became a hot shot. We don't do just one or two dates a night. Now we do three, four, five."

He squeezed harder, but I broke free of his crushing grip. He chuckled and said, "I bet you're glad to be back."

I averted my eyes for a moment. If I looked at him now, I would want to punch his stupid, grinning face. And that would definitely be a safety violation. I waited for my pulse to slow. When it did, I looked up again.

Huxley nodded his head in the direction of the garage and said, "I'll drive."

And so, our night began.

In the old days, Sex Detail had the manpower to cover the entire city. Over the years, budget cuts reduced the department's manpower. They even took away all of the department's desks except for one. Eventually, there weren't enough agents to cover all the married couples and people in long-term relationships. So, the detail focused on dates and new romances. That's where most of the sex violations occurred. The married couples weren't having that much sex.

We caught up with the first couple around nine o'clock as their date was concluding. According to the file, it was their second date, and the girl was "very religious." When she and the guy got to the door, they kissed. The guy grabbed the girl's butt, and she backed away, ending the date in a slap. The guy was left standing on the doorstep. Huxley looked sullen, but didn't say anything. He shifted the van into gear, and we drove to the second case.

This one was between two kids, barely of consenting age. They returned to the boy's apartment. Since this was their fourth date, the probability of them consummating was extremely high. Using the binocular's X-ray function, we were able to see them engage in wild sex. They bounced off the walls in all sorts of incredible positions. But for Huxley it wasn't good enough. They used a condom. They had been safe, which meant we couldn't do a thing. We moved on to the next case.

We caught up with them as they were leaving a restaurant. Their car swerved all over the road. They must have sabotaged the Auto-Driver function, which was illegal. The government mandated all cars, with the exception of law enforcement, be driven by computers to ensure the safety of the populace. We could have arrested them for that, but it wouldn't have been as much fun for Huxley.

When they got to the house, they started going at it almost immediately. This was when Huxley got excited for the first time this evening. The couple was not practicing safe sex.

Huxley panted cartoonishly as he watched the amorous couple. It wasn't the sex that excited him, because he hadn't reacted this way with the previous couple. No, it was the fact they were breaking a safety statute, and he would get to arrest them.

"Huxley, it's been long enough."

". . . almost there."

"I'll take care of it."

I couldn't spend another minute in that enclosed space, in the heat, with Huxley doing unmentionable things to himself. I slid open the van's side door and hopped out. The air outside was cooler and less stagnant. "You will not!" Huxley hissed. "That's an order!"

I paused. I had a choice to make. I could play by the rules, as I always had, or I could ignore them. Years of playing by the rules had burned me. Doing that landed me right back where I started. I didn't care about the rules any longer.

Huxley cursed. I heard him clamber out of the van and race up behind me, his breaths labored. We skulked to the front door of the house. Huxley gave the doorknob a jiggle and found it was unlocked. "Follow me," he whispered. "Quietly."

We pushed into the house. As we neared the living room, I could hear the heavy moaning of the two participants. It was accompanied by the unmistakable sound of slapping flesh. They were still going at it. They certainly had stamina.

We entered the living room. On the couch, two huge masses of flesh gyrated against each other. I couldn't tell where one person ended and the other began. The man started thrusting faster. He raised his head up, and he emitted a high-pitched whine, about to climax.

"Freeze!" Huxley shouted.

He drew his weapon and pointed it at the couple. The woman screamed. The man pulled out of her and tumbled onto the floor with a thud.

"You are both under arrest for violation of Safety Statute 12-34-56, failure to use a condom while engaged in sexual intercourse as a non-married couple without permission to procreate," Huxley said.

He holstered the weapon and took out his handcuffs. He slapped them on the wrists of the man and continued, "You are also in violation of Safety Statute 78-12-22, tampering with your motor vehicle's Auto-Driver function, 69-42-06, driving while under the influence of alcohol, and 82-82-29, failure to lock your residence during evening hours."

The woman kept on screaming, and the man blubbered with surprise. Neither of them registered a word Huxley had just said.

"Ya got anything to say for yourselves?"

They remained bewildered.

"Scumbags," Huxley said. "Smith, cuff her and let's go."

I handcuffed the woman, and we escorted them, naked, to the van. They smelled like sweat and sex. I tried to ignore the odors.

As we drove back to headquarters, a permanent smile was etched on Huxley's face. He had waited all that time just to interrupt them at that precise moment. He was sadistic. A stellar government employee.

2

Returning my equipment at the end of the shift took just as long as picking it up. It was another series of long corridors, name and serial number recitations, and right hand turns. I shuffled out of the building as the day shift shuffled in.

As my car shuttled me home, I reclined the seat three inches, the farthest it would go. The car hummed along the expressway, looping around the city. The sun was a yellow orb, hovering in a pale, cloudless sky. I closed my eyes and tried to drift off, but it was too bright.

I turned on the radio. There were only three stations: Weather, News, and Government. Before the First Government existed, there had been hundreds of radio stations. A study revealed that all those choices were distracting to drivers, and when the First Government came to power, radio stations were eliminated. Soon, people clamored to have them back. While the government was deciding what to do, another study revealed that music could evoke unsafe, passionate emotional responses. So, the government created three channels, none of which played music, and none of which people would be interested in.

I flipped through the stations. As usual, nothing good was on. I turned the radio off and tried to sleep again to no avail.

The car turned off the expressway and entered a quiet, residential district. The electric engine purred softly as the car glided through empty streets. The houses lining either side of the road looked the same: one level (stairs are dangerous), white painted exteriors (to reflect UV radiation), exactly fifty feet apart (minimum safe distance to prevent the spread of fire), faux grass landscaping (to prevent allergies), and gray-shingled roofs (because they looked nice).

I passed row after row of factory-produced boxes. If I hadn't known my address, I'd never be able to tell which house was mine. I hated them all.

I had been much younger when I read my first book on ancient architecture. In the past, people could build a home in any style they wanted. Log cabins, townhouses, three-story homes, and yards made up of stones or real grass. My eyes poured over the photographs in disbelief. This lighted a fire in me to devour as much information about the ancient world as I could. In the decades since, every so often, I dreamed I lived in a log cabin.

The car slowed to a crawl, and then made a gentle right turn into a driveway. The garage door opened automatically, and the car drifted effortlessly inside. When it came to a stop, the engine shut off, and the automatic seat belt disengaged. I got out and entered my house.

The tinny harshness of a canned laugh track assaulted my ears. Two rooms away, my wife was watching television. The volume was so high, it sounded like the speakers were next to my head.

In the living room my wife was sprawled across the couch. Her glazed eyes were fixated on the TV. Her frumpy gray clothes were covered in crumbs. Her belly escaped from beneath her shirt. Her short legs hung off the couch, not quite reaching the floor. Her brownish-gray hair looked like a bird's nest.

"I'm home," I said.

Still affixed to the TV, she replied, "Oh . . . hi."

"I'm going to lie down for a while."

"Oh . . . okay."

"You mind turning that down?"

"Oh . . . sure."

Each time she spoke, I caught a glimpse of her short, pointy teeth. They were the teeth of a troll.

She picked up the remote control and pressed the volume button. The on-screen display showed the volume decrease by a single bar. Not wanting to talk to her again, I trudged into the bedroom.

The sound of the TV was muffled, but I could still make out every word. It was a talk show, and the guest was the star of a new First Government movie. All TV programming had to be approved for safety before it could air. As a result, everything was either about the glory of the First Government or the heroics of the safety agents. Those were good for a laugh. I didn't know any heroic agents. Most showed up just to collect a paycheck.

I drew the shades, and then turned on the shower. I left the door between the bedroom and bathroom open. The running water helped attenuate the noise from the TV. I disrobed and slipped into bed. The room slowly filled with steam. A fine mist settled on the ceiling. I closed my eyes, and pulled the sheets over my face. I turned from side to side with sleep avoiding me. I thought about getting up and yelling at my troll-wife, but that would be pointless. I'd rather sleep badly, or not at all, than have to look at her repulsive face.

Once, early in our marriage, I asked her to do me a favor, and she reacted like I had murdered someone. Another time, I cooked dinner, but accidentally boiled the vegetables too long, making them soggy. She screamed profanities and hurled plates at my head. After that, I never confronted her again. It seemed safer than dealing with someone who was so unbalanced. That was a lifetime ago. Now, we coexisted, passing each other in the hallways with few interactions. I couldn't recall how long we'd been married.

Suddenly, my alarm clock was blaring. I lurched upright in bed. The light behind the shades was dimmer. The raucous noise from the TV still flooded the bedroom. I heard my troll-wife cackle along with the laugh track. The room was hazy, thick with steam from the still-running water.

I showered. Standing directly beneath the shower head, the noise from the TV was drowned out. My mind became a blank. I stood there, water streaming down my body, like a statue. I soaked in this small piece of solitude.

Afterward, I went to my closet to get dressed. My clothes were arranged neatly on a dozen hangers. Black suit jackets, white shirts, black pants. Twelve of each, all identical. On the shelf above rested three bowler hats, black. A rack of identical black ties hung to the far right. Black leather belts were draped over the cross bar. Several pairs of black shoes sat on the floor. This was the official uniform of a government employee. It was important that everyone wore the same black everything. I'm not sure why, but there had probably been a study.

As I walked toward the kitchen, I passed through the living room. My troll-wife was still glued to the TV. The pile of crumbs on her clothes had multiplied. She didn't notice me.

I opened the refrigerator, my stomach growling. Salad, fruit, vegetables, milk, yogurt, and a sandwich wrapped in plastic waited on the shelves. It was the same food as every other day. My appetite started to dwindle. I decided to have a bowl of cereal instead.

There had been a time when people were allowed to eat or drink whatever they wanted. After the entire population developed diabetes, the government banned any consumable deemed a health risk. Cigarettes – gone. Soda – gone. Fast food – gone. Potato chips – gone. Pizza – gone. Processed cheese – gone. The list was practically endless. Prohibition Detail monitored banned consumables. That's where I had worked before my big demotion.

Corn flakes crunched blandly in my mouth. I sat at the kitchen table, shoulders bent forward, facing the glass patio door. I watched the sun slowly descend. Its color oozed from yellow to orange to red. I finished the last bite, and realized something was strange.

My dog hadn't greeted me yet. He usually followed me around the house, tracking me from room to room. It was odd for him to not make an appearance. I had been so wrapped up in returning to Sex Detail, I hadn't noticed his absence. I called for him, but he didn't come.

I walked back into the living room and asked, "Where's the dog?"

18

No response.

"Where's the dog?!" I shouted over the noise.

"Oh . . . he's dead," she said, not taking her eyes off the TV.

"What?"

A shudder racked my body. It started at my feet and rippled up to my head.

"Oh . . . I meant to tell you. I took him to the vet yesterday . . ." she trailed off, more interested in whatever drivel she was watching.

"And?"

"Oh . . . he was sick. Not safe to be around other dogs. They put him down."

My face was hot. Tears welled up behind my eyes. I wiped them back with numb fingers. How could he be gone? He had been with me every day for the last ten years. He was the only consolation I had in my dreary life. And now he was dead. My troll-wife didn't have the decency to tell me before they killed him.

My knees shook. My whole body was tremulous. If I didn't move, I was going to collapse. I bolted from the house.

My troll-wife called after me, "Oh . . . they're sending a new one over tomorrow."

I fell inside my car in a heap. The world had turned to a watery haze. My diaphragm felt heavy, and it was hard to breathe.

I managed to turn the car on and punch coordinates into the computer. It glided backward onto the street, then turned and drove toward the expressway. I instructed it to take me to work, but to go the long way around the city.

Work was no refuge. It would harbor no sympathy or solace. Huxley was not someone who would understand. But the place was so wrapped up in itself, it would take my mind away from this. I needed a distraction.

3

The Central Office was bustling with agents eager to leave. I pushed through them like they were an incoming tide. When I reached the other side, Huxley was already waiting for me. His lapel bore a new yellow stain, and his hair was messier than usual.

"Welcome back. I wasn't sure you'd show," he said.

"Huh?"

"I thought that cushy gig you used to have softened you up. Made it so you couldn't handle Sex Detail."

"The work isn't the worst part of this assignment."

Huxley chortled and clapped his hands together a single time, saying, "Woah-ho! Careful what you say. Remember, I am your superior."

He was getting a kick out of this. He squinted and took a step toward me. "Smith," he said before taking another step, "what's wrong with your eyes?"

My skin started to crawl. I lowered the brim of my hat and stepped back. I could smell his reeking breath on me.

"Yeah," he said with a dawning realization. "They're red and puffy. Have you been crying?"

"Don't be ridiculous," I said. I turned away to break free from his leering gaze.

"Oh, Smithy, what's wrong? Did I hurt your feelings?"

"Go to hell."

"Do you need your bottle, little baby Smithy?"

I snapped back around. I raised my fist. Huxley looked at it with huge eyes. A streak of terror shot through him. I hesitated.

Slowly, I lowered my hand. He wasn't worth the effort. When it became clear that I wouldn't punch him, Huxley's face revealed a smug satisfaction.

Huxley backed away and laughed. Shaking his head, he said, "You're such a serious guy. I wish you'd loosen up."

"Can we just get to work?"

"Not so fast. We're waiting for our new recruit."

"I'm surprised they found another poor sap willing to work here."

Huxley dipped his hands in his pockets and leaned back against his desk. He looked at the ceiling with starry eyes. "Someday," he began. He took his right hand out of his pocket and made a slow, sweeping gesture through the air. "I'm gonna be in charge of this whole outfit. You'll see. Stick with me, and we're gonna go straight to the top."

I couldn't tell if he was serious. It was best not to interrupt whatever kind of fantasy he was having.

"We may be in Sex Detail now," he continued. "But we won't be here long. We'll be moving up soon. Soon as our new recruit shows up." He continued to gaze into the ether and smile contentedly.

As if on cue, someone appeared before us.

"Hello, I'm Lowry, reporting for duty. Is this the Sex Department?"

Lowry wasn't what either of us had expected, because Lowry was a woman. There were plenty of female safety agents, but I had never seen one on Sex Detail before. Huxley goggled at her, and a smattering of gibberish dribbled from his mouth.

She was short and slightly plump. Her face was pink and dabbled with freckles. Her features were perfectly symmetrical. She wore the standard uniform of a safety agent. Her feminine features were subdued beneath her masculine clothes. She had shockingly bright red hair, done up in a ponytail, and providing a stark contrast to the drab uniform. The edge of her hairline was frizzy. Her brown eyes danced hopefully as she looked at us.

Huxley found the words he had been searching for, "Why, yes, this is Sex Detail. Welcome, welcome. I must say, I can't recall ever seeing a Safety Inspector as lovely as you."

"Uh, thanks," Lowry said flatly.

She gave me a disconcerted look while Huxley continued, oblivious, "My name is Huxley. I'm in charge around here. And this is Smith. Don't mind him, he's one of the grunts."

"It's nice to meet you both," she said sheepishly.

"Where did you transfer from?" I asked.

Before she could speak, Huxley interjected, "Smith, don't harass the young lady, she just got here."

Lowry seemed to shrink. Her arms pulled in close to her sides, her head drooped, and all her muscles tightened. The hopeful light in her eyes dulled. She was probably offended by Huxley. Everything about him was offensive.

"So, my dear Lowry, where did you transfer from?" Huxley asked.

"Nowhere. I'm starting today," she said.

"Your first day on the job?"

"That's right."

"Excellent! Then I'll be able to train you the right way. You won't end up with a bunch of bad habits like Smith."

"I see."

"Okay, okay, enough chit-chat. Let's get to work."

Huxley waved her over to the city map. It was displayed electronically on a vertical rolling easel. The digital screen had a line of static running across the top, and a large patch in the middle was darkened by dead pixels.

Huxley pointed out the areas we would be investigating tonight. We had leads on seven dates, and each was considered high risk for safety violations. To cover more ground, we would split up. I would go alone while Lowry would go with Huxley because she was a rookie.

Once the logistics were established, Huxley zoomed out of the Central Office. Since Lowry hadn't thrown herself at him, he'd temporarily lost interest. Lowry and I started toward the garage. She smiled meekly.

"Hi, I'm Smith," I said, extending my hand. We shook.

"That other guy, is he always like that?" she asked.

"No, he's usually much worse."

"Well, at least one of my co-workers is sane."

"I wouldn't say that."

She laughed. It was a sweet, girlish laugh.

As we continued walking, Lowry produced a black bowler hat. She put it on, but it looked ridiculous. Her massive hair kept it perched too high atop her head. She took it off and turned it over in her hands.

"Do I really have to wear this?" she asked.

"Look around. Half the agents don't wear them."

"You're wearing one."

I touched the brim with my index finger and said, "I'm a slave to fashion."

We laughed together. We bantered like that as we wound our way to the garage. I was soon feeling better.

In the garage, a black van was waiting. Huxley rolled a window down and snarled at me, "Smith, c'mere."

I approached the van while Lowry waited several feet back. Huxley lowered his voice and grumbled, "What the hell are you doing? Don't hold me up like this again. Got it?"

"Whatever you say."

Huxley looked over my shoulder and cheerily called out, "Lowry! Get in! We've got lots to do tonight!"

Lowry gave me a cute little wave as she climbed into the van. The second her door closed, the van pitched forward, its tires squealing on the pavement.

Once they were out of sight, I got into one of the smaller cars and drove to my first destination. It was a government vehicle, so I disengaged the Auto-Driver. It was nice to feel like I was in control of something.

I followed my targets to a home in a residential district. The drive took forever. By the time they were inside the house, my second assigned case had already commenced. I wouldn't be making it to that one, and I didn't care in the slightest.

My car was parked on the opposite side of the street. I got out my binoculars and began my voyeuristic work. Things inside the house were dull. They talked, drank some wine, laughed, and seemed to genuinely enjoy the company of one another. I wondered how it felt to be romantically involved with someone you liked.

They retired to the bedroom. They took off their clothes perfunctorily, and the man mounted the woman, the alcohol a substitute for foreplay. The monitoring equipment confirmed he was not using a condom. They were in violation of safety regulations, and I had to arrest them.

I tossed the binoculars aside. I reclined my seat. I kicked my feet onto the dashboard, and dropped my hat over my eyes. It was hard to get comfortable in the car, but I managed.

When I awoke, the sun was rising. I brought my seat to its upright position. I checked on the amorous couple. They were sound asleep, and I felt refreshed.

I returned to the Central Office as it was preparing for another shift change. The sounds of fingers clattering on keyboards and agents muttering bounced from wall to wall, creating an ocean of noise.

People looked anxious to finish their reports and go home. At Sex Detail, Lowry and Huxley were hunched over their terminals. Huxley grimaced and asked, "Where the hell have you been?"

"Work. Where else?"

"You better have arrested all those creeps."

"Not one."

"Not one! Whaddaya mean, not one?"

"None of them had sex."

"That's a lie!"

"I don't know what to tell you, Huxley. At least my reports will be easy," I said with a wry smile.

I opened the department desk and pulled out a terminal. It was tiny and square. The keyboard was half the size of a standard one, and the monitor was minuscule. An electromagnetic device charged the battery. The same technology powered cars and virtually every other electronic device. Electromagnetic fields buzzed across the entire city. Wires had become a thing of the past.

Lowry and Huxley had taken the only two chairs. I sat on the desk with the terminal on my lap.

If no safety statutes were violated, a form would take about five minutes to complete. Safe sex could take up to thirty minutes, requiring information about every detail. Unprotected sex could be an ordeal of an hour or more. I completed my forms with a minimal amount of effort.

Lowry stared intensely at her terminal, and her fingers rattled deftly over the keyboard. She hit the enter key and triumphantly said, "All done!"

"Have Smith look it over. He looks bored," Huxley said.

Lowry brought me the terminal and asked, "Would you mind checking this for me?"

"I'd be happy to."

I grabbed her terminal. Rows of blocky green text set against a black background streamed in front of my eyes. My vision blurred. There were too many words. It would take an hour to read all that.

"Looks good," I said as I handed the terminal back.

Lowry smiled and thanked me. I showed her how to electronically file the reports. They disappeared into space, never to be read by anyone.

Meanwhile, Huxley was typing furiously. He didn't look like he was close to being finished. I checked my watch. It was time to go.

"I'm out of here," I said.

"Is Lowry done?" he asked, not taking his eyes off his work.

"Yeah. The reports were perfect."

"Okay. Show her how to turn in her equipment."

Lowry and I stowed the terminals inside the desk, and then headed down the labyrinth of corridors and checkpoints. For whatever reason, it didn't seem as bad as usual.

"Does it always take this long?" she asked.

"Sometimes longer."

"How do you stand it?"

"Practice."

With the ritual of returning equipment over, we found ourselves outside, in the employee parking lot. We reached my car and stopped. "This is mine," I said.

"I'm parked way over there," she said, pointing to a distant corner of the lot.

"Nice meeting you, Lowry."

"You, too."

I opened the door and started to duck in. Lowry said, "Hey, wait."

I stood back up with a dumb look on my face.

"So, what do Safety Inspectors usually do after work?"

"Go home."

"They don't hang out, you know, like in the movies?"

"I wouldn't put too much stock in those."

"Well, could we pretend we're in one of those movies? At least for my first day?" she asked, trying to hide an embarrassed smile.

I smiled, too. I couldn't help it. "How about a cup of coffee?"

4

We scooted into opposite sides of the booth. The seats were hard, made of old leather, cracked, with tufts of stuffing popping out. Surely, that must have been a safety violation, but neither of us cared.

The sun burned outside, but the restaurant's tinted windows protected us from the UV radiation. We were in an old-fashioned diner, a few miles from the Central Office. I came here often, usually choosing to eat here instead of at home.

A waitress appeared. She handed us each a menu and asked for our drink orders. Coffee for both. The coffee was dark and bitter. It was delicious.

"You know," I said, putting my mug down on the table, "a long time ago, people used to add stuff to coffee."

"What kind of stuff?" Lowry asked.

"Sugar. Milk. Chocolate. Whipped cream sometimes."

"Really? That's so weird."

"I bet coffee would taste interesting with any of those."

Lowry took a long, slow, deliberate sip. When she finished, she said, "Yeah, I could see it being better with milk."

"Not sugar?"

"I've never had it," she said nonchalantly.

"I remember my parents using it. They outlawed it when I was a kid."

I was thirty years her elder. It made sense that she wouldn't know about those sorts of things. To her, they were historical oddities.

"You know how some things, like fruit, are naturally sweet?" I asked.

"Yeah."

"Well, you could add that same sweetness to just about anything. It was this white powder. Scoop it up and mix it in. Any drink. Any food. You could buy it at the grocery store," I explained, feeling older with every word.

"Tell me more about the old days, gramps," Lowry giggled.

The waitress returned and asked what we wanted to eat. I ordered an egg-white omelet. Yolks were a rationed food, and you could only have so many per week due to their high cholesterol content. Lowry ordered toast with raspberry jam. The food was good but plain. I used my entire ration of salt, but it wasn't enough to get my taste buds excited. I left half the omelet on the plate. Lowry inhaled her meal, and then looked hopefully at mine.

"You can have the rest if you like," I said, sliding the plate toward her.

"Thanks," she said. She started to wolf down the omelet. She must have worked up quite an appetite after her first night on the job.

"How do you like Sex Detail?" I asked.

"It's not my greatest aspiration in life."

"Where do you want to work?"

She answered in between bites. "I – want to – get to – the top. Maybe – head of – Healthcare – or some other – interesting department."

"But Sex Detail is only for people under disciplinary action. Usually perverts. Nobody has ever started out there. You must have some pretty bad luck."

"Not really. I requested it. I wanted to start at the bottom. Oh, no offense."

"It's fine," I chuckled. "It's the bottom. Sewage Detail is just about the only thing lower."

New agents took a battery of aptitude tests. A computer algorithm crunched the numbers and spat out an assignment. The whole thing was mysterious, but nobody began their career on Sex

Detail. It was meant as a punishment, not a launching pad. The government never fired anyone, because they thought it looked bad to fire agents. So, they were always demoted to the vilest jobs until they eventually resigned.

"But why would you want to start at the bottom?" I asked.

She tipped her coffee mug and drained it in two large gulps. She set it down and said, "I suppose it will make my meteoric rise all the more impressive."

"You joke about it, but I think you're more ambitious than you let on."

"Maybe so," she said, smiling.

The waitress reappeared and asked if we wanted anything else. "Just the check," I told her. I paid for both our breakfasts.

"Thanks, you didn't have to do that," Lowry said.

"It's my pleasure," I replied.

We scooted out of the booth, and found our way back to the parking lot. Our cars were side by side. We chatted idly for another minute. Lowry stretched her arms high above her head and yawned.

"I'll see you tomorrow," she said.

"Tonight," I corrected.

"Oh, yeah, tonight. I've never worked the night shift before."

"It's great fun," I said, deadpan.

She waved goodbye, and we entered our respective vehicles. As my car idled, I watched hers drive away.

The navigation system's screen was in the center console. "Choose a destination," it read in large black letters. Usually, I told it to take me home, but I didn't want to go back there. Anyplace else would be better. I punched in an alternative, the Archives.

"Thank you," appeared on the screen. The automatic seat belt locked me in place, and the car began to drive.

The Archives were a library, but only for government agents. It was there I gathered all my knowledge about the way the world used to be, before the First Government. It was there I had seen the photo of the log cabin. It was there I first wished I had been born a few centuries earlier.

My car tried three parking structures before finding an open space in a lot four blocks away. I was downtown, and the work day was just getting started. Finding a place to park was always an ordeal. Fortunately, the coffee had my head buzzing, and I zipped along the sidewalk, covering the distance with vigor. When I reached the Archives, I took a moment to take it in visually before springing up the stairs.

It was a behemoth designed in the classic First Government style: straight lines, thick square columns, and flat undecorated gray stone walls. Its windows were completely blacked out by UV filters. It was wide and took up an entire city block. The First Government's taste skewed toward the utilitarian.

Once inside, I was in the atrium. It was a large, high-ceilinged, empty room. In front of me stood a basic wooden desk with a bored looking man behind it. To the right of that was a full-body X-ray scanner. I approached, my shoes echoing on the stone floor.

"Name and serial number," the guard behind the desk said lethargically. He hadn't bothered to look up from his magazine.

I recited both and he entered them into his terminal. A moment passed. He looked at the terminal, annoyed, as this huge amount of work seemed to be inconveniencing him. The terminal's screen flashed. He looked back at his magazine and said, "Hand print identification."

A small, square device sat on the corner of the desk. The outline of a hand flashed red on its screen. I pressed my palm firmly against the cool glass. The device gave a high-pitched chirp and spoke in a robotic female voice, "Identity confirmed."

"Now the scanner," the guard instructed.

I knew the procedure. To go anyplace important required at least three levels of security. Twenty levels had been required for air travel back when passenger planes still existed. I suppose that's why people stopped flying. People only traveled cross-country by train now.

I stepped into the machine and raised my arms sideways. I looked like a bird flapping its wings. Once my body was finished getting blasted with radiation, a light at the top of the machine blinked green, and the guard told me I was free to enter. I moved on, glad to be done with the security checkpoint. My whole life was security checkpoints.

The Archives were massive. The building rose four levels above ground, and dove thirty levels below ground. It was stuffed full of information about the old world. None it could be found on a computer. Everything was a hard copy. A few years ago I discovered why.

I had been reading through some old newspapers, passing the time. One of them, from about one hundred years ago, declared, "Hacker Breaks Into Government Archives!" There was a subheading, "Threatens to Reveal 'Truth' About Safety Regulations."

Subsequent newspapers failed to show him disclosing the truth, whatever that was, to the general populace. I imagine he was going to reveal what the world was like before the First Government became so enamored with safety regulations. Back when people could smoke, drink, eat, and fuck to their heart's content. His silence had either been bought or acquired through more nefarious means.

After that, all digital records pertaining to life before the First Government were deleted. Now, to obtain that information, you had to read the hard copies, the books and newspapers. But in order to do that, you needed to be a safety agent with special authorization. I had been granted special authorization at my old assignment. When I was demoted, they forgot to rescind it.

Sub-level Fourteen had books on architecture. I grabbed a few at random. I carried them over to a bare wooden table and sat down.

The room was dark and quiet, devoid of other people. The numerous stacks of shelves were enveloping, leaving little space between them and myself. The musty odor of decaying books filled my nostrils. It was an acidic smell that I found comforting.

I opened the first book, "Great Architecture," to a random page. The first picture I saw was a fading color image of a beautifully unique building. It was stout, with a stone wall motif worked into the body of the structure. It was in a green, secluded forest. It had several balconies that jutted over empty space, seemingly supported by nothing. There were large expanses of glass. Most fantastic of all, a waterfall appeared to spout from the bowels of the house. The caption below the image read, "Fallingwater, designed by Frank Lloyd Wright in 1935. Mill Run, Pennsylvania."

The building was ancient. In all likelihood it didn't exist anymore. The architect had been a genius. He certainly had more imagination than the bores who designed everything today. A building like that would never pass today's safety inspection codes, with all the glass and balconies and waterfalls and other unsafe things.

I flipped through the book, marveling at the incredible buildings. The minutes lapsed into hours. I worked my way through a second, third, and fourth book. Everything was so different now. These ancient architects would gasp in horror if they could see the prefabricated domiciliary nightmare we live in today.

My ears detected the sound of footsteps. That was strange. I was always alone here. It was probably a janitor emptying waste baskets. The footsteps grew louder. I started to focus more on the steps than the book in front of me. They moved closer still.

A man appeared from behind one of the bookshelves. He wore the black uniform of a safety agent. He was quite pale, of average build, and without a wisp of hair on his head. Our eyes locked, and he gave a single nod. I nodded back. He walked to my table and sat in the chair opposite me.

"Inspector Smith," he said.

"Can I help you?"

He placed his palm on my book. He rotated it toward his side of the table. He casually looked over the page. A large white building with several rounded domes and a reflecting pool was the subject.

"The Taj Mahal," he said, reading the caption aloud. "Fascinating."

"Are you a fan of architecture?"

"I'm a fan of you."

"Have we met?"

"Not formally."

He stared at me with piercing eyes. The hairs on the back of my neck stood up.

"My name is Orwell. I've been admiring your work for some time now."

"What do you want?"

"That's not important."

"It is if you want to keep having this conversation."

"That's what I like about you, you aren't afraid to speak your mind."

He acted too familiar, like we were old pals. He stared at me intensely, but spoke with casual charm. Every nerve in my body was on alert.

"I'm looking for skilled people, and you are exactly the kind of person I need."

"And what kind of person am I?"

"Someone who doesn't always play by the rules."

He was talking about last night. Did he have a surveillance team on me? I didn't like being watched. I liked the idea of him wanting to use me for something even less.

"What do you have in mind?" I asked slowly, cautiously, because I didn't know where this conversation was heading.

Orwell rubbed his chin thoughtfully and said, "It's a bit too early to say outright. Some things are still in the planning stages. But speaking generally, I'm putting together a group of like-minded individuals. There's a lot of corruption in the government, and some policy changes may be in order."

I couldn't believe he was serious. He must have been insane.

"Anyway, Inspector Smith, I wanted to let you know you are a candidate for joining my group. I'll call on you again when I have something more concrete to offer."

Orwell pushed himself away from the table. He smiled smugly and said, "Good day." He sauntered away, his feet landing softly on the floor. His exit seemed to take forever.

Feeling shaken, I couldn't enjoy reading any longer. I returned the books to their shelves and headed for the exit. I left through the front door, going through the security checks again. When I returned home, I went straight to bed. I dreamed of nothing.

5

I listed out of the bedroom, bleary-eyed. My head felt like the receiving end of an anvil. An awful racket came from the living room. It was much louder than the usual noise.

A dog rounded the corner separating the living room from the kitchen. It was squat and pudgy with a flat, wrinkled black face. Its body was tan colored. Its tail was curled twice over, and its eyes looked like they were about to pop out of its skull.

It raced toward me at full speed, its butt nearly dragging across the floor. An incredibly long pink tongue flapped from one side of its giant mouth. As the dog neared, it didn't slow down. It careened into my shins with a thud.

The dog jumped at my face, going almost three feet straight up. It tried and failed a second time. Springs must have been attached to its feet. Then it decided something more fun awaited elsewhere. It skittered around me a final time, and ran full speed back to the kitchen.

My troll-wife was sitting in her usual spot. "When did you get a dog?" I asked.

"Oh . . . they delivered it half an hour ago."

"What is it?"

"Oh . . . a dog."

"I know it's a dog. What kind of dog?"

There was no response. She was entranced by the pulsing light of the TV.

I went into the kitchen. Water and dog food were strewn about the floor. Several stuffed dog toys had been dissected, their cotton innards tossed about. In the center of the floor was a coiled up turd. The dog sniffed it, growled, and barked.

"You're barking at your own shit," I said.

The dog looked at me with a vacuous smile. For a moment it resembled Huxley. Then, the dog shot off, racing back to the living room.

"You want to help me clean up this mess?" I called to my troll-wife.

No response. It was just as well. She would only make it worse. I was the only one that did anything around here. Cleaning, cooking, laundry, maintenance, I did it all. She was a worthless slug.

I got a broom from the closet and began to sweep. I took slow breaths as my head pounded harder. My eyes ached. Every muscle in my body was taught. "Stupid dog," I muttered under my breath.

Dogs were supposed to improve health. A study revealed that pet owners had lower blood pressure and stress levels than non-pet owners. Therefore, it was deemed safer to own a pet, and it became mandatory to have one. People were allowed to choose a dog or a cat. Later, another study came out that revealed cat feces carried bacteria that can harm unborn fetuses. So, every cat was rounded up and euthanized. Did former cat owners have less stress after the government killed their pets?

After I swept up the mess, I went back to the bedroom, showered, and dressed for work. I was looking forward to getting out of the house more than ever. As I was leaving, I said to my troll-wife, "If the dog makes a mess, can you clean it up?"

No response.

"Can you walk him so he doesn't go in the house?"

No response.

I lowered the brim of my hat as far down as it would go. With all this talk about safety, the government had forgotten one thing: it wasn't safe to live with a troll. Sooner or later, one of us was going to snap.

By the time I arrived at Sex Detail, Huxley and Lowry were already working. They scrutinized the electronic map. The black swath of dead pixels had grown bigger in my absence.

"How nice of you to join us," Huxley said.

"Welcome back," I said to Lowry.

"Thanks," she said.

"Okay, time to get to work," Huxley said. "We've got a serious crime going down tonight. If we pull this off, we'll be all-stars."

I wasn't sure what he meant, but I knew he was wrong. Nothing Sex Detail did made any difference.

Huxley continued, "My informant is going to meet us at midnight, here." He pointed to an intersection in the northeast sector of the city. He dragged his finger to a forested area beyond the city's border and drew an imaginary circle around it. "Then we're going to follow him to the party which is at an undisclosed location. But it should be somewhere in this area."

Huxley turned around and looked the two of us over. He placed his hands authoritatively on his hips and puffed out his chest.

"This is a big one. We've gotta do this one completely by the book. That means no fucking around. You think you can handle that, Smith?"

"Sure."

Huxley went on like he was a general addressing his troops, and we were a thousand soldiers hanging on his every word.

"There should be anywhere from eight to twelve perpetrators. So, we'll need to take three vans. We'll each drive one. I'll take the lead, of course."

"When are you going to enlighten us with what we're doing?" I asked.

"I was getting to that. My informant notified me of a huge safety violation. It happens on the same night every month. It's going to take everything we've got to pull it off right."

"Your informant?"

"That's right."

"Who's that?"

"That's confidential."

"Is this even a real case?"

Huxley thrust his finger in my face and screamed, *"Don't fucking question me! I'm in charge! One more outburst like this, and I'll have you working Sewage Detail, shoving chemicals up your ass!"*

"Whatever you say."

Huxley looked at Lowry. Her mouth was agape. He took a step back. He adjusted his tie and cleared his throat. He ran both hands over his hair. The accumulated grease kept it slicked back. When he finally collected himself, he spoke as if nothing happened.

"My informant is very reliable. But he only agrees to work with me as long as he remains anonymous."

Lowry raised her hand and, in a sweet voice, said, "I have a question."

"Go ahead," Huxley said.

"Could you give us a few details? Like who we're arresting?"

"Of course, my dear," he said pleasantly. "It's a swingers' party."

"Swingers?"

"It's a big sex party. Couples go there and swap partners," I said.

"How . . . interesting," she said faintly. I had expected her to be appalled or taken aback, but she was intrigued.

"Like I said, there could be a lot of them, so we'll each be taking a van. And be sure to have your weapons charged and ready," Huxley said.

Huxley stepped toward me and, in a low voice, said, "By the book, Smith."

I replied with a single nod, and we departed.

Our caravan of three large black government vehicles was obvious. Anyone trying to avoid us would have seen us a mile away. Huxley's van was in the lead, Lowry's was second, and mine brought up the rear. When we reached our destination, we parked in a neat row along the curb. To the right was a public park, flooded with bright lights. It was empty.

Huxley got out of his van and entered the park. I stayed put and watched. Huxley waited in the grass, just off the sidewalk that serpentined through the park. He stood in the darkest spot he could find, although he was still partially illuminated.

Parks had been found to be safer, from both crime and accidents, if they were brightly lit. Every city was like this, bathed in bright artificial lights that were always on. Night was almost indistinguishable from day. One had to look at the sky to determine if the moon or sun was out.

Five minutes later, a man approached Huxley. They exchanged a laughable secret handshake and conversed a few minutes. Huxley probably felt like a secret agent. When they finished talking, the man disappeared and Huxley returned to his van. He didn't let Lowry or I know what was going on. So much for going by the book.

A car drove by the caravan. Huxley's van pulled out and followed it. Then Lowry went. I started the engine and pulled away from the curb.

We drove for half an hour, winding our way out of the city and into the forest beyond. Here, it was truly dark. Without the city lights, the natural darkness seemed doubly powerful.

Our caravan pulled off the highway and rolled along a gravel road, moving deeper into the forest. Huxley's voice came over the radio, "Okay, everyone, kill your lights. Once we get over this hill, there'll be a house on the right. That's the place."

I turned off the van's lights, something that would be impossible in a civilian vehicle. The caravan slowed to a crawl. My eyes adjusted to the murky blackness around me, and the world gradually came into view.

As we crested the hill, I saw the building. It was just like every other suburban house, only in the forest. How did they get it out here?

The caravan stopped, and we exited our vehicles. The lead car, driven by Huxley's informant, continued down the gravel road. It was soon out of sight, swallowed by the darkness.

The three of us convened in front of the middle van. Huxley squatted as he prepared his equipment. Lowry squatted near him, copying the pose of her superior. I continued to stand.

Huxley brought his binoculars, set to X-ray mode, to his eyes and inspected the house. Lights were on inside, but heavy curtains concealed what was behind them. Huxley started to breathe heavily. He licked his lips. "Yeah. Oh, yeah. This is the place, all right."

Lowry and I exchanged a disturbed glance.

"Yeah, yeah," he went on. "These guys are some big perverts. Real nasty."

Huxley started fondling himself. Lowry stood up and inched away from him.

"Did he do this last night?" I asked in a hushed voice.

"He was a creep, but not this bad," Lowry whispered.

"Sorry. He's usually like this."

"I'd hate to see what he does when he's off the clock."

I stifled a laugh. The more I hung around Lowry, the more I liked her. I hadn't met anyone else with the same sense of humor as me.

"I guess you shouldn't have requested Sex Detail."

"Why? I haven't had this much fun in a long time."

Huxley, meanwhile, was still lusting at whatever he was seeing. He was so enamored, he hadn't noticed our conversation. Overcome by curiosity, I took out my own equipment, and decided to take a look.

There were ten people in the house. Their figures were transformed into multicolored amorphous blobs. Even so, it was easy to tell what they were doing. Somebody's head was moving rhythmically in front of someone's lap. Somebody was bouncing atop someone else. There was a large blob of three people in one. The others were sitting on the furniture, resting. I put the binoculars away.

"See anything good in there?" Lowry asked.

"Good? Absolutely not."

"Hey! Keep it down!" Huxley whispered excitedly. "You're gonna blow our cover!"

We stood for another few minutes until Huxley was ready. He turned to us and said, "Here's the plan. I go in through the front door. Lowry, you come in after me. Smith, you go around to the other side, and catch anyone trying to go out the back door."

I walked to the rear of the house. Inside, I heard the steady thump of music, the occasional laugh, and a woman moaning happily. I pulled out my weapon and felt its weight in my hand. I looked down at it, and my headache grew stronger. I slid it back into the holster. My headache improved a bit.

Suddenly, there was a bang. Huxley had kicked in the front door. *"Safety Inspectors!"* he roared. *"Down on the floor! Freeze!"*

A woman screamed, followed by the sounds of a scuffle. Something heavy fell over, and the droning music was silenced. Shattering glass. Heavy footsteps running through the house. A man shrieked in pain.

The stomping footsteps came closer. I backed away from the door. The door flew open, and banged sharply on the side of the house. A woman, completely naked except for a pair of running shoes, raced out. She saw me. Her eyes grew wide and her pace slowed. One, two, three steps past me. She looked away. Her pace quickened, and she sped into the forest.

A man came out next, wearing only an undershirt. He didn't look at me or slow down. A moment later, another naked woman with a fat, jiggling belly ran out. Both of them disappeared into the darkness.

I waited a few moments. It didn't look like anyone else was coming. I could hear the sounds of the struggle within the house more clearly now. I decided to go in and lend a hand.

I knew the layout of the house instinctively. It was exactly the same as every other house. The kitchen was first. It was empty. I moved into a connecting hallway, also empty. The living room was next. Six people were here, none of them handcuffed. They sat on the floor, covered in sweat, smelling of wine and sex, and hanging their heads in shame. The stereo was smashed and a table turned over. Broken bottles littered the floor. The carpet was soaking up spilled wine.

I turned right, moving into the bedroom. Lowry and Huxley were there. Each had their weapon drawn, aimed at the lone remaining offender. He was naked and holding a tall brass floor lamp. The shade was gone, and the bulb broken. He brandished it like a weapon.

Huxley told him to put it down. Lowry took a step toward him. He took a slow swing at her. She jumped back gracelessly.

"Last chance, asshole! Put it down!" Huxley screamed.

The offender said nothing. His eyes darted around the room, looking for an escape. He swung the lamp at Lowry, quicker this time, but still missed. Lowry was spooked and gave the offender an opening. He dropped the lamp and punched her in the stomach, doubling her over. He wrested the weapon from her hands, and shoved her into the wall. She thumped to the floor.

"Eat this!" Huxley growled.

He fired.

Two probes leaped from the muzzle of Huxley's weapon. They arced over the offender's shoulder. They buried themselves in the window curtain and discharged. The electric pulse set the curtain ablaze.

"Holy shit!" Huxley cried.

With no means of defending himself, Huxley watched as the offender took careful aim. I could have drawn my own weapon, I had plenty of time, but I wanted to see what would happen next.

The offender fired. The two probes hit Huxley square in the chest. His body filled with electricity. He squealed as he seized and dropped to the floor. The offender threw his weapon down, and turned toward the hallway. His eyes opened with surprise; he was not expecting to see me standing there.

He charged at me like a bull. I side-stepped and stuck out my foot. He sailed through the air, and crashed head first into the wall. His skull left a substantial crater in the drywall. He flopped onto the floor. I put two fingers on his neck. He still had a pulse. "Buddy, you're going to have one hell of a headache tomorrow," I said.

I hurried into the bedroom, and ripped down the flaming curtain. I stamped it with my feet until it turned to ash. Next, I helped Lowry up. "Are you okay?" I asked.

"Aside from a stomachache, yeah, I'm fine."

"I'm sorry I didn't get here sooner."

"Don't be. If you had intervened, I wouldn't have seen that." She nodded toward Huxley who was unconscious and twitching.

Lowry brushed herself off. She retrieved her weapon and holstered it. She used her handcuffs to lock together the ankles of the offender who had given us so much trouble. We went into the living room to inspect the others. Everyone was still there. Some of them were shaking.

"How's this for your second night on the job?" I asked.

"Not bad. Seven's a good catch. You get the other three?"

"Must have missed them."

It took us ten minutes to get everyone packed into the vans. By the time we finished, Huxley had woken up. He staggered outside, rubbing his sternum. He was embellishing, letting us see how much he suffered. "You get that son of a bitch?" he asked.

"Yeah," I said.

"Good."

He went from van to van, scrutinizing the offenders. He counted them all before turning to me. He narrowed his eyes and asked, "Why are there only seven?"

"What do you mean?"

"There were ten. Where are the other three? Weren't you guarding the back door?"

"Oh, them. They overpowered me."

Huxley fell silent. He walked a few paces toward the lead van, but then turned back, saying, "You know what, Smith? I'm citing you for insubordination and dereliction of duty."

I climbed into my van. I wasn't interested in what he had to say.

"Are you listening to me?!" he shouted, red-faced.

I shut the door and started the engine. I pulled away from the caravan and made my way down the gravel road. In the rear-view mirror, I saw him jumping up and down, arms flailing. He looked like a cartoon character. It was then I realized my headache was gone.

6

Two weeks had passed since we busted the orgy. When we returned that night, Huxley looked disappointed. Had he expected a ticker-tape parade and riches lavished upon him? Nothing happened. Nothing changed. Nobody noticed. We booked the offenders and sent them on their merry way without any fanfare. Since then, Huxley had been even more irritable.

I arrived about twenty minutes late. I didn't see the need to show up on time. Besides, my tardiness would delay Huxley from getting the evening's work started, and I derived a modicum of pleasure from that.

When I got to Sex Detail, I found Huxley slamming his fist repeatedly into the electronic map on the rolling easel. Each time he hit it, it rolled away from him, so he pulled it back and punched it again. Each collision caused the screen to flicker wildly.

"His exercise routine is coming along nicely," I said to Lowry.

Huxley whirled around at the sound of my voice. "What the hell took so goddamn long? Where the hell were you?" he growled.

"The bathroom."

"You just save that for when you're off the clock, got it?"

He turned back and looked at the map. The screen was dark, and tendrils of smoke drifted out of it. "The map's busted," he said.

Huxley faced Lowry and spoke to her in a condescending tone. He had dropped the sweet act after he realized she wasn't going to sleep with him. "Lowry, it's time to take off the training wheels. I'm letting you out on your own tonight."

"Great," she said, perking up.

"We've got five dates, all high-risk. We'll divide and conquer like always."

He dug some paper and a pen out of the desk. He scribbled something on each piece of paper. He handed the first to Lowry and said, "You've got these two." He handed me the second and said, "You've got one. Think you can handle that?"

I shoved the paper into my pocket without looking at it and said, "I think I can manage."

He leaned in closer. His hot breath smelled like rotten cabbage. "I can't wait 'til you're gone. It's gonna be so sweet when they kick your ass out," he said.

He stared intently, waiting for fear to come to my eyes. It never did. His face went flat. He huffed and said, "Let's get moving."

I ambled toward the parking garage. Lowry caught up and we walked together.

"You're finally independent. Looks like you've made it to the big time," I said.

"I'm just glad I'm not stuck with Huxley anymore."

"Once you get promoted out of here, it'll just be me and him again."

"How awful."

"Maybe you can do something about him when you're at the top."

"Maybe," she said with a wink.

We said our temporary goodbyes and split up. Inside my vehicle, I wondered what to do next. I had no intention of tracking the date. With the Auto-Driver disengaged, I drove aimlessly for a while. I lost track of time. I simply enjoyed the feel of the road. When I tired of that, I turned into a residential area, the darkest I could find, and parked. I tilted my seat back, closed my eyes, and drifted off.

There was a sudden banging of a fist against glass. Someone was shouting. Their voice was muffled. I sat up and tried to get my bearings. The clock showed several hours had elapsed. Outside, the figure was hammering incessantly. It was another agent.

It wasn't just any agent, it was Huxley. I rolled down the window. His muffled cries became perfectly clear.

"Ha ha! I got you!"

"What? Huxley, what's going on?"

"I caught you, you piece of shit, that's what's going on!"

Everything came together. I had been shirking my duties ever since I started back on this assignment, and Huxley wanted to prove it. He must have followed me to confirm I wasn't monitoring the date. The fact that I was asleep was the cherry on top.

"Your ass is gone! As soon as we get back, I'm talking to the Chief! Say bye-bye, Smithy."

I rolled the window up. I didn't want to listen to him anymore. Huxley grimaced and resumed pounding on the window. I started the car and drove away.

Lowry was already at the Central Office when I returned. She had made an arrest on her first date. The couple from the second date had broken up mid-dinner, so she didn't bother following them home. She was typing on her terminal when I arrived. I relayed the events of the evening to her. Huxley hadn't shown up yet.

"What do you think he'll do?" she asked.

"He'll report it to the Chief. The Chief will talk to me. After that . . ." I trailed off and turned my palms up.

"Will they fire you?"

"Nobody ever gets fired."

"So then what?"

"Probably a demotion to Sewage Detail."

"Huxley," she said, her voice lowering a register. "That son of a bitch."

As if summoned by a spell, Huxley appeared before us. His arms were held wide, and he waltzed around the desk with an invisible partner. "Well, Smith," he said with a manic energy, "your reckoning has finally come. I hope you're ready. Don't bother apologizing, it's too late."

He danced his way to the Chief's office, where he disappeared. Meanwhile, Lowry and I waited in silence. For once, I wasn't sure what to say. Lowry's brow was furrowed and flames burned behind her eyes.

When Huxley returned, he looked like he had won the lottery. "Smithy, Smithy, Smithy," he said, projecting his voice as loudly as he could. "The Chief wants to see you in his office. I hope you're ready to grovel and kiss ass. Not like it's going to help."

I didn't acknowledge him. As I walked toward the Chief's office, Huxley said, "Why don't you come along, Lowry? You won't want to miss this."

This marked the third time I was sent to a superior for disciplinary action. I hoped it was some kind of a record.

Unlike the main area, the Chief had an actual office with a closing door. We entered and Huxley hopped over to stand beside the Chief. The Chief's name was Wyndham, and he sat behind a battered metal desk. The room was cramped, with barely enough space for all of us to fit inside. It was atrociously decorated with faux wood paneling. A rickety ceiling fan spun slowly above.

Wyndham was unbelievably fat. I was amazed that someone could get that fat with all the unhealthy foods banned. He wiped the sweat from his bald head with a handkerchief. The ceiling fan did little to drop the sweltering temperature.

Wyndham was not the Chief of the entire operation. There were several Chiefs, and each presided over a number of departments. Wyndham oversaw Sex Detail, Air Quality Detail, Hair Care Detail, and Sewage Detail. He mostly left the departments to their own devices.

Wyndham looked me up and down and said, "Inspector Huxley tells me he found you asleep at the job. Is this true?"

"This work is so riveting, I can hardly stay awake," I said.

"Please don't joke about this, Inspector Smith. The safety of the public is not to be taken lightly. Do you take your work seriously?"

"Maybe not as seriously as Huxley. He's a pretty serious guy."

"Inspector Huxley also informed me that two weeks ago you purposefully let three sex offenders escape. What do you have to say to that?"

"I didn't."

"He made it up?"

"He's got it in for me, Chief."

"And why would he?"

"I used to have his job. And I wouldn't let him get away with all his sick crap. I suppose this is his way of getting even."

"Sick crap?" Wyndham said, his eyebrows rising.

"Masturbating in the middle of–"

Huxley interrupted, "Chief, please. This is hardly relevant. He's trying to distract you. The fact is he has been insubordinate and shirking his responsibilities. And listen to the way he talks to you!"

Wyndham nodded and wiped more sweat from his bald pate. "Quite right," he said. "Inspector Smith, I had Healthcare Detail run an investigation. A few weeks ago, you reported on a couple that you claim failed to have intercourse. Do you remember that?"

I wasn't sure where he was going with this. "Yes," I said.

"Then how do you explain the fact that the woman is now pregnant?"

"Pregnant?"

"Healthcare took a blood sample from her and dated the time of conception to that night. And now she is pregnant without a license to procreate."

"We got you now, motherfucker!" Huxley said, delighted.

I resigned myself. I would be going to Sewage Detail. At least I wouldn't have to deal with Huxley any longer. With an acquiescent sigh, I said, "I fell asleep. It wasn't a big deal. Who cares if these people have unprotected sex or group sex? How is any of that illegal?"

"How?" Wyndham asked with genuine surprise. "The First Government deemed it unsafe and therefore illegal. That's how!"

"It doesn't make sense."

"It makes perfect sense. The First Government said it makes sense, therefore it does."

"But there's no reason for it to be illegal."

"The reason is that the First Government says it's illegal."

"But why is it illegal?"

"Because the First Government says it's unsafe."

"How is it unsafe?"

"Because the First Government deemed it unsafe and therefore illegal. That's how!"

"Well, they're wrong."

Wyndham coughed and his face turned bright pink. More sweat popped onto his forehead. Flustered, he replied, "Inspector Smith! Under no circumstances is anyone allowed to question the authority of the First Government!"

"How do you know they aren't wrong?"

"Because they decreed they are always right."

While we spoke, Lowry grumbled something under her breath.

Wyndham continued, "This kind of behavior is simply not allowed. For lying, insubordination, and sleeping at your post, I was going to demote you to Sewage Detail. But now, after what you've said, I have to reconsider. Clearly, you are not in your right mind. Only an insane person would speak against the First Government."

The agitated grumbling from Lowry grew louder. Neither Huxley nor the fat man seemed to notice. Something bad was coming.

Wyndham wiped his forehead again and took a breath. There were deep rings of sweat beneath each of his arms. He was exerting himself just by talking. "You must be insane. I'm going to petition for your immediate and permanent hospitalization in the asylum."

"Hold on, Chief," I said, slightly panicked.

"You aren't insane?"

"No."

"Then why are you speaking against the First Government?"

"I'm just questioning it, that's all."

"And why would you question the First Government?"

"Maybe not everyone wants all these rules."

"To question the First Government doesn't make any sense. There's no other explanation except that you're insane."

"Chief, listen—"

He raised a hand to silence me and said, "That's my final decision."

Huxley jumped up and down, squawking, "I finally got you!"

A powerful force pressed against me. I stumbled to my right as Lowry knocked me aside. Wyndham looked at her as if he had never seen a woman before. The sweat poured down his face more profusely than ever.

"I'd like to say something," Lowry said.

"Yes, Inspector, um, what is it?"

"I can't stand here and listen to this. You have to know that Smith is a good person. He isn't crazy. He just made a mistake, that's all. Please don't do this to him."

"I'm afraid we have a zero tolerance policy when it comes to insanity," he said, shaking his head.

"If anyone's insane, it's Huxley."

Wyndham looked at Huxley and frowned. "I'm sorry, but Inspector Huxley is an exemplary government employee. You would do well to act more like him."

"But, Chief—"

He held up his hand, silencing her, just as he had done with me. He looked annoyed. He didn't want to hear any more. "Enough. You're done talking. I've made my decision. Why don't you leave, missy?"

"Missy?"

Her brewing frustration hit its boiling point. Lowry flung her suit jacket onto the floor. She ripped off her tie, and undid the top three buttons of her shirt. Her breasts bulged out, barely contained by the lacy frill of her bra. All eyes in the room zeroed in on her.

"Lowry, please, stop, don't worry about me," I said.

She either didn't hear me or ignored my words. She stepped around to the other side of the desk. She lifted a picture frame. Its back was to me so I couldn't see the photo. "Is this your wife?" Lowry asked.

Wyndham nodded nervously but didn't speak. He was trying hard, and failing miserably, to resist ogling her. Huxley wasn't even pretending. He leered at her like a pro.

Lowry put the picture frame back down and faced Wyndham squarely. She gently caressed the sides of his bald head with both hands. After a moment of this, she shoved his face into the ample curves of her bosom.

"Are you sure there isn't anything I can do to make you reconsider?" she asked.

Wyndham didn't put up a fight. Lowry released him, and he kicked back in his chair, gasping for air. His face was flushed. A lecherous smile stretched from ear to ear. He looked away from her and said, "Inspector, this is very unbecoming. I'm sorry, but my hands are tied."

Lowry walked around the desk again and gathered her tie and jacket. As she buttoned her shirt, she said, "I suppose my hands are tied, too."

"What do you mean?" Wyndham asked.

"I'm afraid I'll have to report you for sexual harassment."

"What?!" he said, his sweat coming down like a waterfall.

"Did you not just throw yourself into my breasts?"

"Y-you wouldn't."

"This has been a very traumatic experience for me, Chief."

"I'm afraid I'll have to report your behavior as well."

"Go ahead. But I'll make sure your wife finds out. I'm sure she won't be as understanding as your superiors."

Wyndham hung his head. His eyes bulged.

"You little bitch!" Huxley hissed. "Don't think you can pull the same shit on me. I saw the whole thing. They won't believe you over me, I'm the head of a department."

"Report me," she replied nonchalantly as she finished putting her outfit back together. "But if you do, I might feel compelled to let everyone know about your activities on the job. It doesn't seem very safe having a pervert on Sex Detail."

"Damn you," Huxley grumbled.

The room fell quiet. The only sound came from the creak of the overhead fan. I was stunned. Lowry was so bold. The way she took on these two guys, she was incredible. She commanded the room.

Finally, the fat man spoke, "All right. Let's just say I gave Inspector Smith a verbal warning. And the rest of this meeting never happened."

Lowry shook her head. With her hands confidently on her hips, she said, "Not good enough."

"What do you want?" Wyndham asked submissively.

"A promotion."

"Oh, yes, yes, good idea. I'll transfer you anywhere you want to go."

"And Smith, too."

Realizing he would be rid of both of us, he said, "Of course, Smith, too."

Lowry turned to me and asked, "Where would you like to go?"

I wasn't sure. Was there an assignment I would enjoy? Any choice would be a shot in the dark. "Healthcare," I said, remembering Lowry's aspirations.

"Yes, no problem. I'll get on it right away," he whimpered.

"Aren't you going to congratulate us?" she asked.

"Congratulations on your promotion," Wyndham said.

Lowry motioned for us to leave. As we exited the room, Huxley spat, "Don't think you'll get away with this, you bitch."

Lowry wheeled around. She marched up to Huxley. Her body surged with power. She buried her knee in his crotch. He doubled over and collapsed onto the floor. He emitted a low, pathetic moan.

Outside the room, I said, "Thanks, Lowry. How can I make it up to you?"

She hooked her hand into the crook of my arm. "You can start by buying me a cup of coffee," she said.

7

We slid into the same booth as last time. The waitress was the same as before, too. Lowry ordered a big meal with her coffee. I had coffee only. Lowry blew on her steaming mug before taking a sip.

"How was I?" she asked.

"Amazing," I said. The excitement from earlier was still pumping through my veins.

She returned a sly grin.

"I've never seen anything like that. You weren't kidding when you said you were going all the way to the top."

Lowry put her mug down. She folded her arms and rested them on the table. The lights above shimmered on her red hair, reminiscent of a halo. "Have you worked Healthcare Detail before?" she asked.

"No."

"What do you think it will be like?"

I sipped my coffee. It was strong and bitter. "The same as every other department. We'll waste taxpayer money to enforce a bunch of rules nobody wants or cares about," I said.

"You don't think the public wants the safety regulations?"

"Maybe they did when the First Government was founded. But not now. I can't imagine anyone wants government perverts spying on them."

"You hate this job, don't you?"

"I didn't always hate it."

Lowry sipped her coffee again and gazed out the window. The world looked dark through the UV-filtered glass. Cars drifted by on the busy street. The city expanded as far as the eye could see. Everything was cast in drab shades of whites and tans and grays.

When Lowry's food came, she devoured the meal. I couldn't believe the appetite she had. I could eat like that once, but not anymore. Watching her reminded me how old I was.

"Hey, Smith," Lowry said. "When did you ever like the job?"

"When I was eighteen, like you, just starting out."

"What happened?"

I leaned back in the booth. The old faux leather crackled under my weight. "Three decades on the job happened," I said.

The rest of the meal passed in silence. I drank two cups of coffee while Lowry finished eating. When the meal was over, we'd part ways, and I'd be back to my dismal life again. Lowry would go off and be young and have fun.

"Lowry, you want to do something else?"

"Like what?"

"Have you ever seen the Archives?"

"Just in the training manual."

"What do you say?"

"Sure. Sounds fun."

It didn't take long to drive to the Archives. We entered the square hulk of a building, and found the same security guard as before. The rest of the atrium was as empty as ever.

The guard leaned back in his chair, eyes closed, with an open magazine draped across his chest. I grabbed his terminal and spun it around. I entered my name and serial number. The computer system cleared me, and I went on to the next step.

The process only allowed one agent through at a time. Lowry wouldn't have clearance, so I'd have to cheat to get her in. The full body X-ray scanner was ready. We stepped in together. She pressed against my back, mimicking my position. The machine scanned us. The light blinked green.

"Come on," I said, glad the deception had worked.

We walked through the other side of the atrium. Our shoes squeaked on the well-polished floor. I took her down to Sub-level Fourteen. She gawked in wonder at all the books.

"Smith, this is the history of . . ."

"Everything."

"I had no idea there was so much."

"And this is only one floor."

"Do you have a favorite book?"

"A favorite subject. Architecture. Pre-First Government."

"Architecture?" she said, cocking her head, and saying the word like it was foreign. "People wrote books on that?"

"I'll show you."

I opened a book and we sat at a table. I was already familiar with this one. It was a famous building. It had a boxy base, and then a steep rise to the top, ending at a huge antenna spire. Lowry read the caption aloud, "Empire State Building. Nineteen thirty one. Wow. I've never seen anything like it."

"Of course you haven't. No one has. Before the First Government, people could design buildings any way they wanted. The world looked totally different."

Lowry shook her head in disbelief. She flipped through the book's pages. The Louvre. The Tower of London. Torre Agbar. The Coliseum. And many more. The sheer diversity of structures was incredible. They looked like something out of science fiction. It was hard to believe they ever existed.

Closing the book, Lowry asked, "What else do they have here?"

"What do you want to see?"

"How about literature?"

The literature section was vast. I had perused it many times. It covered three entire sub-levels. Someone could spend a lifetime there and only get through a quarter of the books. Upon seeing row after row of books, Lowry was enraptured.

She slowly walked from one bookcase to the next. Her index finger traced behind her, touching the spines of the neatly arranged books. She left a trail, a single clean line that had wiped away a thick layer of dust.

She turned back to me and said, "I've always loved books like these. My grandmother had–" She stopped, choking on the words. She hesitated before going on. "My grandmother had a collection of books. She kept them under the floorboards of her house. The books were all ancient, but we'd read them together."

"Your grandmother was into contraband, huh?"

"It wasn't that. She just enjoyed them."

Technically, books weren't illegal. The vast majority published today were non-fiction accounts about the greatness of the First Government. Any literature prior to the First Government carried references to life before all the safety regulations. Obviously, this was considered unsafe and therefore illegal.

Lowry plucked a book from a shelf. Her eyes studied the first page, and her chest swelled.

"Do you have a favorite book?" I asked.

Still looking at the one in her hands, she said, "It seems like the one I'm reading at the time is my favorite."

"Can I tell you my favorite book?" a voice said from behind.

Lowry's book slipped out of her hands and hit the floor with a thump. I spun around and saw Orwell leaning against a bookcase. His hands were in his pockets. He had the same self-satisfied smile as last time.

"What do you want?" I asked.

"It's a great book. It's about the future, and how the government has total control. It's quite fascinating. I forget what it's called, but it reminds me of you, Inspector Lowry."

I took two steps back, and wrapped my arm around Lowry's shoulders. She was visibly shaken. Orwell had overheard her statements about the contraband.

"I'm a fan of yours," he said.

"A fan?" she asked.

"Oh, yes. I was very impressed by your performance last night. I've heard of a few different tactics for getting a promotion, but that one was original."

"Tell us what you want or get out," I said.

Orwell shifted back to his feet and took his hands out of his pockets. "It's like I told you before, Inspector Smith, I want to work with the best. People who don't play by the rules. People who are creative. People who are idealistic," he said.

"Lowry's move earlier was anything but idealistic. Clearly, we aren't the type of people you're looking for."

"On the contrary, Inspector Lowry's actions were most commendable. Was she not standing up for you, her partner? That's idealistic."

Lowry tensed, and I squeezed her tighter.

Orwell continued, "There was no way out of that situation. The corrupt bureaucracy protects scum like Huxley and Wyndham. She came up with a brilliant solution to circumvent that. Plus, I like her initiative."

"For the last time, leave us alone," I said.

Orwell sighed. He turned his palms up, like he was about the catch something. A tense moment passed. He let his arms fall casually to his sides. His smile remained.

"Very well. I'll visit you again when you've had some time to think things over. Inspector Lowry, I just want you to know, that if you want to get to the top, working with me will get you there."

He pivoted and walked away, leaving as silently as he had appeared.

Lowry kneeled and fumbled with the book. Jittering, she placed the book back into the empty slot on the shelf. "Who was that guy?" she asked.

"His name's Orwell. I met him a couple of weeks ago. He tried to recruit me for something, but he wouldn't say what exactly. He's definitely shady."

She took a few deep breaths and her trembling subsided. "He overheard us. About the books. Do you think he'll report me?"

"I doubt it. I don't think he's interested in that. He's too grandiose for trivial things."

"Okay," she said with a wan smile. She looked down for a moment, then up at me again. Her countenance had changed. It was inquisitive now. "What do you think he meant when he said I'd get to the top by working with him?"

"He's planning something. Whatever it is, we'd be best to steer clear."

"Maybe he could be useful? Someone to work with. At least for a little while."

"I'd be careful, Lowry."

The fun of the Archives was over. I decided to leave. Lowry decided to stay. She perused the books, recapturing her earlier interest. When I returned home, I found nothing waiting for me except a mess.

8

Daylight.

I woke up giddy like it was Christmas morning. I felt light, free. As I dressed, my suit seemed airy, the black fabric silky. Everything I touched felt improved.

On my way out of the house, I saw the demon-dog passed out on the couch. A wad of cotton, ripped from one of the cushions, was in its mouth. My troll-wife was asleep beside it. I didn't mind. I was headed to work, and I wasn't going to Sex Detail.

The morning routine was quicker and less annoying than usual. Before I knew it, I had my equipment. I entered the high-ceilinged main room. I looked around until I saw the sign labeled, "Healthcare." The area it comprised was quite larger than Sex Detail's.

Lowry was already there with a dozen other agents. The department head, a woman, lectured them while pointing at a large electronic map. It stood proudly on a rolling easel, brand new and state of the art.

When I approached the group, the woman stopped mid-sentence. A perturbed expression crossed her face. "Can I help you?" she asked.

"I'm reporting in."

"And who are you?"

"Smith."

"Inspector Smith, it would behoove you to show up on time."

"Uh, okay."

"You wouldn't want a demotion to Sex Detail, would you?"

I stared at her. When she realized she wasn't going to get a response, the perturbed look flattened, leaving a blank affect. She looked familiar, but I couldn't place her. I racked my brain trying to remember who she was.

Her dirty blonde hair was woven into a tight bun. The skin of her wide face was pulled back, making it look like a pancake. She was tall and underweight. Her complexion was pasty, like she never spent any time in the sun.

She resumed doling out assignments. Her movements were stiff, her voice monotone. She lacked the spark seen in normal people. At long last, I conjured her name: Atwood, the Icequeen.

Atwood focused her gaze on me again. "That leaves us with our two newcomers. I highly disapprove of two rookies to Healthcare working together. I'd partner each of you with a veteran if I had my way, but the higher-ups requested you work together. So be it. But I'm in charge, so I choose the assignments. And until I know I can trust you two, you are getting easy ones. Got it?"

"Yes, ma'am," Lowry said.

"There's a factory on the north side that makes hats. Apparently, the mortarboards they're producing have edges that are too sharp. Go check it out. Shut them down if you have to."

Atwood dispersed the team, and Lowry and I drove to our destination. The factory, a giant rectangle, was pristine on the outside. Its bland colors were the same as any other building. A sign over the front door read, "Clothing Incorporated." The name was as original as the building's design.

The interior was as bland as the exterior. A short entryway branched into two hallways: to the right was the manager's office, and the other direction was the factory floor.

"Follow my lead," I said.

I pushed through the manager's door without knocking. A lean man, with a dome of curly hair, leaped up from behind his desk. "Oh, my!" he exclaimed with a catch in his throat.

I looked around. The entire office was a throwback. A boxy wooden desk stood in the center with a wooden swivel chair behind it. An art deco style lamp was in the corner, spraying a cone of light onto the ceiling. An ancient oscillating fan purred nearby. It was like an antique dealer's office. Where had he gotten all of this?

"Inspectors Smith and Lowry, here for an official investigation," I said in the sternest voice I could muster.

The man stumbled around his desk to greet us. He shook Lowry's hand. He extended his hand to me, but I glared at him. He looked at his hand to see if something was wrong with it. He then looked back at me with an unconvincing smile.

"H-how may I help you?" he asked.

"We've received several complaints about your products."

"C-complaints? What kind of complaints?"

"That they aren't safe."

"Oh, no!" he gulped.

"Take us to the factory."

"Yes, yes, of course."

He grabbed a set of keys from a drawer. He snatched at an array of papers that was scattered across the desktop. He gathered them up, pressing them against his chest. Chattering nervously, he led us into the factory.

As we walked, Lowry gave me a perplexed look. I winked, hoping she would realize this was all in good fun.

The factory was loud. Machines chugged, lining up fabric, cutting it, and packaging it. Presses, gears, and hydraulics rhythmically pressed, turned, and slid. The various organs of these mechanical beasts created a deafening cacophony.

The room had machines on either side with a pathway in between. A few people walked about with clipboards, checking instruments and making calibrations. Everyone wore safety goggles, hard hats, and ear plugs. The volume in here was a safety violation, but no reasonable agent would cite them on account of the precautions they were taking.

"Where do you make the graduation hats?!" I shouted.

"Right this way!" the manager shouted back, escorting us down the long room.

We reached the rear of the factory. The machine before us was spitting completed mortarboards onto a conveyor belt. After they fell onto the conveyor belt, they traveled a few short feet until they dropped into a large plastic box. The hats were mostly black, but a few were a smattering of other colors.

I picked one up, making a real show of it. I held it aloft, turned it over several times, and scrutinized each corner with a press of my finger. I could feel the cardboard on the other side, but it felt soft enough.

I tossed the hat onto the conveyor belt. I turned to the manager and shouted, "What's the meaning of this?!"

"Of what?!"

"These hats!"

"I don't understand, sir!"

"Why do they have so many sharp edges?!"

"What do you mean?!"

"Why did you make hats with four corners?!"

"They've always been made that way!"

"Since when?!"

He shrugged. "Since always!"

"And if people always drank mercury to treat headaches, would you do that, too?!"

"I suppose!"

I pivoted to Lowry and shouted, "I think we've seen enough!"

With a smirk, she shouted, "Are you sure?! I bet there's plenty more safety violations around here! We should probably look!"

I turned back to the manager and shouted, "She's right! What other safety violations are you hiding?!"

"None! None at all!" His body shuddered, and the papers he clutched spilled to the floor. "You're right, the hats are too sharp! Please write me up for that! That's the only thing wrong!"

Lowry raised an eyebrow. She wanted to know more. If I was a decade younger, I might have torn this place apart after hearing such a suspicious statement. But I didn't have the energy for that kind of thing anymore.

I threw my thumb toward the door and shouted, "Come on, let's get out of here!"

The three of us retreated to the entryway. Once off the factory floor, my ears rang loudly. Voices were muffled under a high-pitched whine.

The manager was wringing his hands nervously. "S-so, what happens next?"

"Those pointed hats are a serious safety violation. They're liable to kill someone. Don't you know people throw those things?"

"Yes, of course, I'm very sorry about that. I'll get them fixed."

"I expect them to be corrected in a timely fashion."

"Yes, sir, right away."

"In that case, I'll let you off with a warning," I said magnanimously.

"Oh, thank you!"

"But if we come back and nothing's changed, we'll arrest you on the spot," Lowry said.

"Everything will be taken care of, I promise," he said, his tense muscles slackening with relief.

Lowry and I exited. This wasn't bad for a first day. I never had this much fun with Huxley.

We strolled outside. The sun shone brilliantly above. The short brim of my hat didn't block the glare, so I threw my hand up to shade my eyes. As I did, I noticed a figure standing at the curb. It was Atwood.

"What did you find?" she asked.

"Everything's fine," I said.

"That's not what I asked."

"There weren't any safety violations," Lowry said.

Atwood slowly rotated her head toward Lowry. "I did not address you."

"The place looks good," I said.

Her head rotated back to me. "Are you certain?"

"Well, there were a couple of minor things, but everyone was using proper safety equipment. And the hats seemed safe enough. It was no big deal."

"We'll see about that."

Atwood walked through the front door. She didn't swing her arms when she walked. She moved quickly, with purpose, and didn't make any extraneous movements. We followed her.

She had already dragged the manager back into the factory. He cowered on the floor, his hands sunken into his dome of hair. The machines had been shut down. The factory was oddly quiet without their noise. Atwood paced up and down the long room, inspecting every inch of the machines. The employees froze when her gaze passed over them. She scrutinized every aspect of them, as well.

She returned, looking down at the manager, her eyes empty. "These ear plugs aren't a regulation size. Where did you purchase them?" she asked.

"I-I'm not sure, I'd have to look—"

"The noise level was several decibels too high. Why haven't you serviced the machines properly?"

"I don't, I don't—"

"Those mortarboards should have one additional millimeter of fabric. Why are you skimping on materials?"

"Well, I-I-I—"

"It's a miracle no one has died in this deathtrap, or was killed by one of your deadly products. It's a good thing I intervened. What do you have to say for yourself?"

"Ma'am, I'm sorry. If you give me a chance—"

"I've seen enough. Inspector Smith, arrest this man."

"This is all correctable stuff. I don't think an arrest is necessary," I said.

She jerked at the waist, aligning herself so both the manager and I were in view. "What you think is irrelevant," she said in her usual monotone. "Violation of any safety statute is an arrestable offense. The law must be enforced."

"I'm not going to play along."

The perturbed look returned to her face. A vein swelled in the middle of her forehead. She struggled to keep her stony edifice from crumbling. "Inspector Lowry, you will obey my orders," she said.

Lowry's eyes shifted from Atwood to me to the collapsed manager and back again. She reluctantly pulled out her handcuffs and snapped them over the manger's wrists. "Sorry, pal," she said.

The other employees watched silently as we left the building. They would all need to find new jobs. The place was officially shut down.

At the Central Office, I helped Lowry with the paperwork. She looked rattled ever since we got back. There was something about Atwood she found unsettling.

The paperwork took about two hours to complete. Atwood instructed me to have her inspect it before I submitted it. She wanted to be sure to point out my mistakes. She hated the first draft. I had to correct eight items. On the second draft, I was ordered to correct three items. And on the third draft, I was commanded to correct five items, two of which were returned to how they were in the first draft. Finally, Atwood approved it.

I got up to leave. Atwood stopped me. She corralled Lowry and I behind one of the desks. A half-dozen other agents sat nearby, typing on their terminals. They didn't look at us, but their ears perked up.

Atwood spoke, her cold demeanor fully returned, "For disobeying a direct order, I tried to demote you to Sex Detail, Inspector Smith. Unfortunately, Chief Wyndham wouldn't approve it, so you're stuck here for now."

"Lucky me."

"You should be ashamed of your behavior. I knew you were a trouble-maker. As a senior Inspector, I had hoped you would teach Inspector Lowry the value of our safety regulations. Since you clearly have no desire to do so, I will have to do it myself. Inspector Lowry, from now on, you'll be partnered with me."

"I believe Smith and I were required to work together," she said.

"I went along with that because it was a request. However, as head of the department, I need Healthcare to run smoothly. I have the final decision when it comes to staffing issues. Therefore, I'm splitting you up."

Lowry became a sculpture. I yawned.

"Inspector Smith, starting tomorrow, you'll be with Inspector Zamyatan. You're dismissed."

I walked Lowry back to her car. I tried to console her, but she wouldn't speak. She took it harder than I expected. Atwood was bad, but she wasn't Huxley. Perhaps Healthcare Detail had been the wrong decision. Karma was laughing at us.

9

Zamyatan was parking the car. We had received a tip about a safety violation in a downtown office building. Upon our arrival, we found the parking situation was as dreadful as always. My partner dropped me off in front of the building, and told me to get started while he found a place to park.

It was early morning, but the sun was already blazing. I started to sweat the moment I exited the car. When he drove away from the curb, I pulled off my hat and fanned my face. I headed inside, through the revolving door, welcoming the cooler air.

The building was a high-rise, fifty stories tall, in the center of the city. The atrium looked like every other atrium: stone floor, a ceiling triple the height of a regular ceiling, and a panel of UV-shielded windows above the entrance. To the right was a small coffee stand. Near the back was a bank of elevators and an unmanned security desk.

Whoever was in charge of security would be in trouble if anyone discovered them absent. I hoped Zamyatan wouldn't notice. I wasn't looking forward to doing any extra paperwork today.

Between the elevators was an office directory. I read it, looking at the myriad companies crammed into the building. Which one were we here to investigate? I had no idea. I hadn't paid attention to Atwood this morning.

There was still no sign of my partner. I walked over to the coffee stand.

The barista, a 20 year-old kid with a minefield of acne on his face, asked, "What can I get you?"

"Irish coffee."

"Irish . . . coffee? I'm not sure what that is."

"It's regular coffee, but with whisky in it."

"Whisky? You mean alcohol?"

"You catch on fast."

"I'm sorry, sir, we don't serve whisky. Alcohol is illegal."

"Red wine is legal. It's good for your heart."

"Oh, I see. Would you like some red wine in your coffee?"

"Do you have any?"

"No."

"Then why did you ask?"

The barista's jaw moved up and down like he wanted to say something, but his brain couldn't process the conversation any longer.

"Just give me a regular coffee," I said, freeing him from his catatonia.

"Yes, sir." He began to fiddle with the coffee equipment.

I heard footfalls echo across the floor behind me. I turned around and saw Zamyatan. "You are already here," he said. "Good."

Zamyatan was a middle-aged man of average height with a ruddy complexion and a thick beard. His brown eyes were sunken deep into his skull. His dark hair was hidden beneath his bowler hat.

If he had any feelings about working with me, he didn't let them show. Unlike Atwood who struggled to stay balanced, Zamyatan had no emotions to convey. He was completely collected, and despite my efforts to engage him in conversation, his only interest was doing his job. He didn't want to make friends at work.

The barista finished the coffee. The cup was steaming. He popped on a secure plastic lid and handed it to me. As he did, I asked Zamyatan, "You want one? I'll buy."

"No. One should be enough," he replied.

"One?"

I hoped he didn't plan on sharing it.

"Yes," he said bluntly, taking the cup from my hand.

He popped off the plastic lid, and it clattered to the floor. Steam rose out of the cup in fat waves. Zamyatan reached inside his jacket and pulled out a long cylindrical device. He dropped it into the steaming liquid. A red digital readout appeared on the device. The first number displayed was fifteen. Quickly, the number began to rise: forty-eight, seventy-five, ninety, one hundred twenty two, and it finally stopped climbing at two hundred and thirty seven.

"Just as we suspected," Zamyatan said.

"What have we suspected?" I asked.

"This vendor is selling coffee that is too hot."

"What?" the barista said with disbelief.

Zamyatan put the cup on the counter. He focused his attention on the kid. He rattled off a series of questions. Meanwhile, I picked up the coffee and sipped it. It was definitely hot, but too hot? I couldn't recall a cup of coffee being too hot. At least not one that couldn't be remedied by cooling down for a minute or two.

"Why are you heating it this much?" Zamyatan asked.

"I'm just doing what I'm told," the kid answered, alarmed.

"Do you realize that overheated beverages violate safety statute 43-04-17?"

"No, I didn't, sir."

"So, what, you were just following orders?"

"Yes, sir, that's right."

"And where is your manager?"

"I don't know. It's his day off. He's probably at home."

"We will talk to him. Until then, your coffee stand is closed."

Zamyatan saw me drinking the coffee. "Smith, what are you doing?" he asked.

"Drinking my coffee," I said.

"That is evidence," he said, snatching it away.

"It won't be evidence once it cools down."

He picked the lid off the floor and secured it tightly over the cup. Meanwhile, the barista turned off his equipment and put up the "closed" sign.

Zamyatan and I walked to his car. I felt absurd. I had gone from sex cop to coffee cop. I couldn't believe my luck.

Zamyatan sat, statuesque, in the driver's seat, his hands resting in his lap while the Auto-Driver chauffeured us to our destination. For a while, I mused about Lowry, wondering how she was getting along with Atwood. After that, my mind lapsed into space.

The car pulled to a stop in a quiet neighborhood. The engine whined down, and I stepped onto the curb. A home, just like mine, stood modestly before us. The smell of fresh air filled my nostrils. Birds chirped in the distance. A gentle breeze blew across my brow. I closed my eyes, taking it all in.

Zamyatan marched toward the house. He rang the doorbell and rapped on the door. A moment later, a short, fat man appeared.

"Mr. Hartley?" Zamyatan asked.

"Yes? How can I help you?"

"We are Safety Inspectors with the Healthcare Department. We would like to ask you a few questions. Would you please come with us?"

"Uh, yes, sir," Hartley said timidly.

Zamyatan turned on his heel and strode past me. "Cuff him," he said brusquely.

Hartley lifted his wrists for the handcuffs. Instead of doing that, I motioned for him to follow me. When Zamyatan reached the car, he helped Hartley get inside. He must have seen Hartley wasn't wearing handcuffs, but he didn't say anything.

Back at the Central Office, we placed Hartley in an interrogation room. It consisted of nothing more than an overhead light and a chair. The walls were padded so suspects couldn't accidentally or deliberately harm themselves.

I stood in one corner of the room, my arms folded over my chest, and one leg kicked back against the wall. My partner began the interrogation. I wasn't interested in participating. This case redefined the concept of a waste of time.

"Were you aware the temperature of the coffee violated safety regulations?" Zamyatan asked.

Hartley shook his head furiously.

"Why did you make it so hot?"

"I was told to make it that way."

"And who told you that?"

"The owner, Mr. Karp."

"Did anyone complain about the coffee being too hot?"

"No."

"What temperature do you usually make it?"

"I don't know. Mr. Karp showed me how to make it, so I taught all of our baristas to do the same. We don't even look at the temperature."

"Why would he want it so hot?"

"He told me people liked it better that way. That it was more European."

"European? What is that?"

Zamyatan wasn't up on his history. Most agents weren't. My days spent in the Archives kept me well informed about all sorts of world history tidbits. Centuries ago, all the continents had different names, instead of the numbers they are assigned today. Continent Three was named Europe. That was before the First Government streamlined everything. It boggled the mind to imagine a time when there was more than one government, more than one language, more than one culture. How did people communicate? How did anything get done? It seemed like a fairy tale.

"I don't know what he meant," Hartley answered.

"Very well. We are going to keep you here until we can talk with your boss."

We headed out once more, the Auto-Driver shuttling us to another identical neighborhood. I checked my watch. It was the afternoon now. This coffee conspiracy was taking all day. We'd have an obscene amount of paperwork to complete.

Zamyatan knocked on the front door and rang the doorbell. We waited. I already knew everything that would happen next. Karp would peer at us sheepishly, Zamyatan would ask him a few questions, and Karp would say he didn't know he was doing anything wrong.

After a full minute, Zamyatan knocked again. I heard a dull scuffling from within the house. Someone was pacing, deciding whether or not to answer the door. Zamyatan knocked a third time.

The door opened. Karp looked out at us. His hair was a mess, and his eyes were fully dilated. His hand, which rested on the door, had a fine tremor. It looked like he was drinking too much of his own product.

"Mr. Karp?" Zamyatan asked.

"Yes?"

"We are Safety Inspectors with the Healthcare Department. We would like to ask you a few questions about your coffee stand."

"Please, come in," he said, swinging the door wide open.

Zamyatan peered inside. His eyes narrowed. He turned the offer over in his mind. He shook his head and said, "You will have to come with us."

Was he serious? Was he expecting an ambush from a coffee shop owner?

Karp stepped outside. "Of course, Inspector," he said as he pulled the door shut.

Zamyatan turned and walked past me. "Cuff him," he said brusquely.

"Let's go," I said to Karp while motioning toward the car.

He walked quickly, his rapid pace fueled by caffeine. Zamyatan had already reached the car, and was opening the back door. Karp was halfway down the sidewalk, headed for the vehicle. I shoved my hands in my pockets and wondered how many more people we'd have to arrest today. How far did the coffee conspiracy go?

Suddenly, Karp broke to the right, running fast, and speeding away.

"Go after him," Zamyatan said calmly.

I raced after Karp. Within moments, my heart was pounding, about to burst from my chest. The muscles in my rib cage tightened, and felt like a knife twisting in my side. I was huffing, already out of breath. The sweltering heat sent sweat pouring down my face.

Karp, about fifteen years younger than me, was gaining distance. There was no way I'd be able to catch him. I kept running, pumping my legs, and trying to ignore the pain that racked my body.

Ahead, the street turned into a T-junction. Karp veered right and shot off with greater speed than before. The guy was getting faster by the second. I was no match for him. I shouted something, but it came out an unintelligible gasp.

I rounded the corner. Karp's body looked small now. He must have been fifty yards ahead of me. My body was screaming. My lungs couldn't fill with enough air. My feet started to drag. My toes caught against the asphalt, and I slammed into the street. For an instant, I thought my face had imploded.

I felt a gust of air blow past my right side. Zamyatan's car zoomed by, quickly gaining on Karp. The car made a hard turn and braked. Karp hurtled into it. He hit the hood and tumbled over the vehicle. He collapsed on the hard pavement beyond.

I grabbed my hat and sat upright, my entire body aching. I stretched my back and heard the pop of vertebrae. I tried to stand up but found my legs would not cooperate. That was fine. I'd wait for Zamyatan to pick me up.

With Karp handcuffed and in the back seat, Zamyatan's car approached. The car stopped beside me. The window rolled down. Zamyatan poked his head out and scratched his beard. "Get in," he said stoically.

I hauled myself up, feeling pain run through my body anew. When I got inside the car, Zamyatan said, "That is why you handcuff them."

"Leg cuffs might have been better," I said.

Fortunately, we didn't have to track down any more suspects. Karp admitted to intentionally overheating the coffee because it would taste better. He said he got a lot of compliments from his customers. We eventually let Hartley go. Atwood was pleased with our arrest, and, as far as she was concerned, the coffee conspiracy was closed.

Even after all that work, Zamyatan didn't crack a smile. We sat across from each other, at a desk, dividing the paperwork evenly. It took hours to complete. We ended up leaving work late. As salaried employees, we did not get paid overtime.

10

I lumbered out to the parking lot. Lowry was nowhere in sight. I stood beside my car with one arm slung across the roof, and watched stragglers trickle out of the Central Office. Most had already left for the day, on time, as there was no reward for extra work.

On the far side of the lot, a larger group of agents were filing into the building. The night crew. Their faces were far less enthusiastic than the ones who were going home.

After a good thirty minutes of waiting, I decided I wasn't going to see Lowry. She must have slipped out before Zamyatan and I had finished our work. Now the only thing I had to look forward to was a night with my demon-dog and troll-wife.

I got in my car and punched in the coordinates for the diner I frequented. I ate alone, slowly chewing a bland piece of meat.

Once I finished choking down dinner, I trudged back to my car. I sat inside for a long time, the engine off. I watched the sun drop below the horizon. The sky turned fiery orange, then dusky purple, then dark black. Fluorescent lights continued to burn over every inch of the city. For the streets and sidewalks, it was always the middle of the day.

I started the engine. The electric motor whirred to life. I input a new set of coordinates. The vehicle maneuvered out of the parking lot and into the street, carefully minding all traffic laws.

Before me stood a solid brick building with an affixed sign reading, "Clothing Incorporated." The windows were dark. I walked toward the dormant factory, looking side to side, making certain no one was watching.

The front door was locked. I stepped off the sidewalk and walked to the right, alongside the building. When I reached what I thought was the manager's office window, I attempted to open it. It was locked, too. I headed to the rear of the building, trying, and failing, to open every door or window I encountered.

The back door didn't budge. I would have been inside already if I had my multi-tool. I would have to take a different approach. There was a long vertical window, at ground level, just to the right of the back door. I took off my hat and pressed it to the glass. I punched the hat as hard as I could.

I reeled back, clutching my hand as it throbbed with pain. The window, meanwhile, stood proudly, undamaged by my feeble attempt to break it.

With my hand still aching, I searched the ground for something to use. It was easy thanks to the bright lights that perpetually shined. Between the seams of the faux grass, I pried a hefty rock out of the ground. I faced the window and chucked the rock like a shot-put.

The rock passed through the glass like it wasn't even there. A dog began barking nearby. No doubt someone had heard that. I scrambled through the shattered window, stumbling inside.

I was in the factory now. The machines were eerie, shadowy hulks, devoid of life. I walked across the factory floor, headed for the manager's office. His office had caught my eye when I was last there. The items it contained were from another time. With his position and salary, he couldn't afford to be an antique collector.

After the manager's arrest, no agents bothered to search his office. It wasn't part of the routine procedure. Typically, offenders were caught in the act and prosecuted based on agent reports. There was little need for further investigation.

The wire cage fan on his desk was made of stainless steel. Its power cord stretched to some kind of homemade battery. I squatted down to get a better look at it. The rubber in the cord was frayed. It would shock anyone unlucky enough to touch it.

The battery was necessary because an old device like this wasn't compatible with the electromagnetic field. Why would someone risk owning such a blatant piece of contraband?

I rummaged through the manager's desk. It was filled with all sorts of ancient stuff: pens, gadgets, snack foods, and other miscellaneous items.

I opened a large filing cabinet and found something even more wondrous. It was a mechanical instrument, like something out of a science fiction story. It was similar in design to the terminals we used at work, except it didn't have a screen. It was a fat box with a keyboard, and a long black cylinder in the back. I slowly pushed down one of the keys, feeling a weighty resistance. As I did, a thin metal rod levered upward. I pushed it harder and the rod clacked against the cylinder. I smirked, amazed.

I walked back to my car, marveling at the manager's contraband. I wondered if Karp had been hiding any contraband with how strangely he had acted earlier. My instincts had panned out so far, so I thought I'd test them again.

Karp's house was on the other side of the city. It took nearly an hour to get there. He hadn't locked the front door when we picked him up, so entering posed no problem.

The inside of the house was clean. The kitchen was sparse save for a few bananas that had turned black with age. I opened the refrigerator but found nothing enticing inside. The living room's furniture was threadbare. Even so, it was nicer than the stuff in my house. There was no artwork on the walls, and there was no TV. Karp had been living a rather Spartan lifestyle.

Just before I entered the bedroom, I heard a noise. I stopped and listened.

Nothing.

"Hello?"

Silence.

It had probably been my imagination.

The bedroom was tidy. He had a twin-size bed with a single nightstand and a small lamp. This room was as plainly decorated as the rest of the house. Karp either didn't spend a lot of time here, or he didn't need a lot of material objects to be happy.

A quick look in the adjoining bathroom revealed nothing. I went back into the master bedroom. I moved toward the closed closet and stopped. I decided against it. There would be no point. His clothes would be just as uninteresting as the rest of the house.

I turned away and faced the portal between bedroom and living room. My hands were slack at my sides. I had hoped to uncover something extraordinary, but there was nothing here. Karp's only vice seemed to have been hot coffee. Too bad, because I had been in the mood for something excit–

My vision flashed bright white. The back of my head erupted like thunder. My balance was gone. I careened to the floor. For the second time today, my face hit the ground. Pain, so much pain. Footsteps thumped around me.

"Uuunnnhhh, hey," I slurred, raising my head.

Two men raced out of the room. Their backs were to me as they flew down the hallway. They disappeared. The front door slammed shut.

Slowly, I gathered myself from the floor. I rubbed the back of my head until the throbbing abated. I saw the closet doors were open. The clothes were pushed off to one side. Karp must have had something, and whoever those guys were, they had come for it.

I swiped my palms around the inner walls of the closet. I banged hard at a couple of places. I searched every inch, slowly making my way to the floor. After another bang, a floor panel bounced. I dug under it with my fingers and pried it open. The slot was just wide enough for a person to fit through. It was dark beneath.

I went in, feet first, slowly lowering myself, and groping blindly for the floor. I slithered in, my paunch barely scraping by. Down and down I went.

My feet hit dirt. It was completely dark except for the shaft of light that came in from the closet above. After a few seconds, my eyes adjusted to the darkness. There was something hanging just before me, a thin chain. I pulled it. With a click, a naked light bulb brightened.

The dugout was approximately twenty square feet in size. The height was about five feet, and I had to hunch forward. The walls and floor were dirt. The ceiling was the foundation of the house. Karp must have excavated this room. It would have taken years.

I looked around, my stomach fluttering with excitement. If those two goons hadn't attacked me, I never would have found this. I walked back and forth, taking in everything.

Shelves lined the dirt walls. Each shelf was carved out of soil with a thin piece of wood added for support. There were scraps of plastic wrapping and cardboard littering the shelves and floor. Whatever had been stored here previously was gone now.

As I made a final survey, my eye caught something. One of the shelves held a cardboard box. Part of the dirt shelf had given way, and soil partially obscured the box. Greedily, I pulled it away and ripped it open with my hands.

Inside, I found a dozen more boxes, colored blue and white. I lifted one out and read the label. They were boxes of salt. A single box was a ration for a family of four for an entire year. Karp had been storing contraband underneath his house.

And now it was mine.

11

I sipped my coffee, wishing it was hotter.

All of Healthcare Detail had swarmed onto Hospital Twelve. The facility was one of the major downtown healthcare centers. It was a gigantic building that served hundreds of patients a day.

Atwood walked at a brisk pace. The other agents hurried to keep up with her. I walked at my regular pace. I couldn't run because I would spill my coffee.

I was so tired from last night's investigation that I bought a cup of coffee from a Central Office vending machine. It tasted a month old and was lukewarm. Even so, I drank the sludge, eager for the caffeine to hit my brain.

At Healthcare Detail, Atwood pointed to the electronic map which displayed blueprints of Hospital Twelve. The map blinked and was replaced with the names and faces of three physicians. Atwood told us they were violating safety regulations and had to be arrested immediately. She assigned us each to a group of four. My team consisted of Zamyatan, Lowry, and Atwood herself.

Before the briefing adjourned, Atwood said, "This is a huge case, everyone. Career defining. Don't screw this up for me."

The other agents nodded in the affirmative. The bevy of people broke up and departed for the parking garage. My team piled into Zamyatan's car. Zamyatan took the driver's seat, Atwood the front passenger's seat, and Lowry and I were consigned to the back.

"Nice to see you again," I said to Lowry.

"Thanks," she said, looking slightly ill.

The Auto-Driver engaged and the vehicle took off. Atwood craned around and looked at me, stone-faced. "Don't get any ideas, Inspector Smith. I only put you with us so I could keep an eye on you. I don't want you ruining this."

"I wouldn't dream of it."

The car slowed as the hospital came in sight. We stopped at the front entrance. The electric motor shut off. Atwood was out of the car in a flash.

All of the agents were here now, clustered near the front doors. A few citizens goggled at our congregation. Everyone turned their attention to Atwood. "Remember your assignments. Do everything by the book and this should go flawlessly," she said.

The teams scrambled into the hospital, each team headed in a different direction. One team was positioned at each of the hospital's main entrances, one team monitored the elevators and stairwells, and one team went into the administration office. The last two teams, including my own, were tasked with the apprehension of our targets.

Despite racing to the elevator, Atwood was forced to wait. I continued my leisurely walk through the lobby. When I caught up with my teammates, the elevator doors slid open.

The eight of us piled in. My shoulders pressed tightly against two other agents. Lowry was squished somewhere in the back. A harmonious ding signaled our arrival on the sixth floor.

Atwood squeezed her way out of the elevator, made a right turn, and walked quickly down the hallway, her arms firmly planted against her sides. Everyone else struggled to get out of the elevator. They scurried after her.

Lowry exited last. I waited for her. "How've you been?" she asked.

"Good," I said. "I don't want you to get in trouble. You'd better catch up with the others."

She gave me a disappointed look, and then ran to catch up with the group.

I resumed my languid pace. I passed a sign that read, "Department of Internal Medicine." Ahead of me, the other seven agents bustled into the ward. They swarmed in and out of rooms. Their shouts echoed down the hallway. I walked around the Nurses Station. The nurses didn't notice me. They were flabbergasted. As I passed the patient rooms, I peeked in. People were in varying degrees of embarrassment or anger. Some were in bed, some were upright, some dressed, some naked. Atwood's raid and privacy infringement must have been a safety violation of some kind.

A crash rang out near the end of the hallway. It sounded like a metal tray hitting the floor. A moment later, a man in a long white coat flew out of a patient room. Zamyatan's arms were wrapped around his legs. The doctor waved his arms to catch his balance. He couldn't. He hit the floor, and his nose crunched. Zamyatan quickly handcuffed the doctor. The other agents surrounded them.

"Doctor," Atwood said in her usual monotone. "You are in direct violation of Safety Statute 99-45-99. You are under arrest."

Two agents hauled the doctor to his feet. The lower half of his face was smeared with blood. He looked dejected. He said nothing, only groaned.

"Take him away," Atwood said with a wave.

They escorted him to the elevator. By this time I had finally caught up with the cluster of agents. Lowry looked uneasy. The others masked their emotions.

"What did the doctor do?" I asked.

"Inspector Smith," Atwood said. "You had better learn the safety codes of this department. Now, let's get going."

Atwood started to walk, but stopped when she noticed a puddle of blood on the floor. With a slight tremble of agitation in her voice, she called out, "Does anybody know the penalty for a biohazard violation? Unless you want to find out, someone had better clean this up ASAP."

Atwood, Zamyatan, and the other two agents marched back to the elevators. A nurse swiftly cleaned the bloody floor. Lowry stayed behind and said, "He was prescribing a medication off-label."

"What was it?"

"He gave someone an antihistamine for sleep." She looked down the hallway and saw the others were nearly at the elevators. "We should hurry up."

I took another sip of my coffee. It had grown cold. I pitched it and followed Lowry.

With only six of us, the elevator was less cramped. Atwood stood across from me. I could see something smoldering behind her eyes. She noticed me scrutinizing her, straightened her posture, and blinked away the emotion.

The elevator dinged and we entered the thirteenth floor. The sign on the wall read, "Department of Geriatrics."

Events repeated themselves. The group ran down the hallway, intruded into patient rooms, and shouted menacingly for their target. I shook my head, still feeling fatigued. I should have called in sick today.

To the right of the Nurses Station was a little alcove. Standing there was a fresh pot of coffee. While the team continued their flurry of activity, I strolled over expectantly.

I began opening cabinets, looking for a cup. There weren't any, so I borrowed a mug that was in the sink. I rinsed it out as I heard a barrage of screams. There were bangs and shouts, and the din of footsteps racing back and forth. I poured the coffee, listening to the sweet sound the liquid made as it filled the mug. I took a sip. It was nice and hot.

Stepping toward the Nurses Station, I heard more commotion. I leaned one elbow against the station's desk. I raised my mug, drinking slowly.

The doctor they were after was causing quite a ruckus. He was yelling and running laps around an old man who stood, befuddled, in the middle of the hall. Another agent was chasing him in a circle. The doctor was knocking over everything he could find to trip his pursuer.

Atwood decided she had watched this display of buffoonery long enough. She drew her weapon and fired. She missed.

The electrodes struck the old man in the arm. He went stiff, and his eyes rolled back in his skull. When the pulse of energy stopped, he collapsed. The absurd circular chase halted. The doctor and agents gawked in disbelief. Atwood dropped her weapon, and then ripped Lowry's weapon out of its holster.

"Take this you bastard!" she shouted.

This time her shot hit the mark. The doctor's body danced with a surge of electricity. He, too, collapsed to the floor, partially over the unconscious patient. His white coat was singed black where the electrodes had buried themselves.

The two nameless agents collected the doctor and dragged him to the elevator. Atwood and Lowry retrieved their weapons. They walked toward me with Zamyatan close behind.

I swallowed the rest of my coffee in a single gulp. It burned its way down my throat. I set the mug onto the desk as the agents walked by.

"Seems like a lot of trouble for a prescription," I said.

"Prescription? Ha! That guy's a murderer!" Atwood said. She marched past me, her arms swinging. Color blushed in her cheeks.

I fell in with the group and walked beside Lowry. She had actually paid attention to the briefing this morning, and she knew the details of each offender. "He euthanized someone," she said.

"How could he? The law is clear that's illegal."

"The patient was ninety years old. Terminal cancer. Awful pain. He just had a stroke. He asked the doctor to end his suffering."

Our pace slowed. Atwood and Zamyatan continued onward, putting some distance between us and them. Lowry lowered her head and spoke more softly than usual.

"I don't know, Smith. I know what he did was a safety violation, but it feels like the right thing. Arresting him for helping someone, it feels wrong."

"I'm sorry, kid. We have a terrible job."

The next elevator ride was more comfortable. With four of us remaining, we had much more room. Above the doors, red digits blinked the floor numbers. As we ascended, Atwood said, "Inspector Smith, I want you to wait in the hallway by the elevator. I want you out of the way. But if you see the suspect, I want you to stop her. Can you handle that?"

"Sure. What's her name?"

"Doctor Bennett."

"What did she do?"

"Abortion."

The First Government, in their infinite wisdom, outlawed all abortions no matter what. Even if a pregnancy could harm the mother, everything had to be done to save the fetus. As far as I knew, no abortions had ever occurred in my lifetime. Now I knew why Atwood considered this a career defining case.

We walked onto the twentieth floor. The sign read, "Department of Obstetrics and Gynecology."

I followed the group until we reached the ward's entrance. I leaned against the wall and watched as the others resumed their hospital raid. With only three of them, it took much longer than before. They moved in and out of rooms, banging, running, and shouting. Atwood must have really wanted a promotion.

Behind me, I heard the whoosh of a flushing toilet. A minute or so later, a figure appeared on my right. She gasped.

I looked over and saw a tall woman with mousy brown hair wearing a long white coat. She had a plain but comforting face. An ID badge hung from the lapel of her coat. It featured a terrible photograph accompanied by her name: Dr. Bennett.

"What's happening, Inspector?" she asked.

I tipped my hat back. She had no idea we were here for her. I pushed myself away from the wall and said, "Don't be alarmed. They're looking for you."

"For me?" she asked, her voice becoming tremulous.

"It's okay," I said in my most soothing voice. "It's because of the abortion."

Her face blanched.

"Listen to me. Those other agents, all they care about are the rules. But I'm not like them. Tell me what happened."

"Well, I was on-call three nights ago. This girl came in. She was only fifteen. She had an ectopic pregnancy. Based on the location, she was going to die. I couldn't let her. I had to do something."

"You're saying that if you hadn't done it, the patient definitely would have died?"

She nodded and continued, "I know abortions are safety violations. I'd never done one before. But how could I just let her die? Isn't that a safety violation, too?"

Bennett had a point. A safety agent could just as easily arrest her for letting the patient die. Given the contradictions, I'm surprised anyone would want to be a physician.

I looked into the ward. The team had covered two-thirds of it. In a few minutes they would turn back. I didn't have much time.

"I'm sorry, doctor, but your career is over. If you want, I can spare you a lifetime in Safety Re-Education."

Her eyes turned to liquid, and she stared at me for what seemed like an eternity. At last, she nodded. With a growing sense of urgency, I said, "First, we need to ditch your clothes. Where can I get one of those hospital gowns?"

"The Clean Utility, down there," she said, pointing at the opposite end of the hall.

"Wait in the bathroom," I said.

I jogged to the end of the hall. The door to the Clean Utility was locked. I pulled out my multi-tool and set the device to its universal key setting. The lock clicked open and I entered.

There were several large bins holding clean sheets, clean gowns, and clean blankets. There were also a series of smaller bins that housed toothbrushes, combs, shampoo, and other personal care items. I grabbed a gown and an electric razor.

As I exited, I saw Atwood had reached the far end of the ward. Her face was bright red, and she was jumping up and down and screaming. She was too far away to notice me. I dashed into the bathroom.

"Doctor Bennett?"

She hesitantly poked her head out from one of the stalls.

"Put this on," I said, tossing the gown to her.

She grabbed it, and I turned around. I stared at the tile wall while she dressed. I heard the soft rustle of clothes. She said something doleful under her breath.

She told me she was finished. I turned back and realized I had grabbed the wrong size gown. It went down to her shins and billowed around her body. Her regular clothes were rumpled on the floor.

"The next part won't be fun. I'm sorry," I said.

I brandished the electric razor. Bennett kneeled in front of a toilet, and I hovered over her. The razor buzzed as it ran over the contours of her skull. Clumps of brown hair floated into the toilet bowl. Once her head was cleanly shaved, I flushed. I worried for a moment that the toilet would clog. Fortunately, it didn't.

I gathered Bennett's white coat, ID badge, and stethoscope. I stashed them in the toilet tank. I grabbed the rest of her clothes and said, "Let's get out of here."

We made our way to the door. Bennett caught a glimpse of herself in the mirror. She froze. The reflection gazing back at her was not the same person she was used to seeing.

"Come on," I said, pulling her out of the bathroom.

I looked down the hallway. Atwood was screaming at several nurses. She was halfway back. We had to move faster. I hurried to the Clean Utility and dropped Bennett's clothes down the laundry shoot. I raced back to the hallway. Bennett was standing in front of the elevator, twisting her hands together. I pressed the call button.

We waited.

And waited.

"Hey!"

Bennett's body shook with surprise. Atwood stormed up to me. "What the hell are you doing?" she shrieked.

"Watching for the doctor, just like you asked."

"And who's your friend?" she asked, eyeing Bennett. Bennett looked petrified. I tried to get Atwood's attention back on me.

"She's a Psych patient."

"Psych?" she asked.

"Wandered off the ward, I think."

"Oh? Well, where's her wrist band?"

All patients wore wrist bands to identify themselves. Atwood was turning back to Bennett again.

"She ate it," I said.

Atwood shifted back to me once more. She wrinkled her nose. "Ate it?"

"Yeah. Right in front of me. Craziest thing I've ever seen."

Bennett burped. The break in the tension made me want to double over with laughter. I somehow managed to restrain myself.

"Why'd you do that? What's wrong with you?" Atwood asked.

Bennett stiffened again under Atwood's laser vision.

"She can't talk," I said. "She's catatonic."

"Catatonic?"

"Yes, I believe that's what it's called."

The elevator dinged and the doors slid open. I grabbed Bennett by the arm and pulled her inside. "I was just about to take her back to the Psych ward. You don't mind, do you?" I asked.

"No, but hurry up. I need you here. We've got to find that damn doctor," Atwood grumbled.

"Yes, ma'am."

Atwood narrowed her eyes. I shouldn't have been so compliant. She must have thought something was up. I smacked the button for the lobby. The elevator doors closed, and the machine started its descent. Bennett and I both breathed sighs of relief.

"Is there a secret way out of here? One the agents won't be guarding?" I asked.

Bennett thought for a moment. "There's no secret exit, but the third floor has a bridge to the doctor's parking garage. They might not know about that."

"It's worth a try."

I punched the button for the third floor.

Bennett's hunch had been right. There weren't any agents guarding this area. We hustled across the connecting bridge and into the parking garage. It was a brightly lit behemoth of concrete walls and floors. Bennett's gray gown blended in nicely. I pointed to a corner of the garage and told her to hide there.

I backtracked, working my way down to the hospital's basement. It, too, was deserted. I went to the laundry room and found Bennett's clothes and shoes in the laundry shoot. I grabbed them and raced back. Going back up again, my luck held out. I didn't encounter any other agents. When I reached Bennett, she quickly changed her clothes.

The back of the garage had a stairwell that led to the street. We descended and escaped into an alley. Ten yards to the right was the street.

"This is as far as I can take you," I said.

"What should I do now?"

"Get a cab. Go to the train station. Get out of town. Pay cash. You'll have to start over, and you won't be a doctor again, but at least they won't find you."

"I can't believe this is happening."

"Do you have any family? Anyone you want to bring with you?"

She shook her head.

"Okay. Good luck."

I offered my hand for a shake. She wrapped her arms around me. She was sobbing. "Thank you. Thank you for everything."

I squeezed her. I couldn't recall the last time I had hugged someone. It felt nice. We couldn't stay here long, though. I pulled away and ushered her toward the street.

Bennett hailed a taxi. She opened the door and put one foot inside. She turned back and said, "I don't even know your name."

"I'm nobody."

Bennett waved before ducking into the vehicle. The taxi drove off. I didn't know how far she would get. I hoped, wherever she went, she would be safe.

Before I returned to the twentieth floor, I had to get a prop. It would help explain my prolonged absence.

The elevator doors opened. I walked to the Nurses Station. Atwood had transformed it into a command center. A dozen agents were present. She ordered them this way and that. Lowry sat in a chair off to one side, cradling her head in her hands, looking dazed. Zamyatan stood behind Atwood like a thick piece of oak.

"Smith!" Atwood shouted as I approached. "Where the hell were you?"

I raised my prop. "Cafeteria. Getting a cup of coffee."

She cursed at me, and then resumed her dictatorship. I stood outside the Nurses Station, drinking my coffee and feeling content. The agents tore the hospital apart. Eventually, Bennett's white coat was discovered. Bennett herself never was.

12

I was starving. It was one of those gnawing hungers. The kind that made me feel like my stomach was going to implode.

I rolled off the couch, still in a stupor. The clock on the wall said it was a few minutes after six. I usually didn't wake up this early, not on weekends. The house was filled with silence. I could have breakfast in peace.

I padded into the kitchen and flipped the oven on. As it heated, I walked toward the bathroom, ready for a shower. I ran both hands through my hair. It was standing upright. Sleeping on the couch always did that to me.

When I got home last night, later than usual, my troll-wife was already asleep in bed. She failed to turn off the blaring TV. The only way I'd get any sleep was by spending the night on the couch.

The hot water was refreshing. It cascaded down my body in waves. Washing my hair, I gingerly touched the back of my head. It stung. As much as it hurt, though, I wasn't mad. Those goons had done me a favor.

I turned off the water and returned to the bedroom. I didn't dare turn on the lights. My troll-wife was slumbering on the bed with the demon-dog beside her, its head resting on her chest. I silently grabbed clothes out of the closet and returned to the living room on tip-toes. I felt like a cat burglar.

Opening the refrigerator, I found a gleaming treasure. The loveliest steak I had ever seen. I bought it last night on my way home. I couldn't buy these things ahead of time. My troll-wife would always eat them.

I pulled out the thick cut of meat. It was a deep red hue with glistening white fat. My mouth flooded with saliva. I put it on the counter, and grabbed a carton of eggs. My body was electric with anticipation.

I seared both sides of the steak, and then put it in the oven. I cracked open two eggs and set them to cook in a pan. The house filled with the aroma of breakfast. I was in heaven.

Once the eggs were finished, I slid them out of the pan and onto the plate. I waited another minute before opening the oven and pulling out the steak. I pressed the meat with my finger. It was soft, medium-rare. I let the steak join the eggs on the plate.

At the kitchen table, I basked in the glory of the meal. But it wasn't quite ready. It needed a final touch. I had stowed something special in my inner jacket pocket. I slowly pulled it out, holding the small plastic cylinder above the plate. And then, I turned it over, shaking it. Fine white crystals of salt fell atop the steak and eggs. Now, they were perfect.

I carved out the first piece of meat. As I chewed, flavors surged to life in my mouth. If I were to die at this moment, it would be in a moment of bliss.

I heard a clicking noise. It was distant at first, but grew louder. I took another bite and looked at the kitchen's entrance. Standing there, short and fat, was the demon-dog.

It took a second for it to register what I was doing. It stared at me dumbly, and then its eyes lit up. It galloped toward me and crashed into my leg. Then it was up, standing on its hind legs. It panted hard. Its long tongue lolled out to one side.

"I'm not going to drop a piece of steak into your mouth, if that's what you're thinking," I said.

It started jumping at the plate.

"No!" I said, brushing the animal onto the floor.

The beast didn't give up easily. It was back, but jumping higher. Its paw hit the plate, making it rattle. I pushed the plate farther back on the table. I shoved the dog away, but it returned again. It was stubborn.

"Oh . . . I thought I smelled food," a voice said.

My troll-wife entered the kitchen. She looked like the walking dead. Her face was swollen and ashen. Her hair was dirty and tangled. Her belly stuck out so far, her shirt could not contain it.

"This is mine," I said firmly.

"Oh . . . I'll just have a bite," she said with her eyes zeroed-in on my meal.

A bite would involve her slobbering on everything. I grabbed the plate, but her hand shot out faster. She clutched the steak and ripped a huge chunk out with her teeth. Juices ran down the sides of her mouth. With a full mouth, she mumbled, "Oh . . . that's pretty good."

The demon-dog was leaping at her now. She dangled the steak in mid-air. "Oh . . . do you want a piece?" she asked.

I bolted from the table and snatched the steak back. I only had seconds to act. The demon-dog and troll-wife were coming back for more. Quickly, I sliced the rest of the meat off the bone. I stuffed all of it into my mouth.

"Oh . . . I wanted some more," she said.

The demon-dog started to bark at me. I turned my palms up, letting it know there was nothing left. This was what my life had become. I couldn't remember the last time I had a relaxing meal at home.

With the food gone, the interlopers lost interest and withdrew. I checked my watch. If I left now, I could reach the Archives by the time it opened.

Even though it was the weekend, I still wore my uniform. Once, I had tried to enter the Archives in casual clothes. They subjected me to an hour's worth of additional scrutiny. It wasn't worth the trouble to try it again.

The weekend security guard was just as lackadaisical as the usual guard. He was sketching something on a piece of paper. He looked at me, disinterested, and returned to his drawing. I passed through the security checkpoint without a problem.

Instead of descending to the stacks, I veered right and headed for the Acquisitions office. It was a small room. The front door was wood with a frosted piece of glass next to it to let in light. I rapped hard on the door. When it opened, I was met by a man who held a mug of coffee in one hand, and a piece of toast dangled from his mouth. "Can I help you?" he asked.

"I'm Inspector Smith. I'm here about your new book."

"Smith? Did you make an appointment?" he asked, the toast still between his teeth.

"No, but I called yesterday. Didn't I speak to you?"

"I don't remember speaking to anyone named Smith."

"Number 1872124482," I said grudgingly.

"Oh, yes, Number 1872124482. Now I remember. You wanted to look at the new acquisition."

"That's right."

"Come in."

He gulped down the rest of his toast, and ushered me into his office. He offered me a chair in front of his desk. He chased the toast with his coffee, and then sat down opposite me.

The desk was fastidious. A terminal was in one corner, a telephone in another, and his nameplate was at the front. Not a speck of dust could be found.

"Let's see," he said as he opened one of his desk drawers. He removed a fat tome and laid it squarely on the desktop. "We got this two days ago. I haven't had a chance to catalog it yet. I'm surprised to hear you're interested in such things. We get historians in here sometimes, but never Inspectors."

The book, hard-bound, had seen better days. The pages were discolored yellow. The binding was coming apart. The cover was crumbling. The title, faded but legible, read, "Contracting and You. An A-Z Guide to Building Everything."

"It's just a hobby of mine. I find pre-First Government architecture fascinating."

"Hmm, yes, I suppose it is. Everything was so non-uniform. The buildings were quite hideous."

Ignoring his remark, I asked, "May I?"

He removed a pair of white gloves from the desk. Once I had put them on, he slid the book toward me. I handled it carefully. The first few pages were no longer bound to the spine. In the

Table of Contents, something piqued my interested. Chapter Seven was titled, "Principles of Log Cabin Construction."

I turned to the center of the book. Although aged and weathered, the text was still readable. It was written in an archaic form of English, but I'd grown accustomed to deciphering this dialect over the years. The book provided a technical overview, assuming the reader already had some basic knowledge of construction work. I found it enthralling.

"What do you think?"

I looked up. In my excitement, I had forgotten about the other man. "It's fantastic," I said.

"I'm glad you like it."

He slid the book back toward him and stowed it. "Obviously, it needs a lot of restoration. If you like, I can contact you when it's finished."

I pulled off the gloves and tossed them onto the desk. "That would be fine."

"It's always nice to meet a fellow antiquarian," he said.

I thanked him and departed. Next, I went down to the stacks to spend some time reading. I thought I would try to find something different today. Perhaps botany. I neglected the science books, and decided I would try to visit them more often.

The bottom floor was as deserted as the rest. The shelves contained a thicker layer of dust here than anywhere else. All this knowledge and hardly anyone was interested. Why did the First Government bother to keep this stuff around?

I walked up and down the rows of books, perusing their titles. I chose a few at random and began to read. When I tired of science, I went to the literature section and read a few more books. There was one book in particular, about a father and daughter, which captured my attention. I read it from beginning to end.

I closed the back cover of the book. The air around me felt icy. I decided to go outside and warm up.

I wandered to a nearby park. A gentle wind ruffled the branches of a tree. Children chased each other around the park, wearing their required helmets and knee and elbow pads. I found a metal bench and sat down. I tilted my head back and let the sun's rays warm my face.

A few children tossed a rubber ball back and forth. A dog ran between them, trying to catch it. They giggled, and the dog barked with excitement.

I sat until my need to talk to someone outweighed my need to sit. I left the park in search of a telephone. Mobile phones had been outlawed ages ago due to their radiation emission. Now, phone booths stood on every street corner.

The booth's rickety metal door slid shut, attenuating the commotion of the outside world. I dialed Lowry's phone number. It rang several times. She answered with a breathless voice, "Hello?"

"Hi, Lowry, it's me, Smith."

"Hey, how are you?"

"Eh, I don't know."

"Are you all right?"

"I'm not sure what to do with myself. Maybe I'm bored."

"Being bored is a problem I wish I had."

"Why, what are you doing?"

"I've got a date later. A friend of mine set me up with a cute guy," she said enthusiastically.

My spirits flagged. I wasn't jealous of the date, I just liked her company. She was doing the usual thing people her age did. I shouldn't have been surprised. Of course she wanted to go out on dates. She didn't want to spend all day talking on the phone to some geezer.

"Okay, have fun," I said.

"Thanks. Have a good weeken–"

I hung up.

Hands deep in my pockets, I trundled along the sidewalks of the city. I walked until my legs burned and I couldn't walk any more. I found a busy restaurant and ate alone. All around me people dined with their families. I ignored them and concentrated on my food. After that, I walked a little farther.

13

The phone wouldn't stop ringing. Each time it squawked, Atwood's lips turned up into a snarl. It was time for the morning briefing, and she was handing out assignments. Each ring of the phone interrupted her concentration. While the other agents were clustered around her, I hung back, leaning against a desk, the phone behind me.

The phone cycled through a series of rings. It had done this three times. It would fall silent for about thirty seconds and then start up again. Like clockwork, when the thirty second interval was reached, it blared again.

She tried to ignore it and continue with the briefing. Agent X would be sent to investigate Location Y. Agent Q would be sent to apprehend Suspect Z. It was so exciting I could barely keep my eyes open.

After the twelfth ring, the phone quieted. Atwood prattled on, going down her list of agents. She went alphabetically. Zamyatan would be last, and wherever he was sent, I would have to tag along. When she reached his name, she said, "Inspector Zamyatan, you and your partner will be sent to Market Street. We've had a report from a dentist of a suspicious increase in cavities in the area. Go interview—"

The phone shouted.

Atwood's eye twitched. She stopped talking. She suppressed whatever emotion was bubbling inside her. She had managed to regain her icy countenance after the debacle at the hospital last week.

"Would someone answer that phone?" she asked.

I leaned back and scooped up the receiver. There was a worried voice on the other end. The caller spilled out information so fast I could barely make out the details. He reported an abnormality in his company's manufacturing system. Safety agents had a reputation for arresting first and asking questions later. Of course he was nervous.

I told him something reassuring and hung up the phone.

"What was it?" Atwood asked.

"Eastern District Wine Company reported a malfunction in their processing system. They think the wine may have elevated alcohol content. They want us to help them."

"Fine. I will take that case."

"I'm sorry, but I believe it's my case."

"Inspector Smith, I am the leader of this detail, and I choose the assignments."

"That's true, but regulations state that the agent who takes a call is assigned to the case automatically."

She quieted again. Her right eyelid fluttered, and the vein in her forehead protruded. She took a deep breath and her tic vanished. "Inspector Smith, I would like you to resign control of the case to me."

"I'm sorry, but you said we had to run this department by the book. So, I'd better take this one."

"Since when have you cared about the rules?"

"Since you taught me how important they are."

Her body quaked like a tree being bit by a chainsaw. The volume of her monotone voice rose slightly as she said, "Very well. But as your supervisor, I will be a part of this investigation."

"I guess the cavity crisis will have to wait until tomorrow."

Atwood dismissed the other agents. She, Zamyatan, Lowry, and I drove to the east. No one spoke during the ride. The winery was nestled against a rolling green hill on the outskirts of the city. It was a building just like all the others. The only difference was sprawling acres of grape vines growing over wood trellises.

The air was fresher here. The sky seemed closer. Being outside the city was always relaxing. These wine growers had a good thing going for them. Maybe I was in the wrong profession.

We trudged up the gravel driveway and entered the winery.

A thin man with a triangular head and a plume of bushy hair greeted us. He looked like a carrot. I recognized his voice from the phone.

"Hello, Inspectors. I'm so glad you're here. We have a terrible problem, and I don't know what to do."

"Your wine's alcohol content is too high?" Atwood asked.

"Yes, ma'am."

"Take me to it."

The carrot man escorted us through the homey front building and into the production area. We weaved a path through a maze of tall metal vats. The ambient temperature dropped the farther we walked. We reached our destination, a cramped room stuffed full of wooden casks.

The carrot man hefted a crate of wine bottles onto a deeply scratched table. "This is the first batch where we noticed it. A few customers called us to let us know they got intoxicated. They were worried about their safety," he said.

Zamyatan craned his neck around, looking in awe at the gallons upon gallons of wine surrounding us. So, Zamyatan had an interest in something, after all. Lowry shivered and rubbed the sides of her arms. I took off my suit jacket and handed it to her. She threw it over her shoulders. Atwood was completely unaffected by anything in the room.

The carrot man continued, "We used our AC meter to check the content. This batch and two others read four percent."

"Double the legal amount," Atwood said flatly.

"We were going to test everything, but our meter broke. It's going to be a month before we can get a new one. Of course, we don't want to send a tainted product to the consumers. I don't know what to do."

"Why not toss the whole lot and start over?"

The man shook with alarm. "No! We can't! We'd have no product for a year! We'd go out of business!"

"You'll just have to shut down production until you get a new meter."

"But, ma'am, that would kill us. Isn't there anything you can do?"

Atwood pondered this. Her bureaucratic mind could only comprehend following regulations. Problem solving was out of her scope.

"We could test it ourselves," I said.

All eyes in the room snapped toward me.

"Let's test each batch. If we don't get drunk, it's a clean batch. If we do get drunk, they can dispose of it. It might take all day, but we could really help these people."

"Inspector Smith, that is a preposterous idea," Atwood said.

"Yes, but we can't knowingly leave contraband behind. You know the regulations."

"Well . . . that's true . . . but . . ."

Zamyatan spoke, still eyeing the wooden casks, "It is not a bad idea."

"I should run this by headquarters," Atwood said.

"You're the head of Healthcare Detail. I'm sure they trust your judgment," I said.

"We do not want to waste time with unnecessary questions," Zamyatan said.

Atwood relinquished. "Very well." She turned to the carrot man and said, "Set us up in the front room. My colleagues appear to be cold."

A small room to the right of the entrance was reserved for wine tasting events. It was decorated with mahogany paneling and a shimmering hard wood floor. The bar was made of fine wood, and stretched end to end across the room. Near the bar were several square tables. Atwood and Zamyatan took a seat at one of the tables. Lowry and I sat at the bar. She took off my jacket and handed it back to me.

"What are you doing, Inspector Lowry? Come over here," Atwood said.

"The bar stool is better for my back," Lowry said, giving me a sideways glance.

"Don't think you can get out of work. I'll be watching you," Atwood replied.

The carrot man returned followed by a train of employees carrying crates of wine bottles. They stacked them in the center of the room. It was a mountain of alcohol. Employees opened the crates, and began to pull out one bottle from every crate. A bottle was placed before me, and I realized I hadn't thought this through. The more wine one drinks, the more intoxicated they become, regardless of the alcohol content. If Atwood had any brains, she would figure that out.

Deep red wine filled my glass. Lowry pulled her glass closer. Across the room, Atwood analyzed her glass. Zamyatan had already drained his first glass thirstily.

"Bottoms up," Lowry said.

We drank.

The Eastern District Wine Company made good wine. This was dry with an earthy taste. Wineries like this were the only operations sanctioned to manufacture alcohol. Red wine was the only legal alcoholic beverage on account of its positive cardiovascular effects.

I swiveled my bar stool and watched Zamyatan pour himself a second glass. He gulped it down as if he were dying of dehydration. Beside him, Atwood wrinkled her nose at the taste. She shook her head and tipped the rest of the glass into a basin.

"Do not waste it," Zamyatan said.

"It's disgusting," Atwood said.

"Whatever you are not going to drink, you can give to me."

"Fine."

Meanwhile, I removed my multi-tool and placed it on the surface of the bar. I pressed a small round button on the top. Although it was quiet, I heard the device click and whir.

Zamyatan was on his third glass. Atwood opened the next bottle and tasted the contents. She pushed the glass away and reached for the next one. Zamyatan took her discarded glass and drained it. This was going to take a while.

Crate after crate was opened. Bottle after bottle was uncorked. Atwood took a few sips from each glass. Zamyatan drank the rest. Lowry drank casually, enjoying the wine, but not overdoing it. I drank one glass and then stopped.

The carrot man came back several times, and each time Atwood shooed him away. The compounding effect of the alcohol was getting to her. She looked looser. She swayed in her chair, her monotone went away, and her words began to slur. Beside her, Zamyatan kept hammering down drinks. He was reeling.

Lowry poured herself another glass. Before she could take a drink, I put my hand on her arm. I shook my head. She looked at the glass, then at Atwood and Zamyatan. When she looked back at me, I could tell she understood.

The hours flew by. The sun arced across the sky, and was now beginning a downward trajectory. The blue sky became streaked with orange hues.

Suddenly, there was a crash. Zamyatan's head hit the table. Several glasses fell over, splashing wine. A bottle toppled, rolled off the table, and shattered on the floor. The carrot man barged into the room. "What happened?!"

"It's the wine!" Atwood bellowed. She tried to stand, but her feet got caught in the legs of her chair. She sat back down with a heavy thud. "Ya guys've been puttin' too much alc'hol innit. We're gonna hafta shut ya down."

"Oh, no!" the man said. "That's why I called you. So you wouldn't shut us down."

"Don't worry, sir, you'll stay open," I said.

"The hell d'ya know, Smith? Ya ain't in charge of this detail. I am. Yer jus' a piece of trash who'll never 'mount to anythin'."

Atwood stood again, knocking her chair to the floor. She shook Zamyatan by the shoulder. He didn't stir. She shook harder, and he began to snore.

"I think he's had too much," Lowry said.

"Shut up, bitch!" Atwood roared, staggering sideways.

"I think this case is closed," I said.

"This is my show, and it's over when I say it is."

Atwood picked up a bottle and turned it upside down. A single drop fell out. Atwood contorted her face and said, "A'right, we're done. Le's go."

I walked over to the table and hefted Zamyatan. The bastard was heavy. He awoke enough to totter, with my support, across the room. On the way out of the building, Atwood glared at the carrot man and said, "You'll be hearin' from us."

When I passed him, I said, "No, you won't."

Lowry grabbed my multi-tool and pocketed it while I slogged outside with Zamyatan. The carrot man was left behind in astonishment. Once we got into the car, the Auto-Driver carried us back to the Central Office.

The vehicle pulled into a parking space and the engine powered down. Zamyatan was snoring in the front. Atwood sat next to him, in the driver's seat. She turned around and said, "Le's get inside. I want yer reports on my desk b'fore the end of shift."

The three of us exited, leaving Zamyatan inside to sleep it off. Atwood took the lead, but she kept listing off course. Had she never been drunk before?

Atwood made it to her desk and slumped into her chair. She cradled her head in her hands. She groaned slightly. No one else was back from the day's assignments. The Central Office was subdued.

Lowry handed me the multi-tool. Turning it over and over in my right hand, I casually walked over to Atwood.

"You know, that was something else," I said.

"Wha?"

"You and Zamyatan getting drunk like that. I've never seen anything like it."

"That place's obv'yusly making their wine too strong. Fir' thing tomorruh, I'm headin' over there to shut 'em down."

"How are you feeling?"

"My head's numb."

"Nothing quite like it, is there?"

"Dammit, Smith. Ya knew this'd happen. I'm writin' ya up."

"Something tells me the bosses are going to be much more interested in my report. The one detailing how you got drunk on the job."

"Who they gonna b'lieve? My record's flawless."

"Perhaps. But my video will change that."

"Vidyo?" Atwood asked with concern washing over her face.

"I'm going to submit my report just like you ordered. And I'll include this."

Lowry had a terminal ready. I plugged the multi-tool into the terminal, and hit a few buttons on the keyboard. A video played on the screen. It was the recording of Zamyatan and Atwood getting drunk over the course of the day. Atwood's already pale face drained to the color of snow.

"The quality on these things is incredible. Oh, this is my favorite part," I said. We watched Zamyatan crash onto the table, and Atwood stumble around and yell at the carrot man. I stopped the playback and tucked the multi-tool into my pocket.

"Smith, wait, ya wouldn't," she said.

"I would."

"Please. My career. Wha' kin I do?"

"I'm sorry, but I have to report your unbecoming conduct. After all, it's regulation."

"Smith. Please. I'll do anythin'," she groveled.

"Sorry. Rules are rules."

Atwood buckled to the floor and cried. When the other agents returned they gave her peculiar looks, but nobody bothered to ask her what was wrong. The rapport she had built with the team was outstanding.

The next day, as expected, I was called into the Chief's office. The Chief's name was London. His office was in much better shape than Wyndham's. It was brightly lit, tastefully decorated, and had recently gotten a fresh coat of paint. His desk was devoid of clutter.

London was impeccably dressed. He wore a pair of small round glasses. His black hair was slicked back. He was reading a report on his terminal when I entered.

"Ah, yes, Smith, please sit down," he said, gesturing to a chair in front of his desk.

The chair was comfortable.

"I read your report. It was very interesting."

"Which part?"

"Inspector Atwood's behavior."

"It wasn't exactly regulation."

London shook his head and said, "No, not at all. I'm afraid I can't tolerate that kind of behavior. Healthcare Detail has a spotless record. I am not about to let someone like that ruin its good reputation."

"What will happen to her?"

"A demotion. I was thinking Sewage Detail."

"If I may, sir, Sex Detail is down two members. They could use another person," I said. I figured Huxley and the Icequeen would get along famously.

He considered this and his face brightened. "Excellent idea, Smith."

"And what about Zamyatan?"

London steepled his fingers beneath his chin and pursed his lips. "He'll have to be dealt with, of course. Perhaps he should join Inspector Atwood in Sex Detail?"

"Sir, Zamyatan is a good agent. He just got caught up in Atwood's debauchery. Maybe you could discipline him, but let him stay in the department?"

"You worked with him. If you think he's good, I'll let him stay. Now, there's the matter of what to do about you."

I felt a little bad about what happened to Zamyatan. He ended up as collateral damage. On the other hand, no one had forced him to drink that much. At least I was able to save him from working with Huxley.

London continued, "Your intuition and dedication to this job is outstanding. I'm pleased to offer you a promotion."

I hadn't expected that.

He went on, "You handled this situation exceptionally well. Your talents are being wasted here. So, first thing tomorrow, I want you to report to Prohibition Detail. Congratulations, Smith."

"Thank you, sir. Can I make a request?"

"Name it."

"My partner, Lowry, helped me with this investigation. She is as responsible for the positive outcome as me. I was hoping she could come along."

London clacked a few keys on his terminal. He pulled up Lowry's file. He perused it and said, "I don't know. She's a rookie. She's not ready for such an important assignment."

A few minutes with London had clued me in on his weakness. I leaned forward and said, "Yes, I realize that. But she's been my partner since her first day. I decided to take her under my wing and train her to be an outstanding agent. I wouldn't want her languishing with another partner. Especially one who may not be as dedicated to the rules as I am."

London folded his hands together. He cocked his head to one side and said, "Very well. I'd hate to see her flounder under the tutelage of a lesser Inspector. Tell her to report to Prohibition Detail with you."

That had been surprisingly easy. Maybe I had been going through this thing the wrong way all these years. Lying and sucking up had gotten me further in a few moments than hard work and honesty had in decades.

14

Lowry was my good luck charm. I had been caught in a downward spiral, but the day she arrived, my life took an upward trajectory.

I was about to enter the Central Office when I turned back and saw her. I couldn't help but smile. She waved enthusiastically. "Hi, Smith," she said as she reached me.

"Ready for our new assignment?"

"I'm ready for anything."

We went inside and performed the morning ritual of collecting our equipment through a nauseating regurgitation of identifying information. When we were finished with that, we adjourned to the central hub of the building.

The room was a sea of black. An incalculable number of people in identical black suits bustled about. I looked over the array of signs that hung from the ceiling. Prohibition Detail was in the farthest corner of the room.

The department was arranged like all the others: an electronic map, several desks, and a collection of disinterested employees. One agent hunkered over a terminal, typing, with dark rings under his eyes. He must have been a holdover from the night shift.

Sitting at a desk was a chubby man with thin hair and thick glasses. He was perusing a magazine. Piles of paper were stacked on the desk, and he ignored them like a pro. A placard read, "Bradbury."

"Agents Smith and Lowry, reporting," I said.

Bradbury looked up at us with casual disinterest. "You need something?"

"We're new to the detail," I said.

"What are your names?"

"I'm Smith. She's Lowry."

"Huh. I'm not sure I got any paperwork on transfers."

"It happened yesterday," Lowry said.

"Okay, I'll take your word for it," Bradbury said. He returned to his magazine.

"Do you have an assignment for us?" I asked.

He sighed and said, "Check the terminal. There should be some open cases. Pick whichever one you want."

Lowry grinned. I thanked our apathetic supervisor before stepping away.

"I like this detail. Let's stay here awhile," Lowry said.

I grabbed a terminal, logged in, and scrolled through the active cases. There were over three dozen pending investigations. Bradbury didn't run a tight ship.

"Any of these cases sound good to you?" I asked.

"Nah. Let's get some coffee."

"I agree, but we should pick one. Last time I went too long without a case load, I almost went crazy from boredom."

Lowry closed her eyes and pointed to the tiny screen at random. Her finger fell upon a case marked, "5534A – Residential – Lawn Equipment."

"Lawn equipment? Nice pick." I tagged ourselves to the case and said, "All right, let's get that coffee."

We drove to our usual diner. The parking lot was deserted. The inside of the building was dark. Affixed to the door was a note reading, "Closed by Healthcare Department until further notice."

"You don't think . . . Atwood?" Lowry asked.

"No, she's history. It's unrelated."

"Well, now what?"

I had an idea, but I hesitated to bring it up. I wrestled with the notion for a bit, and then said, "We could go to my house. I've got coffee there."

"That sounds great. What's the matter?"

"It's just – my wife – she's a little – disgusting."

"After Huxley, how bad can she be?"

I chortled. We got back into the car and drove to my house.

I pushed the door open and peered inside. It was strangely calm within. The TV was off, the demon-dog was absent, and my troll-wife was nowhere to be seen. I checked my watch and saw it was only half-past nine. She never left the house early. Where was she?

"Looks clear," I said.

Lowry followed me, asking, "Why do we have to sneak around your own house?"

"If you meet my wife, you'll understand."

We crept into the kitchen, side-stepping the chaos of trash and dismembered animal toys. My face flushed hot with embarrassment. Lowry gaped at the disarray. I tried to redirect her. "The coffee pot is over here."

I pulled fresh beans from the cabinet. I ground the beans and ran them through the filter. The coffee maker chugged and sputtered. Steam rose toward the ceiling. Deep brown liquid dripped into the glass carafe.

Making small-talk, Lowry asked, "How long have you lived here?"

"Since the required marriage."

"Oh. It's . . . nice."

"It's a dump."

"I was just trying to be nice."

"It's okay, you don't have to. I hate living here. I hate all the houses in this goddamn city. They're all exactly the same."

"Hey, look, coffee's ready," Lowry said abruptly.

A small patio lay on the other side of a sliding glass door. We took our drinks outside. Lowry blew on hers, cooling the liquid. I stared toward the horizon and took a large gulp. A minute passed. Then another. The silence stretched on.

"Do you have any kids?" Lowry blurted out.

"No, but I always wanted a daughter."

"So why didn't you?"

"The marriage."

"You and your wife can't have kids?"

"It's not that."

"Too bad. I love kids. They're so much fun."

There was a sudden bang from behind. We both turned around. My troll-wife came galumphing into the kitchen. She held a bulging paper sack in her arms. The demon-dog was close at her heels, bouncing with excitement. She dropped the sack onto the kitchen counter with a heavy thud. She saw us and walked onto the patio.

"Oh . . . who's this?" she asked, pointing at Lowry.

"My partner," I said.

"Pleased to meet you," Lowry said, extending her hand.

My troll-wife shook her hand and snorted grotesquely. When the handshake ended, Lowry noticed a slimy film had attached itself to her palm. She wiped her hand vigorously on her pants. My troll-wife was oblivious.

"What's in the bag?" I asked, knowing the answer would not be good.

"Oh . . . I just got done grocery shopping."

"What did you buy?"

"Oh . . . they had a sale on ice cream. I was able to get six gallons."

"Six gallons? How? We're only regulated a half-gallon per month."

"Oh . . . I used the rest of the grocery money to pay off the cashier. He pretended each item was for a different customer."

"Did you get anything else? Any food?"

My troll-wife lost interest in the conversation. She lumbered back to the kitchen and tore open a container of ice cream. She ate from the carton, scooping with her fingers.

"Two weeks of grocery money was spent on ice cream and a bribe," I grumbled.

Flummoxed, Lowry asked, "How could you marry . . . *that?*"

"I didn't have a choice. It was the Lottery."

The Lottery was the nickname of the automated government-run marital arrangement system. Numerous studies have shown that married people live longer, happier lives, and have fewer medical problems. It was safer to be married than single. By law, any person who is still single by age thirty-five must enter the Lottery and be paired up with a person of the opposite sex. Divorce carried risks for worsening health and suicide, and was therefore illegal.

"I figured, how bad could she be? But as soon as I saw her, I realized I shouldn't have been so picky when I was dating."

"Yeah. Guess I should think about that."

I took another gulp of my coffee. It had lost its flavor. I poured it onto the faux grass. "Let's get out of here," I said.

I suggested we go back to the Archives. Upon entering the building, I saw the usual security guard was absent. A menacing man, sitting at full attention, was behind the security desk. His eyes locked onto us and never blinked.

"Name and serial number," he said sharply.

I gave mine and he entered the information into his terminal. "Hand print ID," he said.

As I had done many times before, I pressed my palm against the flashing screen. The device's light changed to green.

"Go through the scanner," he commanded.

I stepped into the machine and it blinked green. "You're clear. Next!" he said.

Lowry told him her name and serial number. He punched the keys of his terminal and frowned deeply. "I'm sorry, ma'am, but you aren't authorized to enter."

I stepped back through the scanner and said, "It's all right, she's with me."

"Please stay out of this, sir," the guard said with a scowl.

"There must be a mistake. We're with Prohibition Detail," Lowry said.

He checked the terminal again. "No, ma'am, no mistake. You don't have clearance."

I walked up to the desk and said, "Listen, we're both with Prohibition, and we need to use the Archives for a case. You wouldn't want to be responsible for holding up an investigation, would you?"

The guard stood up, revealing his colossal frame. "Sir, you need to step away from the desk," he said sternly.

Lowry started, "This is a misunderstanding. If you just call—"

"Where's the usual guy?" I interrupted.

"What?" the guard asked.

"The usual security guard. Where is he?"

"Sir, I'm warning you for the last time. Back away. I will use force if necessary."

"You will? I'd love to see that. Those muscles of yours are awfully big."

The guard fumed. His body rippled with tension. His hands squeezed into fists that looked like boulders. He stepped around the desk.

Lowry wrapped her hands around my arm and pulled me away. "We're sorry," she said. "We'll go take care of our clearance issue. Thank you for understanding."

Before I knew it, we were back on the front steps of the building. "What the hell was that?" I asked.

"Smith, that guy was going to murder you."

"I can handle myself."

"I know. But we just made Prohibition Detail. Let's not screw it up yet."

I sighed. She had a point.

"Thanks, Lowry. Come on, let's go get you clearance. Then we can shove it in that jerk's face."

Lowry gave me a reluctant smile.

We drove back to the Central Office. It was still the middle of the morning, so traffic was light. Once we arrived, we descended to the bowels of the structure. We entered the Security Department. It was electric with activity. At the front of the room was a desk with a severe looking woman sitting behind it.

"Can I help you?" she asked, peering over her half-moon glasses.

"I'm Lowry with Prohibition Detail. I need to have my security clearance increased."

"Reason?"

"To enter the Archives."

"Serial number?"

"4471331744."

A palindrome. How odd.

"What's your name again?" the woman asked.

"L-O-W-R-Y."

"Yes, here it is. I'm sorry, but you don't have clearance for the Archives."

Lowry gave a twisted smile and replied, "Yes, I know. I need to *get* clearance."

"You want clearance?"

"Yes."

"Then you need to go to the ID Office. They handle that."

"Okay, thank you."

We headed upstairs. "That was a waste of time," Lowry groaned.

"Of course, it's the government," I said.

On the top floor we found the ID Office. The layout was the same as the Security Department. The only difference was the front desk was staffed by a man shoving doughnuts into his face. Judging by how many he was eating, he was well over the ration limit.

"Can I help you?" he asked, his voice muffled by food.

"I'm Lowry with Prohibition Detail. I need clearance for the Archives."

"Serial number?"

"4471331744."

He clattered at his terminal, leaving sticky doughnut residue on the keys. After a minute or so, he looked up and said, "Sorry, your name isn't associated with that serial number."

"What?"

"You gave me the wrong name. The name attached to that serial number isn't Lawrence. It's Lowry."

"That's me. I'm Lowry."

"I'll need to see your ID."

Lowry started muttering obscenities under her breath. She pulled out her ID and showed it to him. When he handed it back, it was covered in sticky fingerprints. "Well?" Lowry asked, annoyed.

"We only give out new IDs. For the actual clearance, you'll need to go downstairs. To the Security Department."

"We were just there. They sent us up here," I interjected, to prevent Lowry's head from exploding.

"I'm sorry, but I can't help until they clear her first."

"If you knew you couldn't help me, then why did you ask to see my ID?" Lowry asked.

He smiled deviously and said, "I wanted to check your marital status. Would you like to go out sometime?"

Lowry gave a single, hearty, "Ha!" and walked away.

"Sorry, pal," I said.

We tramped back downstairs and met the severe woman again. "Can I help you?" she asked.

"You sent us upstairs, but they said your department needs to change my clearance," Lowry said.

"What? Who are you?"

Lowry's face turned bright red. Through gritted teeth, she said, "Lowry. 4471331744. Prohibition. I need new security clearance."

"You'll need to go upstairs to the ID—"

"I was just up there!" The words shot out of her like bullets from a machine gun. *"They said you change clearances and they print cards! They sent me back to you!"*

"Oh, you want clearance. Fill out these forms."

The woman hefted a stack of paper fifty pages thick and pressed it into Lowry's hands. Lowry's grip tightened, and the pages crinkled at the edges. She freed one hand. It drifted down toward her weapon.

I grabbed Lowry's arm and pulled her away. "Thank you, ma'am. We'll fill these out and bring them back," I said.

I steered Lowry into the hallway. She was breathing heavily. We sat on a bench and waited for her breathing to slow and her face to turn back to its usual color. "Thanks, Smith," she said.

"No problem. Give me half of those. We'll work on it together."

We spent the rest of the morning filling out Lowry's paperwork. After turning it in, Lowry was subjected to several hours of waiting, fingerprint scanning, waiting, picture taking, waiting, going back to the ID Office for a new badge, and more waiting. It was nearly five o'clock when she finished.

She dragged herself out of the main building like a pummeled boxer. "If it's all right with you, I'm going to head home."

"See you tomorrow," I said.

Lowry departed.

I wasn't sure what to do with myself. I couldn't go home for dinner, not unless I wanted to eat ice cream. I drove around the city for about an hour, and then ate at a random restaurant. After that, I returned to the Archives. The security guard from this morning was gone. The night guard barely glanced at me when I entered.

15

"My partner cracked."

"Cracked?"

"Went insane."

"What happened?"

"I don't know. Two days ago, he was doing paperwork, and his terminal froze. He lost all his data. After that, he started smashing everything."

I looked at Bradbury's desk. That explained the foot-shaped dent in the wood. I turned back to Takami, one of the night shift agents. His face was haggard with exhaustion.

On my way into work, I had nodded hello to him, expecting him to do the same and depart. To my surprise, he struck up a conversation. The story gushed out of him. He must have been dying to tell someone. Mid-way through his tale, Lowry arrived and listened with fascination.

"Where is he now?" I asked.

"The asylum, where else?" he said glumly.

"I'm sorry to hear that."

"Anyway, my partner and I were going to bring in a suspect today. We've been working this case for a couple of weeks. I want to finish it."

"Yeah, you should. Good luck."

"You think you could help?"

The last thing I wanted to do was lend a hand to a sleep-deprived night shift agent who was depressed about losing his insane partner.

"It won't be hard," Takami said. "I just need a hand bringing in the suspect."

Lowry was beside me, grinning and nodding. She wanted to help. I couldn't imagine why.

"Okay," I said, relenting.

"Great, thanks a lot."

"But you'll do all the paperwork."

"Yes, of course."

"So, where are we headed?"

"Central Corridor. Church Four."

Lowry was beaming for some reason. It couldn't have been the work. It must have been something else.

"What's wrong with you?" I asked.

She tilted her head and replied, "It's nothing."

We piled into Takami's vehicle. He used the Auto-Driver. I sat in the back, and Lowry and Takami sat in front. She kept asking him random questions, some about his case, some about himself. He responded in grunts and half-hearted answers.

The Central Corridor was the downtown part of the city. It was teeming with people hurrying about their mundane lives. Most of the buildings were skyscrapers, designed in the same blocky, utilitarian style.

Nestled between two towering buildings was a much smaller structure. It was only two stories tall. It was, of course, a large, flat rectangle, but it had a round stained-glass window above the entrance. The design on the window was the emblem of the world's religion.

The interior of Church Four was sparsely decorated. There were pews on either side of a long, narrow aisle. At the end was a raised dais with a table that held a few religious artifacts. Takami stalked down the aisle with powerful energy, fueled by the excitement of closing his case.

"Safety Inspectors!" Takami shouted.

He reached the dais and banged the table with his fist. He shouted again. A door opened somewhere. Footsteps echoed off the stone floor as someone approached. A man, wearing the typical religious garb, appeared.

"Yes?" he asked.

"Are you the head of this church?"

"The First Government is the head of the chur–"

"Shut up. You know what I mean," Takami barked.

"Yes, Inspector, I'm Clergyman Dick, head of Church Four."

"We're going to conduct a search. Show us your chambers."

Dick escorted us to the rear of the church. His office was a small, warm room, pleasantly decorated with a plush red carpet, thick gold curtains, and a wooden desk. A substantial bookshelf, filled to the brim, stood proudly behind the desk. A well-worn couch sat along the right side of the room.

Takami made a beeline for the bookshelf. A few feet behind him, I squinted, trying to make out the small titles on the book spines. They were all standard religious texts. Some historical, some philosophical, but all state approved.

Takami whirled around. "Where are the rest?"

"The rest?" Dick asked.

"The rest of the books. The contraband."

Dick turned his palms up and said, "I'm sorry, Inspector, but this is all I have."

"Smith, Lowry, watch him. I'm gonna look around," Takami growled.

He stormed out of the chamber. With starry eyes, Lowry said, "I'm going to help him."

She floated out of the room.

Dick turned to me and asked, "Would you mind if I had a seat?"

"Go ahead."

He walked around his desk and sat in a swivel chair. He offered me a seat in one of the two chairs opposite him. I sat on the couch instead.

"She seems quite taken with your partner."

"I suppose. It won't work out."

"And why's that?"

"She's not his type."

"A playboy?"

"You could say that."

"If I may, your partner seems a bit volatile."

"He's had it rough. His partner got sent to the asylum. I'm just filling in."

I reclined, sinking into the worn fabric. I looked around the room. It was spotless. He spoke again, "Are you quite sure you've got the right church?"

"I don't know. It's his case."

"Inspector, you seem uncomfortable."

"Quite the opposite."

"No, I mean being in here. I can see it on your face. When was the last time you attended service?" he asked.

"Every week," I said. "Just like the law requires."

"Inspector, you're going to lie to me? In a church?"

"All right, it's been a couple of years."

"And why's that?"

"I don't see the point."

"You should know better than anyone. Those with religious beliefs have lower rates of depression and medical problems. They live longer, healthier lives."

"Going to church and having religious beliefs are two different things."

"Perhaps. But why take the risk?"

"I'm not going to worship a state mandated deity just because they say so."

"Do you see the irony, Inspector? One who enforces safety regulations but doesn't follow them himself?"

"Are you going to turn me in?" I asked nonchalantly.

"Of course not. I'm just worried about you. We're children of the First Government. I want what's best for all of us."

The chamber door slammed open. Takami rushed in with Lowry at his heels. He shoved his index finger into Dick's face. "Where is it? Where's the contraband?"

"Inspector, please, as I told you before, I don't have anything illegal. I'm a law-abiding citizen."

Takami held out his other hand. Lowry slapped a pair of binoculars into it, set to the X-ray function. He examined every molecule of the room. As he did, Dick started to look nervous. Takami's gaze settled on the bookshelf.

"You can see for yourself, all those books are legitimate," Dick said nervously.

"There's another bookshelf behind this one!" Takami said with equal amounts of anger and glee. He dropped the binoculars and asked, "How do we get back there?"

"I don't know what you're talking about."

Takami cursed. He grabbed a book with each hand and flung them backward. One almost hit me in the head. I shouted at him, but he didn't hear me. He tore out the books, trying to claw his way through the bookshelf.

The back of the shelf was made of flimsy wood. Takami raised a fist and sent it crashing through. When he drew his fist back, it was scraped and bleeding. He left behind a hole which revealed a secret room.

Takami reached in with both hands and began to tear out the flimsy wood. Soon, the secret room came into full view. Takami kicked at the paneling, knocking out huge chunks. He gave a triumphant roar and pushed into the secret room. The chamber looked like a construction site. Books, fragments of wood, and dust were thrown about.

Dick stood and and inched his way around the desk. I didn't have the energy to chase after him. I rose and blocked the exit.

Enough light from the chamber poured into the secret room to make its contents visible. Lining each of the three walls were bookshelves. Takami ripped books out of their resting places and screamed, *"This shit! We've got you now, you bastard!"*

Takami flung book after book into the chamber. They landed haphazardly. They were texts on all the world's defunct religious cults: Christianity, Judaism, Islam, Buddhism, Hinduism, Voodoo,

Taoism, Shintoism, and more. There were so many. It was a library full of the history of world religion.

Takami walked up to Dick and threw one of the texts at him. "What were you doing with all this contraband?"

Dick winced as the book glanced off his shoulder. "I was studying them."

"You can't study these. What good are they? Some weird, ancient religions."

"It was purely for academic interest."

"Yeah, well, you're still in violation of safety statute 16-49-93. You're in big trouble."

"All right, Takami, stop badgering him," I said.

"Stay out of this, Smith."

I grabbed Takami by his arm and spun him around. I shoved him against an undamaged part of the bookshelf. It rattled, and a book fell to the floor. "Listen, you're acting like a maniac. We've made the arrest. That's enough."

Takami looked at Dick and then back at me. He huffed, "Fine. Let's bring him in. Lowry, call a crew to haul out this contraband."

"Sure thing," she said, chipper.

I let Takami go. He blustered out of the chamber muttering something.

"Inspector," Dick said fearfully. "What's going to happen?"

"Takami will process you."

"Can't you do it?"

"Sorry. It's his case."

"I see. And what about Church Four?"

"It'll be shut down until they can find your replacement."

He hung his head. I escorted him out of the building. The four of us climbed into our vehicle. A large government truck pulled up behind us. A half-dozen agents piled out and swarmed the church.

"They're fast," Lowry marveled.

No one else had anything to say.

At the Central Office, Takami opened his terminal and started his paperwork. "Thanks for the help today," he said. He was calmer. He had transformed back to his normal self.

"Glad we could help," Lowry said.

"See you around."

"Sure. Maybe you and I could grab a bite to eat sometime?"

"Oh, uh, yeah, that would be okay," he replied unenthusiastically.

"Come on, let's give him a chance to work," I said, pulling her away.

We walked through the labyrinth of the building until we were back outside.

"What's Takami's situation?" Lowry asked.

"I don't know. He was probably upset about losing his partner."

"No, I mean his relationship situation."

"He's single, I think."

"He's cute."

"Don't waste your time," I chuckled.

"Why not?"

"He doesn't enjoy . . . the company of women."

"He's gay?"

I nodded.

"How would you know?" she asked, incredulous.

"When I was one of the higher-ups, he worked for me."

"And he told you?"

"Not in so many words, but it wasn't a big secret."

"But how could he? It's illegal."

"Lowry, if every safety agent who did something illegal lost their job, we wouldn't have any safety agents."

She looked deflated.

"Don't worry. The right guy will be around the next corner."

We walked farther away from the building. We rounded a corner. There was no one, only the parking lot. "Well, maybe the next one," I said.

16

I awoke with a jolt. I was draped over a table. I sat upright, the bones in my spine creaking. Something was attached to my face. I peeled it off. It was the newspaper I had been reading before I passed out. It was a crinkled mess now. I flattened the page as best I could, and returned it to the massive rack of newspapers. It didn't matter what they looked like, nobody else read those things.

I knew I would be late for work, but I left without any sense of urgency. After leaving the Archives, I bought a cup of coffee and drove to work.

Lowry was waiting for me, tapping her foot. "You're late."

"Overslept."

"I'm ready to get out there and deliver safety to the masses," she said sardonically.

"Okay then, let's go."

We left the Central Office, and I punched our destination into the car's computer. As I wheeled out of the parking lot, Lowry asked, "How do you work this thing?"

She smacked the computer, located in the center console, hitting keys at random. With enough trial and error, she was able to connect to the caseload server. Plain green text appeared on the screen.

"A surveillance van picked up an illegal exhaust signature," she said.

Surveillance Detail, the top of the food chain for safety agents, was the source of most of our information. Their vans rolled silently down every street, prying into homes and businesses with ultrasonic, infrared, and X-ray technology. If anything suspicious was found, the information was passed to the appropriate department and investigated. Almost everything they saw was considered suspicious, so we were never lacking work.

She read the final line, "Suspected to emanate from lawn care equipment. Storage shed in back of property."

We rolled up to the house and got out of the car. I followed Lowry to the front door. She knocked. There was no answer. "Must be at work," she said. "Should we take a look around back?"

"Lead the way."

We entered the back yard. The grass crunched softly beneath my feet. I stooped over and brushed it with my fingers. It was soft and smooth, not stiff and bristly like usual. This yard was planted with real grass.

When I stood back up I saw Lowry was already at the storage shed. She opened the lock with her multi-tool. The inside was saturated with the sharp smell of burned chemicals. Lowry crinkled her nose and said, "Ugh, what is that?"

The shed wasn't large. The back wall contained a series of gardening tools, flecked with dirt. The wall to the right was home to piles of miscellaneous junk: old rags, hoses, and a rickety piece of furniture. In the back corner stood a mysterious, bulky item covered by a brown tarp.

I pulled the tarp back. Beneath it stood the strangest thing I'd seen in a long time. It was a squat mechanical device with four small wheels and a slender metal handlebar that shot upward at an angle. Another handle, small and black and attached to a cord, rested on the device. I grabbed it and pulled. Something turned within, and the machine sputtered. Nothing else happened. I lifted the contraption. Its underside housed three thick metal blades, matted with green pulp. I set the machine back down on its wheels.

"I found what smells," Lowry said.

An orange canister filled with liquid sat in the opposite corner. I squatted beside her and took a whiff. It was pungent.

"It must be fuel for whatever this thing is," I said, pointing to the machine. "Let's get out of here, I need some fresh air."

Outside, Lowry asked, "What is it?"

"You see the grass? It's not artificial. That thing must be used to cut it."

Real grass didn't exist in the city. The allergens it created were too numerous to be considered safe. It did grow wildly on the outskirts of the city, and I had seen it from time to time when cases took me out there. But I had never seen it like this.

"Why would someone want real grass?" Lowry asked.

"Why don't we ask the owner?"

An odd tingling circulated in my veins. Excitement? I couldn't be sure. I hadn't been excited in years. Feeling a surge of energy, I drove faster than usual through the city. The speedometer rose above fifty miles per hour and started to flash red. I ignored it.

The search for the owner didn't take long. Boye, an accountant, was at her desk. She was trying to work while batting away the advances of a male co-worker. When we introduced ourselves, the co-worker immediately retreated.

"Can I help you, Inspectors?" Boye asked nervously.

"Ms. Boye, we'd like to ask you a few questions," I said.

"Of course. What's this about?"

Several other co-workers were standing in the hallway, eavesdropping. I shot them a glance and they scattered like cockroaches. Lowry closed the office door.

"I'll get right to it. We just came from your home. We found a contraption in your shed. Clearly, it's an unauthorized lawn care device. Tell us about it."

"Yes, you're right, it's for my lawn. It's called a lawn mower."

"Why do you have it?"

Boye started to breathe quickly. Trying to stay collected but failing, she said, "I don't know. I like old technology. Plus, I can adjust it. I can cut the grass any length I want." She froze. Every pore in her body simultaneously exploded with sweat.

"It's okay, we already know about the grass. Who sold it to you?"

"Which?"

"Both."

"Um, oh, I don't know."

"She's lying," Lowry said.

"No! I'm telling the truth. I don't know the person's name!"

"Then where did you get those things?" Lowry asked.

"There's this guy, he goes by the name Mr. X. He sold it to me. But I never saw his face. Everything was pre-arranged. I paid, and picked up the lawn mower and a big, fat bag of grass seeds at a neutral location. I never saw anyone."

"Who arranged it for you?" I asked.

Boye looked at me with liquid eyes and said, "This client of mine. He set it up. I helped him with his taxes, and I didn't charge him."

"And your client's name?"

"Karp," she said, trembling.

"Tell me one more thing. Why did you want real grass?"

"I like how it smells."

"That's weird," Lowry said.

Boye collapsed into a blubbering lump of flesh, with her arms spread across her desk. She whimpered and shuddered. We hadn't been that hard on her. Flirting with the black market seemed too much for her conscience to bear.

"Do you know who she's talking about?" Lowry asked.

"There's an urban legend about a guy named Mr. X who can get any item for you on the black market. Nobody has ever seen him. He probably never existed. I'm surprised the legend has lasted as long as it has."

"So, we're chasing a ghost?"

"Not necessarily. I know where to find Karp. He might be able to give us a lead."

Lowry handcuffed Boye, and we drove back to the Central Office. I instructed her to give Boye a minor contraband charge.

She stayed upstairs to do the paperwork while I took Boye to a holding cell. She would be released in a day.

The holding cells were in an ancillary building attached to the Central Office. At most, criminals were kept for a month before sentencing. The worst offenders, about five percent, were sent to Safety Re-Education. The rest were released. Given the fact that Karp ran from us, there was a good chance he was still here. After depositing Boye, I looked for him.

"Mr. Karp," I said, approaching his cell. It was a small rectangle, separated from the hall by a plate of thick security glass.

"Yeah?" he said, lifting his head off his cot. "Oh, it's you."

"I have a few questions."

"I already confessed. What more do you want?"

I stepped up to the glass. It was almost touching my nose. "It turns out there's something else you can help me with."

"Help with what?"

"Tell me what you know about lawn mowers."

I caught a glimmer of recognition on his face. He dropped his head back on his cot and said, "I don't know what that is."

"I think you do. Ms. Boye said you helped her find one."

"Whatever."

I needed to push him harder. "And what about your little warehouse?"

"I don't know what you mean," he said with feigned disinterest.

"You know, if anyone was stupid enough to leave something behind, like a stolen supply of salt, their sentence could be increased."

Karp stood up. He hesitantly approached the glass. He looked worried. He gulped and asked, "And what if someone was smart enough to help in any way they could?"

"Then their coffee charge would be the only thing they'd have to worry about."

"You're blackmailing me?"

"No. I'm trying to keep charges off your record."

"Okay, fine, what do you want to know?"

"Who's your black market contact?"

"I don't have his name."

"How do you contact him?"

"The west side central park. A message is left for him once a week. Midnight on Sunday. The next week he leaves instructions and a price. Then we provide payment and he lets us know where the goods can be picked up."

"Where are they picked up?"

"Any number of neutral locations. He keeps items stashed in warehouses until they are ready to be moved."

"Like the one under your house?"

"Yeah."

"How many are there?"

"I'm not sure. He has warehouses all over the city. Dozens."

"How long have you been involved?"

"About three years."

"He must trust you."

"I don't know that he trusts anyone."

"He must trust you enough to live on top of one of his warehouses."

"Even so, I always went through intermediaries, and they paid me in cash."

"Okay. I'd like to set up a meeting."

"Weren't you listening? Nobody knows who this guy is. I worked with him for three years and I haven't even heard his voice. It's impossible."

"Maybe, maybe not. But I have an idea. And if you want to get out of here," I said while tapping the security glass, "you'll help."

I walked back to Prohibition Detail. Lowry was typing the report. I peered over her shoulder and saw she was entering the bare minimum necessary. I had taught her well.

"Did you learn anything?" she asked.

"Karp will contact his man in the black market."

"What did he want in return?"

"That's a secret."

She frowned at me and said, "Okay, fine, but when we catch Mr. X, I'll do the interrogation and you can do the paperwork."

"It's a deal."

I walked over to the electronic map. A few quick taps on the screen brought the map to the Western District. A few more taps zoomed in on the park. It was fairly small. Working together, we'd to able to surveil the entire area.

"Hey, boss," I said, turning toward Bradbury. He slumbered with his legs kicked onto his desk and his head dangling over the back of his chair.

"Boss!"

He remained asleep.

I picked up Bradbury's terminal and let it fall on the desk with a heavy thud. It didn't matter if it broke. He never used it.

The sound startled him awake. He keeled backward and crashed onto the floor. The chair flipped over and landed on top of him.

"You okay?" I asked, pulling him to his feet.

He straightened his glasses and tucked in his shirt. "Yes," he said. "I don't know what happened. I must have dozed off for a second. I've been putting in a lot of hours lately."

"Sure, sure, of course you have."

I righted the chair and Bradbury sank into it. The metal supports creaked. He blinked at me, obviously perplexed. "Sorry, you're Inspector . . ."

"Smith."

"Smith, right. I heard you do good work."

"I wanted to let you know that Lowry and I are working on a big case. We need to do surveillance Sunday night."

"Oh, my, it sounds like a doozy."

"It might be. So, we won't be here Monday on account of working Sunday night."

Bradbury picked up a magazine. Flipping through the pages, he said, "Fine, fine, whatever you need."

I walked away and found Lowry grinning at me. "I told you I liked this assignment," she said.

"Let's go. Coffee's on me."

Lowry and I strolled out of the Central Office. Bradbury was oblivious to us departing despite it still being morning. We had put in enough work for one day. This was the government, after all.

17

The minute hand snapped to the top of my watch, perfectly overlapping with the hour hand. I looked up from it and stared into the park.

The sky was black, but fluorescent lights were placed strategically to eliminate any patches of darkness. A pristine sidewalk snaked its way through the artificial grass. A few empty park benches dotted the sidewalk's path.

Beneath one of the benches was a neatly folded envelope, pinned under a rock. That was our message to Karp's black market contact. Lowry and I waited at opposite ends of the park, watching it.

I sat behind a tree, trying to conceal myself as best I could. The tree's wide branches afforded little shade. Hopefully, the suspect wouldn't notice me.

I took out my multi-tool and set it to the binocular function. It didn't have the range or the ability to use X-rays or infrared like the dedicated binoculars, but it was smaller and lighter. I looked across the park and saw Lowry, hunkered behind a tree, looking back at me. She waved. I waved back. Then, she pointed at something.

I panned right and saw a man walk across the grass. His hands were tucked in his pockets, and his eyes were locked onto the bench. When he reached the bench, he knelt down, grabbed the envelope, and quickly walked away.

Lowry and I followed him. We kept our distance, and we didn't speak. He weaved a path through the city. His movements were memorized, and there was no indication he was onto us.

Eventually, he entered a parking garage and got into a car. Lowry noted the registration number. The Auto-Driver casually carried him away while we hurried back to our vehicle, which was two blocks from the park.

We dove inside. I started the engine, and Lowry punched our suspect's information into the computer. The screen changed into a map with his car at the center. He was driving south, toward the outskirts of the city. With the Auto-Driver disengaged, I raced down the street. My heart was pounding. I felt giddy. After all this time, I finally had a real case.

The target had stopped about twenty miles south of the city. We would catch up to him in about ten minutes.

"He must be at one of the way stations," I said.

"Do you think he'll be armed?"

"Maybe. But nothing dangerous."

It was astonishingly dark here, away from the neon blast of the city. There were no other lights except for our car's headlamps. While cities were brightly lit beacons, the wilderness beyond was untamed. Rumors abounded of people who lived out here, apart from society, living without safety precautions. They were lunatics.

I turned the car right and slowed to a crawl. We left the road with a heavy bump. We crept through the edge of a forest, the car jostling over rocks and tree roots. The target was close now. I killed the headlights and stopped the car.

Just in front of us, lurking in the gloom, was the other car. It was turned off. I pulled out the dedicated binoculars, set to infrared mode. The only heat signature out here was from the engine. The rest of the car registered in cool blues and greens. No one was inside. I scanned the nearby area. Nothing.

Lowry popped out of the car. Using our multi-tools set to flashlight mode, we inspected the area, but saw nothing but forest. The inside of the car was in immaculate condition. It was rarely used.

"What, he just disappeared?" Lowry asked.

I leaned against the suspect's car with one hand and said, "He must have gone on foot."

"Then we're screwed."

"Not necessarily. He left the car here. I imagine at some point he'll want it back."

"So, we wait?"

"Looks that way."

Lowry looked frustrated. She had wanted a more thrilling conclusion to our chase. So had I. At length, I said, "I have a feeling he won't be back for a while. Why don't you head to the city for supplies? I'll stay here."

Lowry drove off leaving me alone in the darkness. I found a place to sit a good distance from the target with a clear line of sight. I clicked off my flashlight. It was quiet here. Peaceful. It would be the perfect place to build a log cabin.

About an hour later, Lowry returned. She parked our car deep in the forest, out of sight. She brought coffee and snacks.

"Anything happen?" she asked.

"No, but I noticed this." I clicked on my flashlight and swept the beam from side to side. The light illuminated a pair of tire tracks that curved toward the main road. "There was a second car here. It must have been waiting for him," I said.

"Clever bastards."

I took a sip of my coffee. It was already getting cold. There wasn't much else to do, so I drank it and mindlessly watched the idle car.

My eyes blinked open. Birds chirped in the distance. Sunlight streamed into the forest as individual shafts of light. It was morning.

The target car was still there, untouched. Beside me, Lowry slumbered. My bladder bulged. I rose from the forest floor and brushed dirt off my pants. I walked away and relieved myself.

The day passed uneventfully. Lowry and I spoke in fits and starts. As the day stretched on, the sun slowly set on the horizon. Our shadows grew longer until we were once again plunged into darkness.

I heard a faint rumbling. It grew ever louder. Whatever it was, it was getting closer. Lowry heard it, too. It was coming from the direction of the road. It must be a vehicle of some kind, but what? No car was that loud.

The sound reverberated in my chest. A pair of bright lights swung at us. The crunching of rocks and fallen branches heralded its arrival. Lowry and I peeked out from behind thick trees.

The lights were incredibly bright. This new vehicle pulled up beside the other one and stopped. I made out the silhouette of a battered truck with enormous wheels.

The passenger door opened and a man stepped out. He quickly got into the car and started the engine. As its electric motor whirred, its headlamps switched on. Lowry and I were flooded with light. It would be a miracle if they didn't see us.

Both vehicles pulled away. They shrank as they retreated from the forest.

"Lowry!" I said in a harsh whisper. "We need to follow them."

Crouching, we hustled to where she had stashed our car. I reversed out of the forest, headlamps off. Lowry turned on the computer. The target car was a pulsing blip on the screen.

"He's headed back to the city," she said.

"He's not the one I'm interested in," I said.

My car's tires hit pavement once again. I swung my head in each direction. I could see both vehicles. It was dark, but their taillights glowed bright red. They drove away from one another, gaining distance. I turned the wheel and drove south.

"That truck, it won't have a tracker. This is our only chance to see where it's headed."

"I've never seen anything like that. It must be a hundred years old."

"Hundreds, probably."

"Why was it so loud?"

"It has an internal combustion engine. Runs on gasoline. Like that lawnmower thing."

"Have you seen one before?"

"Not in person."

Like many things, I had read about the history of automobiles in the Archives. The technology was ancient, before even the basics of fusion reactors had been invented. It was mind-boggling to think about the primitive technology of ancient humans.

I drove fast enough to get within a comfortable distance of the truck. I continued to drive without my headlamps, using the truck as a beacon. We drove for about an hour when the truck suddenly swung hard to the right and accelerated down a patch of desolate earth. It kicked up huge plumes of dust. It bounced up and down as it raced over the rocky terrain. We were well beyond the forest now. This area had little vegetation. It was called the Wasteland.

I was forced to slow down. My car wasn't designed to go off-road. The truck's lights blinked off. I grabbed the binoculars again. The internal combustion engine glowed red-hot under the infrared scan. It was easy to follow. We drove after it for another half an hour. The vehicle swung right again, headed north for a few minutes, and then disappeared. I hit the brakes. Lowry lurched forward. Her body jerked to a stop by the seat belt.

I scrutinized the area. There, just to the right. The truck was moving forward at a slight decline. It was descending into the ground. It continued on that trajectory, its heat signature disappearing. It looked like half a vehicle. And then, it was completely gone.

I slung the binoculars around my neck and opened the car door. Lowry and I raced across the barren ground, following the tire tracks. They turned off into a gaping hole in the ground. Wooden planks had been set down as a makeshift ramp. The vehicle had driven into a cave.

"You think Mr. X is in there?" Lowry asked.

"Only one way to find out."

I stepped onto the ramp.

The maw of the cave was dotted with the occasional naked light bulb strung up with random bits of junk. Deep within the bowels of the cave was the low rumble of a motor. Some kind of generator powered the lights.

Lowry and I gradually descended beneath the earth. The farther in we went, the greater the rumble of the generator became. Sound ricocheted along the rocky walls. Soon, we could hear the voices of men.

We both walked as quietly as we could manage. The tunnel curved to the right. We followed the turn. The gentle grade stopped and we now walked along a flat surface. The tunnel turned and turned. The voices, shouting raucously, grew louder.

We turned again. The tunnel opened into a spacious cavern. Directly ahead were rows upon rows of cargo. The truck sat at the far end. Men hauled boxes off the flatbed, and packed and unpacked crates filled with unknown treasures.

We ducked behind a crate. I used the infrared scanner again, peering through the crate at the men on the other side. "There are four of them," I said.

"What should we do?" Lowry asked.

I hadn't thought that far ahead. I looked at her and saw she was trembling.

"This is just like that raid on the orgy," I said, realizing how ridiculous the statement was. "We've got our weapons. We'll be fine."

"So, we're gonna . . ."

"Ask them where we can find Mr. X."

"Smith, I'm not sure."

"These guys are like everyone else. Once they see a safety agent, they freeze up."

"Smith . . ."

"Let's introduce ourselves," I said with a smirk.

I casually walked out from behind the crate. I stood in the center of the cavern. The men continued to work. They hadn't noticed me.

"Evening, gentlemen."

The men stopped. All their eyes locked onto me.

"Who're you?" one man growled.

"Smith, Safety Inspector."

"Shiiit. Get him."

Two of the men approached. I opened my jacket, revealing my holstered weapon. "Now, now, fellas. You don't want to get yourselves hurt, do you?"

They stopped. They looked back at their leader. The growler said, "You ain't fast enough to shoot us all."

"Aren't I?"

"That thing takes time to recharge. No way you can get every one of us."

"Care to try?"

"Get him!"

All four of them raced toward me. It was time to reveal my ace in the hole.

"Lowry, now!"

I snapped my weapon out and shot the nearest man in the chest. He convulsed as he hit the ground. My weapon's fire indicator turned red as it recharged. They continued to converge on me. The next guy should have dropped by now. Why hadn't Lowry fired?

"Lowry, what are you—"

She was pinned to the ground. A fifth man had a knee in her back. He pressed her face into the dirt. She squirmed to break free, but he had a hundred pounds on her.

The other men were almost upon me. The indicator turned green. I fired. The thug on top of Lowry toppled backward. When I looked back again, I saw a fist flying at my face.

I managed to dodge it. I let my weapon fall and raised both hands. I drew back my right fist, and then swung forward. I caught air. He had dodged me. I readied my other hand.

Suddenly, the back of my head exploded with pain. Pulsating lights danced in my vision. I reeled forward. As I fell, I caught a glimpse of a sixth man behind me.

I hit the ground, hard.

18

I awoke with a mouthful of dirt. I opened my eyes but no light came. The room was pitch dark. I pushed up onto my hands and knees.

"Lowry?" I coughed.

No answer.

I groped around the floor, not sure what I was searching for. My fingers brushed against a hard object. I picked it up. It was my weapon. I was still in the cave. The generator was off, and the cave was eerily quiet. Like a tomb.

"Lowry?"

Nothing.

I pulled out my multi-tool and clicked the button for the flashlight. It didn't turn on. The battery was dead, and I was too far outside the range of the city for it to recharge.

I remembered my binoculars. They were still slung around my neck. I tried turning them on. Infrared – nothing. Night vision – nothing. I felt the front of the device. The plastic casing was deeply cracked. I was going to have a hell of a time getting out of here.

I quieted my mind, listening with my lesser used senses. I heard nothing except my heart. I had hoped to hear Lowry breathing, unconscious somewhere. Either she wasn't here or she was dead. In either case, I had to move.

I rose to my feet and turned one hundred and eighty degrees. Hopefully, this would point me toward the cave's exit. Hands reaching ahead, I began a slow walk forward.

The world felt like a bottomless chasm before me. My heart kept trying to leap into my throat. My mind kept trying to switch into panic mode.

My hands pressed against hard rock. Finding something flooded me with relief. I was no longer adrift in empty space. But which way to go? I moved right, shuffling along the wall, sidestepping and keeping my hands planted against the cool rock. I must have moved right for an hour. I traversed the entire space of the cavern. Eventually, my hands felt the rock wall curve away. At last, the tunnel!

Keeping a single hand against the wall, I walked forward. The tunnel turned and turned, moving me up at a gentle incline. Farther and farther, I crept upward through the winding tunnel. Then, I saw a pocket of light. It was a tiny square, like a dollhouse window, high above me. My heart leaped again.

I moved faster now. Baby steps turned into strides. My firm grasp of the wall loosened to almost nothing. The square of light grew ever larger. My feet hit wooden planks, and I ran the rest of the way.

Daylight burned my eyes. I shielded my face from the blinding sun above. The barren landscape, blurry at first, came into focus. My car was still in the same place with tire marks curved in the dirt around it.

There was no sign of Lowry anywhere.

I took the vehicle's emergency flashlight. There was only one thing to do, head back inside. I gulped hard, clearing my throat of dust. I flicked the light on, and reentered the cave.

The cavern had been cleared out. The vehicle, generator, and contraband were gone. Several large crates were smashed to pieces. Among the wreckage was a dark, vaguely human lump.

I turned Lowry's body over, expecting the worst. Her face was smeared with dirt, and she emitted a raspy breath. I shook her gently and said, "Lowry, hey, Lowry, wake up."

She groaned and her eyelids fluttered weakly.

"Come on, we've got to get out of here."

I pulled Lowry to her feet. She was lethargic, and threatened to pull me back to the ground with her. I righted us both, and slung her arm over my shoulder. We walked side by side, although I dragged her more than she walked. We retreated from the cave and returned to the car. She quickly fell asleep in the passenger seat. I had to get her to a hospital.

I blasted back toward the city. I had never driven so fast. Klaxons blared and red lights flashed, warning me about my dangerous speed. I ignored them as I weaved through traffic, the rest of the cars seemingly at a standstill.

The hospital staff admitted Lowry. While she was rushed off for imaging procedures, I was escorted to an exam room. A doctor entered and examined me.

"Nasty bump on your head," he said.

"Yeah, I know. I'm fine."

"What happened?"

"I got hit there. Twice."

"Really?"

"Occupational hazard."

He asked me a series of memory questions and had me perform some neurological tests. He shined a penlight in my eyes and tested my reflexes. He told me I was going to be fine.

"What about my partner?"

"I don't know. I'm not her doctor."

Hospital staff shuffled me out to the waiting room. I sat in an ergonomic plastic chair. I was covered in dirt. The wait to hear about Lowry felt like an eternity.

Eventually, a doctor appeared. "Are you Ms. Lowry's partner?" she asked.

"Yes," I said, standing up.

"She had to go into surgery. It's going to be quite some time before she'll be up for visitors. Why don't you go home and get some rest? Come back tomorrow."

"Okay. Thanks, doc."

I left the hospital with my head down. I couldn't meet anyone's eyes. A thousand pounds rested on my shoulders. A tightness in my chest made it hard to breathe. Tears tried to gather behind my eyes, but I willed them back inside.

When I returned to my vehicle, I saw the lower half of a business suit waiting for me. My eyes tracked up to see Orwell's disgusting face. "What the hell do you want?" I asked.

"Sounds like you had quite the scuffle."

"How'd you know?"

"I like to keep an eye on people who interest me."

"Are you through? Because I'm going home."

I pushed Orwell aside and opened the car door. From behind me, he said, "If you were so intent on meeting Mr. X, you should have told me."

I scrutinized him, unsure if this was just hot air he was spewing. Skeptical, I asked, "You know Karp's black market contact?"

"We're acquainted."

"It's not you, is it?"

"Oh, no, I'm not Mr. X. But we have had some business dealings. I could set up a meeting if you like."

"First of all, stop calling him Mr. X. What's his real name?"

"I'm afraid I don't know it. They simply go by Mr. X."

"Fine, set up a meeting. I need to pay him back for what he did to Lowry."

"I can't have you doing anything rash. It would be bad for my goals."

I was frozen. Rage left me wanting to thrash at everything. I envisioned myself smashing the car, smashing his face, smashing the world. I didn't know what to target first, so I stood there, unmoving, impotent.

Orwell ran his palm over his smooth head and asked, "Well?"

"I suppose if you arrange this, you'll want something in return?"

"Perhaps."

"Money?"

"Nothing as pedestrian as that. I'll want a favor."

I clenched my fists. With a stern voice I said, "Set up the meeting."

"Wonderful," Orwell said with a wolfish smile.

I entered my car and drove off. My skin was covered in grime. I rolled up my sleeves and wiped the dirt away. It didn't help. I still felt as if I had crawled through mud.

My house was in shambles. Pictures were cracked, and the drywall behind them was torn. Huge chunks of plaster sat like rocks on the floor. Spoiled food was everywhere. The refrigerator was on its side, doors open. The demon-dog had its face buried in a bag of shredded cheese. Water was pooled around the kitchen.

My troll-wife was in the living room. The couch was ripped in half. More trash littered the carpet. There was a huge crack in the TV's screen. She was on the couch with frizzy hair and unkempt clothes, and she was stuffing her face with food.

"What happened?!" I screamed over the noise of the TV.

"Oh . . . redecorating," she said with her mouth full.

"What? How?"

"Oh . . . I tried. It was hard. I quit."

"Are you going to clean this up?"

Another fistful of food entered her maw. She crunched it and said, "Oh . . . you're better at cleaning."

My vision went red. My head emptied. I drew my weapon, slowly and smoothly, and fired into her chest. Her body went stiff. She tottered on the edge of the couch, and then flopped onto the floor. Food spilled to the carpet. Tendrils of smoke rose from where the electrodes had burned her shirt. Her eyes rolled up.

I stood over her, and slipped my weapon back into its holster. I kicked over the end table and snapped off one of its legs. I lifted the leg high and, without hesitation, swung it hard against her head. It hit her skull with a dull thwack. Her eyelids closed and her limbs twitched. I swung and hit again. And again. After the third strike, her limbs stopped moving.

I dropped the table leg on her chest, turned off the TV, and went to take a shower. The grime and blood washed off me, circling into the drain. Once I was clean, I felt lighter. I dressed in a fresh set of clothes. I pulled a clean bowler hat down from the top of the closet. I checked myself in the mirror. I looked like a new man.

In the kitchen, the demon-dog had finished the cheese and had torn into a bag of frozen peas. I picked the beast up, its face still buried in the bag. I opened the front door and tossed it outside.

The demon-dog landed on its feet, and took off running with the bag of peas in its mouth. It bounded across the lawn, into the neighbor's, and kept on going. It ran at full speed without taking a look back. I hated that thing, but I had just done it a favor.

I stood on the front porch. My skin soaked in the warm rays of the sun. I breathed deeply. My lungs filled with sweet fresh air. The neighborhood was deserted. Silent. Calm. I straightened my jacket, and then drove back to the Central Office.

Bradbury was dozing at his desk. The rest of the huge, open-air room was subdued with most agents out on cases. I rapped hard on the desk. Bradbury awoke with a stifled choke.

"Hey, boss," I said.

"Oh, uh, hello. Err, um . . ."

"Smith."

"Yes, Smith. How did your case turn out?"

"Terrible."

"What happened?"

"Lowry and I got jumped."

"Lowry?"

"My partner."

"Oh, yes, yes. Where is she?"

"The hospital. She might die."

"Thaaat's," he yawned, "too bad."

"I'm going to visit her. Not sure when I'll check back in."

"Okay."

Talking to him was like talking to a rock. I walked away. Bradbury called after me, "You make an arrest?"

"No," I said, still walking, not turning back.

"Okayyy," he said while yawning again. "Let me know if you do."

I kept on walking. I didn't return my equipment. I was well beyond the time limit for returning it. There was no point.

I returned to the hospital. The people at the front desk wouldn't tell me where Lowry was on account of me not being a family member. Divulging healthcare information was unsafe. I flashed my badge and informed them of all the safety statutes they were violating, most of them I made up. The receptionist, scared out of her wits, quickly told me where I could find Lowry.

Her head was wrapped in bandages. A tube was shoved down her throat, attached to a machine that breathed for her. Unidentifiable liquids were feeding into her through an IV line. She was pale and disheveled. She could have been a corpse.

The nurse let me sit in the room. I kept my distance from Lowry's body. The clock on the wall became fuzzy. Time lost meaning. I stared at her comatose body, and my thoughts drifted to Mr. X. I invented a face for him. I destroyed the face over and over again.

The room gradually became orange. The apparatuses in the room cast ever lengthening shadows. The nurse returned. "Sir, are you planning on staying overnight?"

I was shaken back to reality. "Oh, uh, no."

"In that case, the hospital's regular visiting hours are over."

"All right. Thank you."

I rose from my chair and made my way outside. The city had become cold. Faces turned away from me. The looming skyscrapers were darker than usual. The sprawling size of the city widened. I drove for an hour in random directions. When I tired of that, I got out and walked.

I found a diner, just like the one Lowry and I had frequented. It was in much better condition than the other. The leather booths were crisp, the tables spotless, and the fixtures sparkled. I set my hat down across from me, and I looked at the menu. Nothing sounded good, but I was feeling lightheaded so I had to eat.

A waitress appeared. "Evening, Inspector. How ya doin'?"

I shrugged weakly.

"Rough day?"

"You could say that."

"What can I getchya?"

"Eh, surprise me."

She smiled and walked off. I eased back into the booth and sighed. Behind me, I heard the faint jingle of a bell. Footsteps approached. A man in a suit slid into the opposite side of the booth. I frowned and said, "Seeing you twice in one day is too much."

Orwell folded his hands together and placed them on the table. "I thought you'd be happy to see me," he said.

"That's not the word I'd use."

"Not even if I told you I had arranged a meeting with Mr. X?"

"When can I meet him?"

"Tomorrow night."

"Where?"

"Slow down, Inspector Smith. We have something to discuss."

"The favor?"

Orwell finally had me. He grinned slyly and said, "Like minded Safety Inspectors feel we are in a position to affect change at the national level. We'd like to overhaul several government policies."

"More statutes?"

"I'm not interested in statutes."

"What then?"

"The First Government is a dinosaur. It's been mired in outdated methods for centuries."

"Things seem to be working."

"Working? Have you ever seen a session of the Senate?"

"No."

"Pigs. They're all pigs. Corruption and idiocy is destroying our country. But I can fix it. I've installed trusted agents in high-level positions. Together, we'll take charge and work from behind the scenes."

"And you'll turn the First Government into a puppet show. So what do you need me for?"

"I'm one person short. I like your disregard for the establishment. You'd be most useful. Once you're in place, things will be set in motion."

"You were interested in Lowry, too."

"You're fond of her. I was going to let you bring her along. I want my people to be happy."

"It will never work."

"Perhaps not. But if you agree to help me, you'll have your meeting."

If I wanted to avenge Lowry, I needed to play his game. But I didn't need to pretend that I liked it. "Fine," I spat.

"Wonderful. This is for you," he said, sliding a slip of paper across the table. "I'll be in touch."

Just then, the waitress reappeared. She placed a steaming plate of meatloaf in front of me. She asked Orwell if he wanted anything. He ignored her as he rose and exited the diner.

"Enjoy, hon," the waitress said.

I flipped over the slip of paper. Scrawled across it was the following, "Tomorrow. Midnight. South parking garage 16. Level 4."

I crumpled the paper, my body filling with heat. Tomorrow night that bastard would pay. I looked down at the meatloaf. I took a bite.

19

I arrived early. I didn't want to get sapped a third time. After scouring the parking garage, and finding it nearly empty, I felt satisfied I wasn't walking into a trap. A few stray cars dotted the rows of parking spaces. The floor was a solid sheet of gray concrete. Thick square columns stood like monoliths supporting the roof. Fluorescent lights buzzed above me.

I leaned against my car, waiting. My watch now read five minutes 'til midnight. I heard a heavy clunk. A segment of lights at the far end of the garage turned off. Then, another segment, closer to me, went dark. Then another. The darkness was moving toward me. Finally, the last segment turned off. I was enshrouded in inky blackness. I stood fully upright. My hand crept to my weapon.

A pair of headlamps flipped on. Two cones of light sprayed onto me. I squinted.

Two silhouetted figures stepped in front of the lights. Their faces were obscured, and they threw long shadows across the concrete floor. "You Smith?" one of them asked.

"That's right."

"C'mere."

"Are you Mr. X?"

"We're takin' you to see him." The man held up a small fabric bag. "Get over here."

"I don't think so."

"Suit yourself," he said. The two men turned back to their car. "Wait."

They stopped. The bag man said, "Yeah?"

"What assurance can you give me that you're not going to kill me?"

He let out a hoarse chuckle, "You gotta trust us."

I steeled myself for whatever was about to come. "Okay," I said.

I walked toward the men, hands up. The first man forced my hands behind my back, snapping them in handcuffs. He jerked my weapon out of its holster. The second man shoved the fabric bag over my head. It was stifling. They shuffled me around and pushed me headfirst into the back of the car.

The two men dropped into the front seats, and the car sprang to life. I felt the turns, the accelerations, and the stops. There were so many twists on our journey, I had no idea where we were. I wasn't sure how long we drove for, but it must have been close to an hour.

Once we arrived, I was man-handled out of the car, dragged outside for a bit, and then pulled, stumbling, inside a building. It was cooler in here. It smelled damp.

I was forced to my knees.

"Is this the Safety Inspector?" a female voice asked.

"It's him."

"Did he put up a fight?"

"Nope. Came along, no problem."

"Pull off the bag."

"You sure that's a good—"

"I said pull it off."

The bag ripped away. I gulped fresh air. I blinked and let my eyes adjust to the light. The room was murky. It was long and narrow with a high ceiling. I was in the middle of an aisle, flanked on either side by rows of wooden benches. In front of me was a raised dais with a cracked stained glass window behind it. A woman sat in a chair on the dais.

"Welcome, Mr. Smith," she said. She had a small frame, thick raven hair, and dark eyes.

"Where are we?"

"That's not important."

"Where's Mr. X? He's the one I'm here to see."

"Don't be so hasty. I have a few questions for you."

"I'm not answering anything until I see Mr. X."

A metal object slammed into my upper back. I doubled over, and my forehead cracked against the floor. I turned my head and saw the bag man behind me, holding a metal bat. He gave another hoarse chuckle.

As I raised myself back up to my knees, the woman said, "You are hardly in any position to make demands, Mr. Smith. Now, will you answer my questions, or shall we send you back?"

I cast my eyes to the floor. It was dirty, covered in dust and splintered wood. I took a slow breath and calmed myself. I looked back at the woman and said, "Ask your questions."

She shifted in her chair. On the dais, she looked like she was sitting on a throne. "How did you find our storage facility?" she asked.

"I tailed one of your men."

"How long have you known about our operation?"

"Not long."

"And yet you're already here. You work fast, Mr. Smith."

I grunted.

"What's your relationship to Mr. Orwell?" she asked.

"We don't have a relationship."

"I doubt he would set up this meeting for a stranger. He must have a compelling reason."

I looked side to side. There were six men, three on each side, plus the two guys who brought me in were behind me. Two of them had automatic weapons slung over their shoulders. The others, no doubt, were armed. If I didn't play along, I wasn't getting out of here. So much for my great plan.

"He wants me to work for him. He set up this meeting to get me to do whatever he wants."

"And what is that?"

"He has some crackpot idea about controlling the government."

The woman laughed. It was a deep, sultry laugh. She leaned back in her chair and crossed her legs. The dim light accentuated her body's natural curves. "That old scheme?" she said, bemused. "He still hasn't given that up?"

I stared at her.

"Very well. And why do you want to meet Mr. X?"

"His goons put my partner in the hospital."

"And you want what exactly?"

I narrowed my eyes. "That depends."

"On what?"

"If she lives."

The woman laughed again, although not as convincingly as the first time. She uncrossed her legs and leaned forward in her throne. "Mr. Smith, what if I made you an offer?"

"Such as?"

"Mr. X has vast resources. If you did him a favor, would you be willing to forget your little vendetta?"

"Maybe you don't understand how favors work."

Another slam from the bat sent me reeling forward. I groaned and uprighted myself once more.

"You'd be paid handsomely, of course. Enough to forget all your troubles. You're in a unique position to help us. Mr. X and Mr. Orwell have had many dealings in the past. The way Mr. X sees it, their partnership is at an end. If you could help us bring down Mr. Orwell's organization, Mr. X would be grateful."

"And what about Orwell?"

"Do whatever you see fit."

"You know, it's been great chatting, but I'd like to deal directly with Mr. X."

The woman frowned. "Mr. Smith, I thought you were smarter than that." She looked to her men and said, "Send him back."

I repeated my journey through the bombed-out sanctuary in reverse. The bag went over my head, I was hauled through the dank, unseen world, driven back to the parking garage, and thrown out of the moving car like a person cast out of the ocean.

The car sped away. I picked myself up and pulled off the bag. My hands were scratched and bleeding. My hips, shoulders, back and head all cried out. I was too old to endure this kind of punishment.

My weapon had been tossed out, and lay on the concrete next to me. I holstered it and looked myself over. My clothes were filthy. A long tear crossed the knee of my pants. My hat was long gone. I stood up, feeling my body ache, and meandered to my car.

I sat inside, basking in the processed air. What had I gotten involved in? I was stuck in the middle of some crazy underworld power struggle. And I had no idea what my next move should be.

Before I did anything else, I drove home to collect a few belongings. The house was dim and quiet. A shape lay on the living room floor with a congealed red puddle around its head, and a few dark flies clinging to it. I went to the bedroom and packed a suitcase. I changed into a new suit, and grabbed my last bowler hat.

I drove back to the hospital. I slept in my car, waiting for morning. Once it was time for visiting hours, I returned to the ICU. Lowry's room was empty. I panicked and grabbed a nurse. She told me Lowry had gone back to surgery. I couldn't wait in the hospital any longer. Being there made me suffocate.

I went back to my car. The vehicle's communication system was blinking. I answered it. The screen read, "Audio Only." The speaker piped in a call from the equipment department. A man on the other end asked, "Is this Inspector 1872124482?"

"Yeah."

"You're overdue on returning the equipment you requisitioned several days ago."

"I'm out on a case."

"Please return your equipment by the end of business today."

"What if I don't?"

"You may be suspended from work until the equipment is returned."

"Is that supposed to be a punishment?"

The voice sputtered. While he was stammering a response, I turned off the communication system. I breathed deeply, trying to let the chatter in my head subside.

A moment later, the passenger side door of my car opened. Orwell fell into the seat and closed the door behind him. It looked like my mind wouldn't get a chance to rest after all.

"I trust your meeting went well," he said.

"It was interesting."

"How so?"

"They want me to kill you."

Orwell clapped his hands a single time and said, "That's what I like about you, Inspector Smith. You always speak your mind."

"What kind of arrangement do you and Mr. X have?"

"They procured equipment necessary to help with my reorganization strategy."

"Weapons?"

"Various items."

"So, what do you want from me?"

"I've set the gears in motion to have you work directly for me. But I can't move you without cause to do so. I need you to work a case. Once you complete it, I'll have you promoted."

"Fine," I said. "Now, get out."

"Of course," he said. Orwell evaporated, leaving me in silence.

My head pounded. I wanted to kill Mr. X and now I was working for him. I hated the sight of Orwell and I was working for him, too. I was a double agent, and each side knew it. What the hell was happening?

I headed back to work. Prohibition Detail was empty. Not even Bradbury was there. It was better this way. I wouldn't have to talk to anyone.

I logged into a terminal and pulled up the vast list of pending cases. I had to find one that would be quick and easy. Sixty items down I saw a case that looked promising. A residence was in violation of noise regulations. Normally, this would be Healthcare's case, but it was shifted to Prohibition because the noise was rumored to be caused by a contraband item. Perfect.

I drove to the residence. I rapped on the front door and waited. It creaked open, and a small man emerged from the other side.

"Mr. Lewis?" I asked.

"Yes. What can I do for you, Inspector?"

"There have been several noise complaints. I need to have a look around."

I shoved the door open and walked inside. Everything looked to be kept within regulations. Lewis followed me, wringing his hands, nervous that I would find whatever he was hiding. After a good ten minutes of searching, I went to the back yard. His patio housed three hulking shapes, each covered under a gray tarp.

"What's this?" I asked.

"Nothing, sir."

"Take the tarps off."

"Yes, sir," he said reluctantly.

Lewis pulled each tarp away in turn. Beneath each was an automobile. They didn't look anything like a vehicle on the road today. They were relics. Yet, they had been restored and maintained.

"What are these?"

"Cars, sir."

I gave him a sinister glare.

He twiddled his fingers and said, "Uh, Duesenberg Model J, Cadillac El Dorado, Dodge Challenger."

My eyes were drawn to the third. It was a large, angular beast. Four eyes in the front floated in the large black grill. The long hood swept back, meeting the acute angle of the front windshield. It had two doors, each with a narrow window. The vehicle was gleaming white with a solid red stripe running up the center of the hood and stretching to the rear. It had thick tires with a trace of red outlining the rims. It looked like it would eat any other car on the road.

I put my hand on the body and swept it toward the driver's side door. I looked inside. All black leather interior. A series of four analog dials sat in the dashboard. A rounded knob shifter was in the center console. It was a far cry from the fully digital displays and touch-sensitive screens of today's vehicles.

I turned back, hoping Lewis didn't notice the starry look in my eyes. "These must be a thousand years old. Where did you get them?" I asked.

"Er, um, collectors."

"How are they so well maintained?"

"There's lots of collectors. Usually, we trade services."

He blanched white. He realized he was about to implicate his fellow aficionados. I didn't care about them.

"Where do you get fuel?"

"Um, Inspector, uh . . ."

"Where?"

"There's a network. All over the country. If you know where to refuel, you could drive across the continent. Ocean to ocean."

"Do you have any other contraband?"

"Uh, yes, sir," he said, hanging his head shamefully.

"Go get it."

He disappeared into the house. While he was gone, I marveled at the cars. I knew why he collected these. He was fascinated by the ancient world, just like me.

Lewis returned carrying a box filled with greasy machine parts and tools. He was sweating profusely. He knew the law. This much contraband was going to send him to Safety Re-Education.

"Anything in this box you can't replace?" I asked.

He wrinkled his face, confused by the question. "Uh, well, no, sir."

"Okay, Mr. Lewis. I'm going to charge you with violation of Safety Statute 39-32-14."

"What's that?" he asked, on the verge of tears.

"Improper storage of mechanical parts. Dispose of these immediately. There will be a fine."

His legs wobbled, and his lips trembled.

"I won't mention your two cars," I said.

"Two?"

"Right. You don't own the Challenger any more. You just sold it to me. Now, get the keys."

His faced turned to a bizarre mixture of relief and distress. He disappeared into the house again. He returned with a jingling set of keys and a folded piece of paper. Lewis handed them to me and said, "Fuel depots for the whole continent are on the map. Thought you might need it."

"Thanks," I said, tucking the map into my jacket pocket. "Now, what's a fair price? Twenty thousand?"

"Fair? I don't know. I'm not sure, sir."

"Let's say twenty-five. I'll transfer it to your account."

"Err, yes, okay. Thank you, Inspector," he said, barely able to stand upright.

I opened the Challenger's door and sat inside. I turned the key in the ignition. The engine roared to life. The windows of Lewis' house rattled. I maneuvered out of the back yard and onto the street. I revved the engine. People on the sidewalk turned their heads.

I gripped the steering wheel with one hand, shifted into gear with the other, and hit the accelerator. The engine screamed and the car shot down the street like lightning. As I raced away, I glanced in the rear-view mirror. The quiet, computer-controlled government vehicle I had arrived in was already a small dot behind me.

The next day, I was handed a letter. It was brief but to the point. As a result of my stellar service on Lewis' case, I was being promoted to Surveillance Detail at the national headquarters. Orwell worked fast.

I handed it across the desk. Bradbury spent exactly one second looking at it. He tossed it aside and said, "You're outta here, huh?"

"That's right."

"You ever been to the Capital?"

"No."

"Me neither."

"So, boss, if you could just finish that paperwork for me."

"When are you leaving?"

"Tonight. Just be sure to get that paperwork—"

"I'm kinda surprised. Usually, people are agents for years before they go national."

Bradbury had no idea I'd been a safety agent for decades. He probably hadn't even looked at my personnel file. Or anyone's for that matter.

"Anyway, put in a good word for us when you get over there, okay, Jones?"

"Smith."

"Right, Smith."

I stood up and tapped the top of his terminal. "Please finish that paperwork," I said.

He yawned and nodded.

I sauntered through the maze of desks. When I reached the exit, I turned around for a final look. I had spent decades toiling away here, working with sloths, psychos, morons, and assholes. Once I stepped through the door, I would never see this place again. Good riddance.

Next, I went to the hospital. Lowry didn't look any better. She was entangled in a mass of wires. A monitor beside the bed displayed a series of lines showing her heart rhythm, respiratory flow, and oxygen saturation. She still looked like death.

I stood beside her and gripped the rail of her bed. "I'm working on it, Lowry," I said. "I won't forget what they did to you. I'm going to the Capital for a while. I'm not sure when I'll be back, but I will. I promise."

Part of me hoped my impassioned words would stir her into consciousness. But she lay there, comatose.

I let go of the bed rail. My knuckles had blanched white. I flexed my fingers and let the blood flow return.

There was nothing left for me in this city now. I returned to my car, fuel map ready, and departed.

As I passed through the Central Corridor, an idea occurred to me. I swerved to the right and parked in the emergency lane. I exited the car and looked up at the Archives.

The usual guard was kicked back, snoring behind the security desk. The body scanner stood to the right. There was a slight space between it and the wall. I sucked in my gut and tried to slip through. The machine and the wall pressed hard against my chest and back. I inched along. I grabbed the far side of the scanner, and pulled myself out.

I looked back. The guard was still asleep. I headed down the hall to the administrator's office. It was slightly ajar. I could hear his voice from the other side. I had hoped he'd be out. I knocked and entered.

He looked up from his phone. "I'll call you back," he said before hanging up. He looked at me quizzically. My face registered in his memory, but he couldn't recall how. "Can I help you, Inspector?"

"I'm looking for a book. I need it for an investigation."

"Of course, I'm happy to help. Which book is it?"

"Contracting and You."

"Ah, yes, you had asked to take a look at it a few weeks ago."

"That's right."

"And now you need it for an investigation?"

"Yes."

"What a strange coincidence." He raised his palms and said apologetically, "I'm sorry, but that book is currently undergoing restoration. No one is allowed to touch it until the process is finished."

"You'll need to interrupt it. That book is of the utmost importance."

He cocked his head to the side. He scratched his chin and said, "I've never heard of a Safety Inspector needing a book. This is highly irregular. What did you say your name was, Inspector?"

"Huxley."

"And your ID number?"

I made one up.

"Thank you, Inspector Huxley. Let me make a few phone calls. If everything checks out, I'll make an exception."

"Thanks."

He showed me out. As I pulled the door shut behind me, I read the multitude of directional signs. That was one of the benefits of being in a safety-obsessed nation; there were always a million signs to prevent people from getting lost. I followed the signs, walking through a maze of hallways until I reached my destination.

The room was marked with a plaque that read, "Artifact Restoration – Authorized Personnel Only." I knocked twice and waited. There was no answer.

I fished out my multi-tool. I opened the lock and entered the lab. There were rows of fluorescent lights, upside down, so the light projected onto the ceiling instead of down onto the artifacts. Long tables displayed a variety of books, magazines, and newspapers in varying states of disrepair. I stalked up one side and down the other. Halfway down the second table, I saw an open book with a blueprint of a bathroom. I flipped the cover over. It was my book.

I stuffed it into my jacket pocket. It barely fit, bulging, stretching the fabric. I quickly made my way out of the room, through the winding corridors, and back to the lobby. I walked out of the Archives casually, with a smile.

I fired up the Challenger and drove east. It would take several days to reach the Capital. Fortunately, I had a map of the fuel depots. They would have to be right, or I would be stranded.

Within an hour, I was out of the city. The buildings parted ways, opening onto an expanse of wilderness. Half an hour after that, the wilderness gave way to arid desert. Between the cities there was virtually nothing; no towers, no people, no life, just the Wasteland.

20

The smoothly paved road soon came to an end, and I merged onto the old highway system. The concrete was dilapidated, and the car jostled over the bumps. Even so, the road was in good enough shape for me to keep driving. My vehicle was the only one on the road. I felt like the last man alive.

I checked the map unfolded on the seat beside me. The first fuel depot was about one hundred miles away. I settled into the seat and relaxed my arms, keeping one hand lightly on the steering wheel. I checked the radio, but found only static. I switched it off and listened to the hum of the engine. I pushed the accelerator down, and watched as the needle crept up to one hundred miles per hour. My eyes flicked back to the empty road before me. I let my mind wander, and the time passed more quickly.

An hour passed, and I slowed the car, panning my head, looking for signs of the fuel depot. The Wasteland expanded in all directions, nothing but flat, desolate plains. Then I saw it. A large oval sign stood in the distance. As I neared, its orange letters came into view. "Westlook Motel," it read. The sign was cracked and dirty. The neon had died long ago.

This had to be the place. There was nothing else around for miles.

I pulled off the highway. There were a couple of abandoned jalopies in the parking lot. The concrete was cracked, and weeds shot up haphazardly. I brought the Challenger to a stop alongside the motel and killed the engine.

Wind blew dry air in from the west. A plume of dust kicked up and sent me into a coughing fit.

I walked to the front door of the building. It was locked. The lock was an ancient contraption. I tried the multi-tool, but the fittings were completely different. I proceeded to walk around the building. I made a full loop but found nothing.

I scooped up a hunk of broken rubble and hefted it through the front office window. Glass crashed inside. Within, the building was dark and musty. Motes of dust danced in the light that came through the now-broken window. I called out. There was no response.

I checked the front desk and the back office. I rummaged through every drawer and file. There was absolutely nothing. I sat for a bit in the back office. I swiveled back and forth in the dusty manger's chair. Who would have thought finding an illegal fuel depot would have been so difficult?

I went outside again and made another pass around the building. I inspected the ground, looking for anything that might resemble a trap door or secret compartment. Again, nothing.

When I returned to my car, I checked the map. This had to be the right location. Whatever was here at one point in time was gone now. The next location was one hundred and fifty miles away. I had enough fuel to get there, but if I couldn't find it, I'd be walking the rest of my journey.

I revved the engine and set off down the highway. I drove fast and let time slip away again.

The next location looked more promising. I entered one of the old settlements. Hundreds of these pre-First Government towns dotted the landscape. They were remnants of the old world, before the unification. They were all abandoned now, with no utilities or services running to them. The First Government made certain all its citizens lived within the confines of the few, massive cities. It was safer that way; they could monitor and regulate everything for the people.

The settlement had multiple buildings: stores, a hotel, a shopping complex, and houses. As I entered the town, I checked the map again. Written in pen next to the location was the letter "S" circled twice. What did that mean?

I slowly drove down the main street, looking both directions. This place was just as deserted as the last stop had been. I kept looking for an S. Was it an abbreviation? Code? Damn. I didn't have a clue.

I turned right and drove down another wide thoroughfare. At the far end of the street, I saw a low, wide building. It looked like a grocery store. A fat red S stood proudly above the main entrance. Faint outlines of other letters were beside the S, but I couldn't make them out. My heart quickened with excitement.

I parked in front of the store. The entrance was a pair of sliding glass doors covered in a thick layer of grime. I wrapped my fingers around the edge of one and pulled to the right. The door ground hard in its track, but gave way.

My multi-tool's flashlight cast a wide beam. The store hadn't been used in years. Rows and rows of empty shelves lined the room. Fossilized garbage littered the floor. I passed the light side to side as I made my way down each aisle. I searched for something, anything useful.

My excitement dwindled. A gnawing sensation grew in my stomach. If I didn't find anything soon, I would be in serious trouble. I had no more fuel and no provisions. I wouldn't survive the rest of my trip. My only choice was to turn back. I could probably cover half the return journey, but then I'd have to walk the rest. Why had I been so foolish?

I scoured the store from front to back and still found nothing. Dejected, I returned to the car. I looked at the ruined town. The houses were nothing but empty husks. The hot wind blew again, sliding debris across the empty parking lot.

I drove in a random direction. I reached an intersection and felt an odd sensation, a strange urge to turn right. I tried to brush it away, thinking it was meaningless. Yet, something was there, beckoning me. I turned the wheel to the right.

The car crawled down the street. Stillness was all around me. At the corner was an abandoned liquor store. It was worth a try. I parked at the curb and approached the building.

My ears perked up. I heard a muffled sound. It was followed by the scrape of a shoe across cement. The building next to the liquor store, a defunct sporting goods store, was the source. It was dark inside.

I walked over, keeping my hand on top of my holstered weapon. I peered inside. Nothing but inky blackness. "Hello?" I said. No response. Still, I had heard something. I stepped into the store. I felt a presence. Frissons raced through me.

I clicked my flashlight on. The interior of the store was filled with rubble. I panned around slowly until I faced the door, but saw nothing. The other corner, I hadn't checked it yet. I swung the flashlight, aiming the beam on the front corner of the room.

A man was crouched there. Every muscle in his body tensed. He brought a knife up to a young girl's throat. His other hand was clamped over her mouth.

"Get the fuck outta here or I'll cut her throat," he growled.

"I don't think so," I said. I drew my weapon and took careful aim.

"What're you doing?" he asked, surprised. "I'll kill her, I swear."

"If you do that, then I'll kill you."

He pressed the knife harder against her throat. A trickle of blood seeped from her flesh. She let out a subdued cry. Her eyes went wild.

Holding my multi-tool in one hand and weapon in the other, I focused. I adjusted my aim slightly. I breathed slowly, steadying my body. "You know," I said, while fine-tuning my aim, "You could just let her go."

"I'll give you to the count of three, then I'll kill her if you don't scram."

"Okay."

He looked confused. He growled again, trying to appear ferocious. "One."

"Two," I said quickly.

"Hey, what're you do—"

The electrodes hit him in the forehead. He pitched backward. The knife clattered to the ground. His body convulsed in large, slow spasms. The moment the girl was free from his grasp, she bolted outside.

I found her huddled in front of the store, shaking. I advanced slowly. I didn't want to scare her off. I knelt beside her. She rocked back and forth, trembling, her eyes fixed on infinity. "Are you all right?" I asked softly.

She didn't say anything.

"My name's Smith. What's yours?"

No response.

"Do your mom and dad live around here?"

To my surprise, she raised an arm and pointed down the street.

"Okay, let's go find them," I said.

I took her small hand in mine, and we walked side by side. She led the way, turning here and there. It wasn't long before we reached an old school. It was two stories tall, wide, with faded yellow paint, and boarded windows. The wood appeared fresh.

"Here?" I asked.

She nodded.

A woman burst out of the building. She shouted the girl's name as she raced toward us. The girl ran to her mother. They met in an embrace, crying happily. The mother dropped to her knees and stroked her daughter's dirty blonde hair.

Behind them, a man, probably the girl's father, walked toward me warily. He was at least a decade younger than me, maybe more. But his long beard and weathered face belied a lifetime of hardship most would never know. Once he had gotten between his family and me, he asked, "Who're you?"

"Smith."

"What do you want, Smith?"

"Just passing through. Looking for some fuel."

"What were you doing with my daughter?"

He looked angry. I raised my hands and said, "I saved her. There was a guy with a knife who had her hostage. In the sporting goods store."

"Who was it?"

"I don't know. Some crazy pedophile."

"A raider?"

"Maybe."

"This true, honey?" he asked, keeping his vision on me. His daughter blubbered out an affirmative response while cradled in her mother's bosom.

The man waved his hand and four men emerged from the school. They brandished a variety of crude weapons: a pitchfork, a shovel, an ax, and a sledgehammer. They locked suspicious eyes on me, as well. The man said to them, "The old sporting goods shop. A raider. Check it out."

Then, to me, he said, "Sorry, but we don't get a lot of strangers around these parts."

"I didn't know anyone lived out here."

"That's how we like it. We don't want to be bothered. Now, you're going to wait right here until those guys get back."

Fortunately, the sporting goods store was close. A few minutes later, the four men returned, carrying the unconscious raider between them. They dropped him to the ground. A large puff of dust billowed around his body. With the charge I'd given him, he wouldn't awaken for several hours.

For the first time since my arrival, the man took his eyes off me. He looked at the raider and said, "I'll be damned. Looks like your story checks out. So, it's fuel you're looking for?"

"Yes."

"You're lucky. We usually don't trade with outsiders. But considering what you've done, I'll make an exception."

"Thanks."

"Are you hungry?"

Just then, my stomach growled. I patted it and said, "I could use a bite."

"Why don't you stay the night? Let us thank you properly for saving my daughter. You can leave tomorrow morning."

"That sounds great."

The small tribe welcomed me into their home. The interior of the school had been converted into a village. Each classroom was a single-family apartment. Some of the rooms doubled as workshops and others as storerooms for supplies. It was dim without electric lights, but candles and reflected sunlight provided enough illumination.

The man introduced himself as Levin, and he gave me the full tour of his community. Men, women, and children came out to greet me. They stared at me like I was an alien. Outsiders were rare here, and outsiders welcomed into the school even rarer. I was given a thousand thanks for what I had done. I smiled and nodded and told them it was nothing.

The day wore on and the sun began to set. The community moved out to the playground behind the school. A series of barrel fires were struck up to provide warmth and light. The various families had prepared a variety of dishes, most I had never heard of. The flavors were incredible. Salt, spice, lard, and all manner of delicacies I had never tasted. My taste buds exploded jubilantly.

"Is every night like this?" I asked between bites.

"No," Levin said. "But my daughter is back. And we captured a raider. These are things worth celebrating."

"What's going to happen to the raider?"

"Hmm, do you really care?"

"Not especially."

"Then concentrate on eating," he said with a laugh.

The people of the tribe played music on homemade instruments. The sounds of woodwinds, strings, and drums floated from the earth to the heavens. The people played and danced and laughed. The sound must have carried on for miles. All of my senses were enveloped by the festivities.

"I'm amazed," I said.

"By what?" Levin asked.

"All of this. That you have this community. And you all seem so normal."

"What did you expect? That we would be mutants?"

"No, not that," I laughed. "In the city we have rumors that people live in the Wasteland, and they're all crazy. To be honest, I didn't think anyone lived out here. I didn't think it was possible."

"Humans are surprising. We can live just about anywhere."

The sun had set, and people were illuminated by the orange glow of the fires. Long shadows were cast across the ground.

With a bloated stomach, I eased back and belched. Levin stretched himself out, too. His daughter laughed and played with the other children. He watched them with a twinkling joy in his eyes.

"How long have you lived out here?" I asked.

"All my life. I grew up here."

"Is it hard?"

"Hardship is relative, don't you think? The city may have abundant food and shelter, but the people are like cattle. Docile and stupid. Contained."

"The freedom you have here is – I don't know – but I'm envious."

"Why don't you stay?"

"I don't think I'm ready yet. Besides, I still have a few important things to take care of."

"This life isn't for everyone."

"No. And neither is the other."

Levin and I sat there with full bellies, talking and laughing. Around us, the other tribe members sang and danced and clapped. They had more fun than I thought possible. As the night grew later, the full moon rose. I had never known how bright the moon was before now. It had always been drowned by the fluorescent lights of the city.

That night, sleep came easily.

The next morning, Levin took me to the grocery store with the S on the front. Around back, hidden beneath the façade of an obsolete electrical junction box, was the town's supply of fuel.

Via hose and funnel, Levin transferred the golden liquid into a pair of aged canisters. As the fuel spilled into them, he asked, "How far are you going?"

"The Capital."

"And you're sure you have to go? We could use a good man like you."

"Thanks, but I've got business there."

"Fair enough."

"Any idea where the next depot keeps its fuel?"

I held up the map and tapped the location, circled in red.

"Sorry, no clue."

Levin pulled out the hose, careful not to spill any fuel. We each took a can and walked to my car. Levin brandished the funnel again as he poured fuel into the car's tank.

We stood quietly. The air blew gently from the south. I gazed out over the flat, arid ground. I had never been so far from civilization before.

The last bit of fuel drained from the canisters. Levin shook each one, trying to extract every drop. He pulled out the funnel and snapped the car's fuel door shut. He extended his right hand. I grasped it firmly. Then, in silence, he turned and walked back to the school.

I didn't stay to ponder my surroundings any longer. I hit the road. When I reached the next fuel depot, I found the stash easily. I refueled and resumed my journey.

The following evening, I pulled up to the next fuel depot. It wasn't even a town, just a small, crumbling gas station from the ancient world. Two enormous floodlights were placed on either side, blasting against the growing darkness.

I stopped at one of the gas pumps and grabbed the fuel nozzle. Before I could use it, I heard the tinkle of a bell and turned around. A man was exiting the gas station holding a rifle.

"What kin I do fer ya?" he asked while chewing on something.

"I need to fill up."

"Dat'll cost ya."

Something told me he had been through this routine before. He seemed well practiced.

"I don't have any money," I said.

"Well, naw, I don't have iny fuel fer ya."

I put the fuel nozzle back into the pump. "There must be something I can do."

Ignoring that, he asked. "Where ya from? Ya ain't dressed like nobody I know."

In my usual attire, I had become the best dressed man in the Wasteland. "I'm from the city," I replied.

"Which 'un?"

"Western."

"Ya look like a city boy wit' dem clothes. Too bad I don't make no deals wit' city boys."

"What about Safety Inspectors?"

He leveled the muzzle of the rifle at me. A jolt of fear electrified my nerves. I quickly raised my hands. "I'm just driving through, that's all. I'm not interested in anything else."

He considered this, slowly chewing on whatever was in his mouth. Then, he called, "Hey! Git out here! Need ya!"

Another man, dirtier and greasier than the first, emerged from the gas station. He stood beside the first man and asked, "What's his story?"

"Inspector from de city. Wants fuel. Whaddaya think?"

"Hmm. Kill him?"

"What 'bout de udders? Dhey might come lookin' fer 'im."

I seized on the chance. "That's right. They will. I'm expected in the Capital in a few days, and they know the route I'm taking. They'll definitely look for me."

The second man said, "All right, then. Get the hell out of here."

"But without fuel, I'm not going far."

"And he ain't got no money," the first man said.

"So, he can do us that favor," the second man said.

"Dat 'un?" the first man said with surprise.

"Okay, sounds good, whatever you want," I said.

The second man waved the first to lower his rifle. He took a step toward me. The crags in his face were deep, accentuated by the shadows thrown about from the spotlights. He gauged me and said, "There's a raider camp about five miles south of here. They keep killing our livestock. And they hit the supply truck that comes to us every three months."

"And you want me to . . ."

"Stop them. Kill them. Whatever it takes. You do that and you can have as much fuel as you want."

I didn't have much choice.

"Deal," I said.

We stared at each other until the first man barked, "Git goin'!"

With a nod, I turned and entered my car. I headed off-road, bouncing over the cracked earth. I couldn't drive fast for fear the tires would blow. The drive took an eternity.

The encampment was easy to find. A semi-circle of tents was clustered beneath a jagged rock formation. I would have expected a group of raiders to be living more discretely. On second thought, what did they need to hide from?

I exited with my weapon drawn. I cocked the brim of my hat up, to let in the last few rays of dwindling sunlight. Ahead, a figure emerged from one of the tents. They were too far away to discern any physical details.

My shoes crunched over hard gravel. The figure watched me intently, not moving. Soon, a second figure appeared, then a third. Now, there were ten people scouting my approach. I felt silly holding my weapon. I didn't stand a chance.

"Hold it," a female voice called.

I stopped.

"Who are you?" she asked.

"Smith. I'm from the city."

"What do you want?"

"Just to talk."

"We've got nothing to say to you."

"I need fuel. I'm almost out. Can you help me?"

There was a lengthy pause. Eventually, the woman said, "Drop whatever you're carrying and walk forward, slowly."

My weapon rattled when it hit the ground. I walked forward at an even pace. The encampment grew larger and the people came into view. They were the sorriest looking souls I had ever seen. Men, woman, and children were dressed in rags. Their bones bulged through their sallow skin. Their lips were dry and cracked. The children were muddy-faced.

A woman, with a face like hardened leather, standing in the center of the group, spoke up, "We don't have fuel. Did those two men send you?"

"Yes."

"Bastards. Why did they send you?"

"They told me if I could stop you from raiding them, they'd give me fuel."

"Bastards," she repeated. "They're the raiders, not us."

I wasn't sure how to respond.

"Do we look like raiders?" she asked with a sweeping gesture.

The tents were moth-eaten, a swarm of flies buzzed around a skeletal goat, and the rest of the people were huddled around a tiny fire. Their cold, ragged bodies were cast in an otherworldly glow. They didn't conjure up images of rough and tumble outlaws.

She continued, "We have to take their livestock. We stole that goat last year. Without it, we'd die. And we've lost several good people over the years trying to deal with them."

The sight of the encampment had left me speechless. She kept talking, "They used to sell us provisions. It was good for a while, but then they started raising their prices. Pretty soon, we couldn't afford anything. I tried to negotiate a deal, but they weren't interested, said they didn't want to trade with us anymore. That's when we started stealing, it was out of necessity. They've killed a few of us in the process. But they sentenced us all to death when they stopped trading."

By now, the other people were losing interest. They had heard all this before. They returned to their duties mending clothes or looking after their children. Soon, only the woman and I remained.

"When they told you to stop us, what did they want?" she asked.

"They told me to kill you."

"Well, mister, as you can see, there aren't many of us. And we're already dying. You probably could kill us if you wanted."

The idea left a metallic taste in my mouth.

"I'll make you a deal. You kill those bastards, we'll take over their operation, and you can have all the fuel you want."

I took a step back. "I'll think it over," I said.

She narrowed her eyes and said, "The next time I see you, I'll know what you decided."

I walked back to my car, retrieving my weapon along the way. The moon had risen now, casting a pale light on the desert landscape. It looked like the surface of the moon.

I sat inside the car, pondering my choices. Whichever side I chose, someone was going to die. If I did nothing, someone was going to die. I racked my brain. No matter what happened, the outcome would be terrible.

I drove back to the gas station. The small compound was bathed in artificial light. The two men were waiting for me as I pulled up to the building.

"How'd it go?" the second man asked.

"They're dead."

He clapped the first man on the shoulder. "Excellent! Some good news for once!"

The first man gave a half-smile, but still held the rifle in his hands, ready for any wrong move on my part.

"So, about that fuel," I said.

"Did he really do it? Or is he jus' sayin' dat?" the first man interjected.

"Good point," said the second man. "Why don't you spend the rest of the night with us? In the morning, you'll take us to the encampment and show us their bodies. After that, you can have your fuel and our blessings."

"If it's all the same, I'd rather head out now."

"Nonsense! You're our guest tonight. Come inside and join us for a drink."

Reluctantly, I followed the two men into the gas station. The inside was stuffed with so many provisions it was difficult to move around. The cramped space was littered with racks of foodstuffs. A makeshift stove and steaming bucket of water, a sink perhaps, stood on the crumbling countertop. Four chairs, a tiny square table, and a bed were in the center of the room.

The first man offered me a chair. As I sat, he yawned. He propped the rifle against the table, the muzzle pointed toward the ceiling, and sat down across from me. Meanwhile, the second man rummaged around one of the racks. He returned with three dusty glasses and a bottle of brown liquid. He sat and poured three drinks.

"Cheers," he said, pushing a glass over to me.

I lifted it, holding it up in the dim light. The brown liquid glinted. "What is it?" I asked.

"Whisky. Give it a try."

It burned my throat. I leaned forward and coughed. The second man laughed. The first was disinterested. He drained his glass in a single gulp. He leaned back in his chair, folded his hands over his chest, and closed his eyes.

"My first time was like that," the second man said. "Coming from the city, the only alcohol you've ever had is wine. This stuff packs quite a punch."

"Have you always lived out here?" I asked.

He refilled my glass and said, "Not me. I'm from the Capital originally. I lived a boring life just like you." He nodded to the first man and said, "Him, he's a native. He's lived in the Wasteland his entire life. I met him about thirty years ago."

"Why did you leave the city?"

"I was run out. I had one of the more egregious safety violations. As an Inspector, I'm sure you can imagine. So, I grabbed my son, and we left. We wandered for about a year. Then, he and I hooked up, and three of us took over this gas station."

I took another sip of whisky. It still burned, but not as badly as it had at first. "So what happened with these raiders?"

"What do you care?"

"I'd like to know exactly why I killed a bunch of women and children."

He nodded and drained his glass. "We used to trade with them. We have a vendor from the city. He comes out every three months or so to resupply us. Costs in the city went up, and so did ours. The raiders couldn't pay, and we can't afford to run a charity."

"What happened next?"

"They broke in here, tried to rob us. We didn't have weapons at the time, so we couldn't defend ourselves. We were scared to death. The next time, though, we were ready."

He rose from his chair. He stood behind the first man, who was dozing. He leaned forward and kissed his bald head. "It was hard living in constant fear. To be honest, I felt bad for them. But not anymore."

"What changed?"

He walked over to the rack of supplies and rummaged around. His voice quavered as he spoke, "Our son. They killed him. He tried to stop one of their raids and they killed him. I can never forgive them for that."

"Those people were starving."

"Good. They deserved to starve."

He found whatever he was looking for and started to turn back. He held a different bottle of liquor in his hand. The first man let out a long, deep snore. Time slowed to a near standstill. I had to choose. The starving people or the old men. Right, wrong, good, evil, none of it applied. I had to pick one or the other.

I stood up and drew my weapon. I fired into the second man's chest. As his body contorted, he dropped the bottle of liquor. It smashed apart. The first man awoke. He was disoriented, but reached for his rifle. I didn't have time for a second shot. I lunged and grabbed the rifle by the barrel. I swung it around, and smashed the stock into the side of his head. He tumbled to the floor.

The men slumbered, almost peacefully. Now, all I had to do was fill up my car and get out of here. I stumbled outside and filled the gas tank. I wanted to get out before they woke up.

"You did it," said a nearby voice.

My heart skipped a beat, and I whirled around. The woman from the encampment and two men were standing behind me. They were dusty and looked like ghosts beneath the white flood lamps. They must have followed me from the moment I left them.

"We could hear it from out here. Sounds like you did a number on them."

"Yeah."

"They're dead?"

"No. If that's what you want, you'll have to do it."

"Sounds like a treat."

"Be careful what you do."

The woman had grown tired of me. "You got your fuel, mister. It's time you hit the road. But before you go, I brought something for you."

She offered a brown paper bag. I inspected the contents. There was a foul smelling mass of herbs inside. I crumpled the bag closed. I didn't want to smell it any longer.

"The last fuel depot is a hundred miles from the Capital, so you'll have to stop there. The man who lives there, he hoards his fuel. He knows me. Give him this and he'll let you fill up," she said.

I ducked inside the car, and pulled the Challenger back onto the highway. The tires hit pavement, and I pushed the pedal down hard, racing over the empty road. The farther I drove, the more the feeling grew that I had left an awful mess behind.

The rest of the cross-country journey was uneventful. I filled up again at another vacant fuel depot. At night I stopped driving and read my book, pouring over the chapter about log cabin construction. Soon, I came to the final location marked on the map.

Before me was a squat cube of concrete. There was a heavy metal door with thick rivets running along the sides, tarnished with age. In the center of the door was a small window, with what appeared to be a camera on the other side, looking out.

A voice, layered with static, barked at me through an intercom, the location of which was hidden. "Who are you?!"

"My name's Smith."

"What do you want?!"

"I'm driving to the Capital. I need fuel."

"No fuel here, go away!"

I held up the bag of herbs and waved it in front of the security camera. "A friend of yours told me to give you this."

The voice abruptly became pleasant, and said, "Well, why didn't you say so? Come in, come in."

There was a loud metallic clack. I put a hand against the door and pushed inward. I was met with a steep staircase leading down into a black abyss. There was no light. There was no railing. There was only a precipitous drop into darkness. I slowly made my way down, feeling like I was descending into Mr. X's cave again.

When I reached the bottom, I pushed through another heavy metal door, as thick as the first but not tarnished by weather. I entered a square room, a command center by its appearance. It had a woodsy, burned smell. At the far end were a Spartan bed and a stack of canned food. On the adjacent wall was a desk with a bank of terminals and half a dozen monitors. None of them revealed anything except the vast expanse of the Wasteland. Sitting at the desk was a hump-backed man, bald, with pale skin. I imagined he hadn't been to the surface in years.

He beckoned with one hand. When I was within arm's reach, he snatched the paper bag and buried his nose in it. He reveled in the odor. Then, he realized I was still present. "Over there. There's your fuel. Hurry up. I want you out of here in ten minutes," he said.

I saw a reservoir, covered with a metal lid, with a beaten metal bucket beside it. I lifted the lid and was greeted by pungent gasoline fumes. I dropped the metal bucket and filled it by hand. I lugged it up the flight of stairs and carefully poured its contents into the Challenger. I did this several times until my car's fuel tank was filled.

I returned the bucket and pulled the lid back over the reservoir. I was exhausted. I tried to sit for a moment, but the man snapped at me, "Get out of here!"

I jumped to my feet and hurried out of the bunker. It was probably for the best. There was no telling what that guy was up to. As soon as I was back outside, the heavy metal door slammed behind me and locked.

An hour later, I met the bright lights of the Capital. Here, things were clean, smooth, and orderly. I had returned to civilization. I had expected more, a sense of awe perhaps, but it didn't come. The Capital was a mirror image of my home city. It had the same drab colors, the same cubic buildings, and the same flood of fluorescent lights. It was as if I had driven days to end up exactly where I started.

21

It felt like I had never left home. The only difference was the Capitol Building in the center of the urban sprawl. It was a cubic monstrosity like all the other buildings, except for a vomit-colored dome rising from the top.

Last night, I slept in my car. When I awoke, a note was pinned beneath the windshield wiper. I grabbed it and tore it open.

"Inspector Smith,

Meet me in my office at the Capitol Building first thing in the morning.

– Orwell"

I crumpled the note and tossed it to the ground. He must have known the minute I arrived.

When I entered the Capitol Building, several heads turned at the sight of me. My suit was wrinkled and dusty, my skin was dirty, thick scruff covered the lower half of my face, and I emitted a foul odor. A week without a shower did much to make me conspicuous.

The lobby swarmed with people. Dozens of them spoke and walked such that the sound became an unintelligible hum. The floor was made of unforgiving stone. A series of large windows above the entrance let in streams of morning light. Two lines were formed with people shuffling single-file. The first was for civilians, the second was for safety agents. The dark suits and bowler hats were a dead giveaway.

I entered the second line and trundled mindlessly toward the front. When I reached the security desk, the guard eyed me suspiciously. I continued with the routine check-in procedure. When I passed through the body scanner, lights above me flashed red and an abrasive klaxon blared.

"Hold it!" shouted the guard. His face bore a scowl, but his eyes betrayed a feeling of joy, a chance to finally do something. "Arms out!"

I spread my arms like a bird's wings. He patted me down. His hands stopped when they found the bulky object in my inner jacket. He reached in and pulled out my weapon. It was heavily scratched from being dropped too many times.

"What's this?" he asked.

"Standard issue weapon," I replied casually.

He radioed for backup. Soon, six more guards surrounded me. Behind me, I heard the groans of people in line. They were going to be late for work.

"How'd you get this?"

"It's mine."

"It's a safety violation to possess one of these."

"Well, I don't own it. It's the one that was issued to me."

"Explain how you still have it."

"I forgot to return it."

My deltoid muscles quivered with fatigue, and my arms began to descend. When they came to rest at my sides, the burning in my shoulders subsided. Meanwhile, the guard continued to scrutinize me. No doubt his pea brain was having difficulty comprehending the situation.

"Why are you so dirty?"

"I haven't had a chance to do my laundry."

"You always have this bullshit attitude?"

"Only when it suits me."

The guard's face turned red. He grabbed a fistful of my shirt and roared, *"You're coming with me, smartass!"*

He started to pull me away when a sharp voice said, "That won't be necessary."

The guard stopped. Orwell walked toward us, his suit immaculate and his bald head shimmering. He flashed his identification. The guard let me go.

"It's all right," Orwell said. "He's one of mine. He's new and a bit hard-headed. Please, excuse us."

The guard stepped back without a word. I straightened my mangled shirt and tie. I stooped and retrieved my weapon. When I stood again, I met Orwell's eye line.

"To my office," he said.

We took the elevator to the fiftieth floor, the top of the building. Orwell escorted me down the hall to a room with a small black placard that read, "Surveillance Department."

It was quite different than the open-aired office to which I was accustomed. The department was subdued. It was a winding labyrinth of offices and cubicles. Many doors were shut. People spoke in hushed tones. The lights were dimmed. The walls were thick with sound-proof material. We wound our way through the maze until we reached Orwell's office.

The windows overlooked the city. From this height, the world below looked like a model. The edges of the Capital could be seen with the Wasteland in the distance.

Orwell sat at his polished desk and offered me a plush chair. I sat across from him.

"I wish you wouldn't have driven. It would have been much faster for you to take the train."

"You wish I had taken the train so you didn't lose track of me."

"Actually, no, I'm on a time-table. I have a job for you that should have been completed three days ago."

"What's the job?"

"A low-level bureaucrat is holding up a piece of legislation I need passed. As I said before, all my other people already have assignments. This can't be completed without you."

I watched him. When he realized I wasn't going to speak, he continued, "This bureaucrat is trying to extort me. He knows the legislation is crucial for my department's future. So, he wants me to pay up, or he'll keep the bill bogged down for eternity."

"What's the bill?"

"It lets my department have independent control of our finances in case of a government shutdown. I could go into the details if you really want."

My eyes had already begun to cross with boredom. "No thanks. So, I find this bureaucrat, then what?"

He waved his hand as if shooing away a fly. "Do whatever it is you do. Work your unorthodox magic. Just make sure he sends the bill through."

Was that it? His master plan? His reason for harassing me to join his ranks? I rose from the deep-cushioned chair. "Does this bureaucrat have a name?" I asked.

"Benson. He's on the thirty-fourth floor."

I exited Orwell's office, and soon found myself on the thirty-fourth floor. It looked more familiar than the fiftieth. The hallways were searingly bright. Beams of fluorescent light bounced across the polished walls and waxed floor. The room was open-air with small cubicles expanding in every direction. Each cubicle had a nameplate, and walls that only rose to waist-height so as to not obstruct any views. I walked up and down each aisle until I found my target.

I knocked on the padded wall. The sound was nearly inaudible, and the man inside didn't flinch. I cleared my throat. Still nothing. I guess I wasn't going to make a subtle entrance. I reached out and tapped his shoulder.

Benson swiveled around. A half-dead look was in his eyes. He scrutinized me, no doubt confused by how dirty I was.

"Benson, right?"

"Yeah."

"Inspector Smith. We need to talk."

He gestured to a folding chair neatly tucked into a corner. I sat down, my legs sticking halfway out of the cubicle. I looked at him and waited. He stared at me. It seemed like I would have to start.

"You have a bill for Surveillance Detail."

"Yeah."

"It's come to my attention that it's being delayed."

Nothing.

"I need you to push it through."

Nothing.

"What can I do to help you move this bill along?"

"Talk to Mr. Orwell."

"He sent me."

"Then you already know."

"Help me out here."

"Mr. Orwell knows my price. When he pays it, I'll move the bill to the voting process."

"Why won't you move it along now?"

"The bill is a big one. It's a small price to pay for what Mr. Orwell gets in return."

"It's your job."

Nothing. I could taste bile rising to the back of my throat. Were all bureaucrats like this?

"Blackmail is illegal."

Nothing.

This guy was maddening. "Look," I said. "It's beneficial to everyone if you just push this thing through. I'll talk to Orwell. We'll get you a promotion at the very least. How does that sound?"

Benson turned his sleepy eyes away from me and returned to his work. I checked my watch. It was going to be a long day.

I folded my hands behind my head and leaned back. I watched Benson go about his morning routine. He typed in short bursts. He checked his messages. He drank coffee. He filed miscellaneous documents. He repeated this over and over. A normal person could have completed his duties in a quarter of the time. He worked in slow motion.

When noon finally came, he excused himself, squeezing by me to leave the cubicle. I stretched my stiff limbs and followed him. He ate lunch outside, on the large covered patio. He had brought his own food: a sandwich, an apple, baby carrots, and water. The lunch, while perfectly safe, was as bland as him.

When the lunch hour ended, we returned to the cubicle. Neither of us had said a word to one another since the initial exchange. The afternoon was the same. Typing, reading, filing, etc. Only he worked even more slowly now. He seemed to be moving backward.

My mind was on fire. I was screaming at him to move faster or speak or screw up or do something interesting. My muscles ached. I could feel them atrophy minute by minute.

Around three o'clock, my eyelids felt heavy. I leaned farther back in the chair and dozed. I awoke as Benson squeezed past me again. It was five o'clock, and he was leaving for the day. I followed him down the long aisle of cubicles, all the way to the elevator.

He turned around and asked, "Will I see you again tomorrow?"

"I sure hope not."

"Then tell Mr. Orwell to pay me."

He slipped into the elevator as the doors were closing. Not that it mattered. I didn't want to ride with him. Another moment with him would be torturous.

Benson hadn't made any mistakes today. He followed all safety regulations to the letter. He was a model employee, apart from the blackmail. Finding a reason to bring him in was going to be difficult.

I walked back to his desk. The entire floor had cleared out. It was ten minutes after five, and not a single bureaucrat remained. I reached into my jacket and removed the salt container, a ration too large for any one person to possess. I hid it in the filing cabinet, low and out of sight. Benson may follow the safety regulations, but blackmail was illegal. That's what I told myself so I didn't feel so disgusting.

I returned to the top floor. Orwell was still at his desk, reading a document on his terminal. He looked up as I entered.

"Well?" he asked.

"Have someone search his office."

"Excellent," Orwell said. "You look exhausted. Go and get some rest."

"I need a place to stay."

"Of course. Talk to Nabokov on your way out. He'll fix you up."

The second to last door on the right held a severe-looking man. Aged, stern, and pock-marked, he would be frightening to children. He was a bit frightening to me.

"Yes?" he asked.

"I'm new. Orwell said you could help me with a place to stay."

"I've anticipated your arrival." He handed me a key card and a slip of paper with an address. "I hope you find everything to your liking."

"Thanks. Good night."

He gave a single nod and stared intensely until I left the room.

There are two types of standard domiciles. The first, the house, was reserved for married couples. Single people could live there under the condition that they were widowed. Everyone else lived in standard one-bedroom apartments. Normally, a man of my age would never be seen in an apartment as everyone is required to be married to a member of the opposite sex by age thirty-five. Exceptions were made, such as for extended business stays.

The building was a high-rise. It looked exactly the same as the one I lived in as a young man. My apartment was located in the middle of a long hallway. I would have neighbors on either side, above, and below. I opened the door. The motion sensor automatically turned on the light. Crisp, conditioned air met my nose. I inhaled deeply.

Clean beige carpet welcomed my weary feet. Tan walls were sparsely decorated with paintings of nature. The living room had a couch facing a small television. To the right was a cramped kitchen and tiny bedroom. Altogether, the apartment was about five hundred square feet in size.

I tore off my clothes and left them in a pile by the door. I climbed into bed, and read the construction book until my mind drifted off to sleep.

Nabokov had five suits waiting for me. The next morning, after I showered and shaved, I slipped into a freshly pressed suit, along with a stiff pair of shoes, and a new bowler hat. I ate breakfast rapidly. Nabokov had seen to it that my fridge and pantry were well stocked. After eating, I went back to the Capitol Building.

Orwell's office was filled with people. He sat at his desk, the morning sun glowing behind him, but subdued by the UV-filter. Two agents flanked him, and four more stood around the perimeter of the room. Sitting in a chair in front of the desk was Benson.

Orwell noticed me and said, "Come in, Inspector Smith. Mr. Benson and I were just having a chat."

"About what?" I asked, poorly faking ignorance.

"Mr. Benson was discovered with an illegal surplus of salt. As you well know, this is a safety violation. I'm afraid he may have to be sent to Safety Re-Education."

Benson looked at me with burning eyes. It was the most emotion he had ever displayed. Orwell continued, "Mr. Benson disputes the charges."

"That's right!" he shouted. *"This bastard planted it!"*

"Do you have any proof?" I asked.

"You spied on me all day!"

"Safety Inspectors do that sort of thing routinely. How else are we supposed to find safety violations?"

Benson grumbled something to himself, and then said to Orwell, "Check the security tapes. You are Surveillance Detail, aren't you? You'll see him plant it."

"Do you mean this footage?" Orwell asked, turning his terminal around.

There were two angles on Benson's cubicle: one directly above and one from the aisle. In both, it showed a man removing the salt ration from his suit jacket and placing it in the filing cabinet. The motions were mine, but the face belonged to Benson.

"You bastards!" he cried. *"You forged that!"*

He leaped out of his chair, his hands aimed for my throat. Before he reached me, two sets of powerful hands grabbed him. Two agents pulled him back and pinned him on the chair.

"Mr. Benson," Orwell said. "It seems to me that with the illegal salt ration and attempting to assault a Safety Inspector, you have forgotten what it means to be a safe citizen. I have no choice but to send you to Safety Re-Education."

Benson's breathing slowed. The fire in his eyes died. His eyelids became sleepy. His taut muscles relaxed. "Fine," he said complacently. "I'll push the bill through."

Orwell grinned slyly and said, "I'm glad to hear you are so reasonable." He looked at the agents holding him and said, "See that he does it, then let him go."

In an instant, the room cleared out. Only Orwell and I remained.

"You got a new suit. It looks very good on you," he said.

"Yeah. Thanks. So, about Bens–"

"I'm glad we got that all straightened out. I appreciate your efforts. Why don't you take the rest of the day off?"

After that bewildering display, I wasn't about to argue with him. On my way out, I stopped by Nabokov's office. I thanked him for setting up my apartment, and I asked him where I could get a good cup of coffee. He directed me to a place two blocks away. He had been right. They served fantastic coffee.

22

It was raining. Traffic had come to a standstill. Precipitation forced the Auto-Driver function to stop moving cars, because driving on wet roads was unsafe. Rows of white lights stretched out before me. Red lights stretched the other direction.

I had decided to walk to work as my apartment was only a few blocks from the Capitol Building. The rain had started as a few sprinkles, but my face stayed dry beneath the brim of my hat. By the time I had my coffee, the rain had reached a steady downfall.

I stood on the sidewalk, beneath the coffee shop's awning. The hot coffee was welcome against the chill morning air. People walked by with umbrellas, or ran if they did not have one.

Tiny tendrils of smoke drifted up from the concrete where the raindrops hit. A man raced from the street into the coffee shop. He rubbed his face, trying the ease the pain from where the water had pelted him. While the structures of the First Government were kept in excellent condition, if one looked closely, one could see the pock-marks of corrosion left behind from the rain.

I was waiting for the rain to let up. I wasn't in the mood to get drenched, and I didn't want to have my new suit ruined in the process. I didn't care if I was late to work. I sipped my coffee again, and felt warmth radiate through my chest.

Now that I had joined Orwell's ranks, I had to figure out a way to help Mr. X bring him down. Then, once I was in Mr. X's good graces, I could kill him. But how would I do it? It could take years to learn the inner workings of Surveillance Detail. I didn't have that much time. I had gone far in life on luck, and I hoped that Fortune would smile on me again.

The rain relented, and I left the safety of the awning. I walked the next two blocks quickly, only getting damp in the dissipating mist. Street lights were reflected in the puddles along the road. I reached the Capitol Building and started up the front steps. As I entered, the cars began to move again.

Orwell wasn't in his office. I wandered aimlessly through the department, finding most of the doors locked. Eventually, I found myself in Nabokov's office.

"I'm looking for Orwell," I said.

"He's watching the proceedings for his new bill," Nabokov said.

"How do I find him?"

"He'll be in the upper gallery of the Senate Hall."

"The Senate, huh? What's it like?"

"Turbulent, I suppose."

I finished my coffee, and tossed the cup into a nearby waste basket. I caught Nabokov's eyes following me. They radiated a look of distrust.

"Do you need directions?" he asked.

"No thanks, I'll find it."

I followed the plethora of signs to the Senate Hall. I had never seen the First Government in action, no one outside of politics had. News of the First Government's accomplishments permeated radio, television, and film, but there was never a candid look into what they actually did. Politicians were cloistered. With each step toward the Senate Hall, my pulse quickened. My stomach fluttered. I felt like I was in a dream.

I reached the entrance. A red lighted sign reading, "Senate in Session – Do Not Enter" blazed above the thick wooden doors. Farther right was a second set of doors with a placard reading, "Observation Gallery – Open." I entered the second set of doors.

Before me was a dark tunnel with a pale square of light at the end. In the distance I could hear a subdued roar, almost like static. I walked toward the light, feeling like I was either about to be born or about to die. The light grew bigger and the noise ever louder. Finally, I emerged on the other side. The sound was almost deafening. Hundreds of voices shouted, clamored, and screamed at each other simultaneously. Amid the din, no single voice could be distinguished.

I stood on a balcony. Below me, about fifty feet down, was the Senate Hall. A steep staircase led from the main entrance down the center of the room. The room was crescent-shaped. Desks were crammed together. Aisles between desks were exceedingly small. At each desk sat, or stood, a politician who was screaming, gesticulating, and sometimes throwing objects at the other politicians. They appeared to be children in the midst of tantrums. The desks were pointed toward the far wall of the room. Standing there was a man who flapped his arms in distress. A few objects were hurled at him, but he ducked below them like someone who dodged objects professionally. Above him was a digital display that read, "Bill 14823674942 – In Favor: 0, Against: 0 – 3:23 Remaining."

The balcony held a smattering of onlookers, other safety agents, but it was mostly empty. To the far right was Orwell, who watched the proceedings with a placid expression. My footsteps were masked by the noise below. I sidled up to him, and he jerked with surprise. He wasn't used to people sneaking up on him.

"Is this your first time in the Senate?!" he asked with a shout.

"Yes!" I shouted back.

"What do you think?!"

"It's loud!"

Orwell laughed.

"What are they doing?!" I asked.

"Voting!"

"It sounds like arguing!"

Orwell rolled his eyes playfully.

"There aren't any votes yet!" I said, nodding to the display which showed only two minutes left on the clock.

Orwell pointed to the hapless man beneath the digital readout and said, "It's the foreman's job to tally the votes!"

"But with everyone shouting, he can't hear them!"

"Precisely!"

Thirty seconds remained. The countdown for the bill was almost over.

"Is it usually like this?!" I asked.

"Always!"

"So, nothing ever gets done!"

"On the contrary . . ."

A thunderous horn blared. The congregation quieted instantly. They settled into their chairs. Airborne paper floated to the floor. The shift from noise to silence made it seem like I had suddenly gone deaf. The foreman spoke, "Deliberation has ended. Votes are zero to zero. The motion passes."

I gave Orwell a perplexed look.

"You see," he said, no longer shouting, "in the matter of a tie, the proposed bill is automatically passed."

"How many end up like this?"

"In all the years I've been here, every single one."

The digital readout changed. It now read, "Bill 1114561132 – In Favor: 0, Against: 0 – 30:00 Remaining."

Instantly, the politicians were back on their feet, spewing noise and launching objects. A fight broke out between two of them. They traded punches, grappled, and soon one was having his head slammed into a desk by the other. No guards came to their aid, and no one else seemed to notice.

"This is our bill, Inspector Smith!" Orwell shouted.

"And they only get thirty minutes to debate it?!"

Debate wasn't the right word to describe the disarray below, but it was the only word that came to mind.

"That's right! Thirty minutes per bill! Every bill gets passed! How's that for efficiency?!"

The chaos continued. The people moved in waves, there was a rhythm to their entropy. Mesmerized, I lost track of time. Every safety statute went through this process. The invasiveness, the overreaching, the overprotectiveness, the conflicting laws, the idiocy of the regulations all made sense now. All one had to do was draft a bill and it would become law. The politicians couldn't compose themselves long enough to consider whether or not a bill was logical. And even if one politician could, it wouldn't matter with all this gridlock.

"Pay attention, Inspector Smith, this is a big moment for you!"

I looked at the digital readout. The final ten seconds drifted by. When the clock hit zero, the horn blared again, and the congregation hushed. The foreman spoke, "Deliberation has ended. Votes are zero to zero. The motion passes."

A few moments later, the circus began anew. Orwell turned to me with a pleased look on his face. "Congratulations, your first bill passed!"

Orwell ushered me out of the balcony and back to his office. I collapsed into the plush chair in front of his desk. Outside, the clouds had broken up, and the gray sky was turning to blue. As the light brightened, his features became cast in shadow.

Orwell pushed a button on his desk. "Two cups of coffee," he said into the intercom.

A few minutes later, Nabokov brought a tray with coffee, cream, and sugar. He slid it onto the desk. Once he left the room, I said, "So, is he your . . ."

"No, but he is quite an asset. He can acquire anything. A remarkable talent, truly. I hear he used to be a top field agent in his younger days."

I looked at the foreign objects on the tray. The dreamy sensation came back to me.

"A token of my appreciation for your hard work. Have you ever had coffee with cream and sugar?"

"Never."

"Then you're in for quite a treat. Go ahead."

I let the sugar crystals slide off the tiny spoon like grains of sand. I wasn't sure how much to add, so I stopped after the third scoop. I poured cream from the tiny carafe, watching with astonishment as it puffed into a brown cloud. A quick stir of the spoon made the entire drink change color.

Orwell, a creepy voyeur, watched me, and I tried my best to pretend like I didn't notice. I raised the cup to my lips and sipped. The bitterness I had expected wasn't there. A sweet, creamy flavor met my tongue. My mouth puckered involuntarily. "Too sweet," I said.

Orwell chuckled and fixed his own cup. "Once you drink it this way, you'll never drink it black again."

"How could this be illegal?"

"The government's stupidity knows no bounds."

"And that's why you want to change things?"

Orwell drank from his cup and let out a satisfied "ah." He set the cup back down and replied, "Exactly."

"What would you do?" I asked.

"First, that circus downstairs would have to go."

"They can't get anything done."

"You already have a good grasp of politics. Without the Senate, we could have actual officials scrutinizing, debating, and voting on real legislation."

I drank more, and let him continue.

"The Second Government, as I like to call it, would have specifically appointed politicians. Qualified individuals who will sort out matters, vote, and run the government far more efficiently."

"An oligarchy?"

Orwell waved the notion away. "No, no, nothing quite so dramatic."

"How would your system be any different than what we already have?"

"You see, the Second Government will have an official leader, a president, like of a corporation. He would preside over all the decisions. He would appoint the politicians. He would sign bills into law or veto them. The office would also hold powers letting him act independently in case of political gridlock, which, as you can see, can be a serious problem."

"And I suppose you would be the first president?"

"If I must," he said, feigning humility. He was a bad actor.

"Quite a sacrifice."

Orwell didn't react.

"I'm not sure the people will go for it. They like electing those guys, even if they don't do anything. The taxpayers like to pretend that their voice matters," I said.

"The measures I enact will be temporary. Only until the system is corrected enough to hand the reins back to the people."

"How long would that take?"

"How long does it take a boy to become a man?"

"I don't know, but I'm sure there's some kind of legislation about it."

Orwell had grown cold. I slurped down the rest of my coffee and banged the cup on the tray. "Any new assignments for me?" I asked.

"Yes," he said. He put his cup down, and the contents sloshed onto the tray. He turned his terminal toward me. It showed a woman's dossier. "This is a mid-level bureaucrat named James. She's working on a special project of mine. Check on her progress and report back to me."

I exited the office without another word. I had enough of Orwell for one day. Working in close proximity to him was testing my patience. His scheme was ridiculous. While the First Government didn't work, installing this guy at the top of the food chain was only going to make things worse.

On my way out, I stopped in Nabokov's office. "I heard you can get anything," I said.

"Within reason."

"Could you get me some cream and sugar?"

"Easily."

"How much will it cost?"

Nabokov frowned at me and said, "Nothing. You are a member of the Surveillance Department."

He returned to his work. He didn't bother looking at my pleased reaction. I knew Surveillance Detail had its perks, but I didn't realize to what extent. Life as a safety agent had sucked me dry for years, and it was time I got a little something in return.

23

The lady James was not much to look at. Her hair was stringy and matted with dirt. She wore a dingy gray blouse that barely contained her bulging belly. She sat with her back to me, typing on her terminal with one hand, and holding a sandwich with the other.

As a mid-level bureaucrat, she had her own office, not unlike Wyndham's. The décor was dated, several pieces of trash lay on the floor having missed the waste basket, and the shades were drawn to keep the room dim. A stack of papers leaned precariously on her metal desk, ready to topple over.

The office door was halfway open. Before I could knock, she said, "Come in."

I entered. She took a bite of her sandwich. Still looking at the terminal, she said, "So, you're Orwell's new errand boy?"

"I'd like to think not," I said to the back of her head.

"He's been trying to get you for a while now. And now you're here and doing whatever he asks. What would you call that if not his errand boy? His stooge?"

"I'll stick with errand boy."

James turned around. She stuffed the rest of the sandwich into her mouth and swallowed without chewing. She eyed me suspiciously and said, "And now he's sent you after me."

"I have no idea why I'm here."

"Checking up on the project?"

"That's right, but I don't know what the project is."

She belched. The stench wafted over to me. I tried not to react.

"He's consolidating his power. He has me working on a bill that will give Surveillance Detail control of utilities in a national emergency," she said.

"I take it you have a problem with this."

"You really are nothing more than a blunt instrument, aren't you?"

"I'm a government employee. They don't exactly select us for independent thinking."

She hurled a few more insults my way. While she did, I managed the work out the implications of Orwell's two bills. Her reason for concern was well founded, but didn't align with my goals.

"If you're done snooping for your master, would you please leave?"

"Let me ask you something. You already seem to know a lot about me. So, you probably know I'm no fan of Orwell. What if you and I worked together? What if we finished the bill, but worked out a way that Orwell wouldn't gain any real control?"

She considered this for a moment, then narrowed her eyes, and said, "Get out of my office."

I obliged. It was good to get out of there. It smelled like a wet dog.

I rambled back to the top floor. Nabokov was waiting for me by the department's entrance. His face was made of stone.

"Mr. Orwell needs you for a job tonight," he said. "He needs you to supervise someone on a sensitive assignment."

"Sounds fascinating."

"You'll be on Surveillance Van Sixteen with Safety Inspector Wells."

"Great."

"Do you need directions?"

"No thanks, I'll find it."

I reversed course, headed downstairs. Talking with Nabokov was disquieting. He was always around. There was something unsettling about a man who never left his job.

I spent the rest of the day in the cafeteria. I lounged in a chair in the farthest corner, and picked at some food while watching streams of people file in and out. Some spoke quietly, others laughed raucously, others ate alone, and others escaped quickly, not wishing to linger.

While the sun set, and the light outside grew pale, the fluorescent bulbs above grew brighter. Shadows disappeared beneath the harsh, artificial light. Darkness had no chance to gain a foothold.

By the time night had fallen, only a handful of stragglers remained. They, too, eventually left, only to be replaced by the night shift, shambling in to get cups of burned government coffee. I checked my watch. It was time to go.

The second sub-basement of the building was a parking garage for government vehicles. Vehicles had to be parked in designated areas, partitioned by department. With a multitude of signage in front of me, it was easy to find Van Sixteen.

A very tall, wiry young man stood outside the van. He had one foot kicked back against the wheel, his arms folded over his chest, and his weight transferred against the van's door. For the start of the shift, he already looked like a wreck. His hat was missing, tie pulled halfway down, and shirt crumpled.

"Hey," he said. "You Smith?"

"Yeah."

"I'm Wells. Nice to meet'cha."

We shook hands.

"What do you say we hit the road? The sooner we get done with this, the sooner we can go home."

I liked him already.

We clambered into the boxy vehicle, and Wells punched some coordinates into the computer. The Auto-Driver eased us onto a long ramp, which we ascended until emerging onto a surface street.

"What are we in for tonight?" I asked.

"We have to vet a new informant."

Wells explained the process. I had been an agent long enough to know how it worked, but I didn't interrupt him. Despite having a significant presence with surveillance cameras, vans, and airborne drones, there simply wasn't enough infrastructure to know what everyone was doing at all times. Therefore, agents relied heavily on the use of informants. Usually, they were angry neighbors or disgruntled spouses. The government didn't mind. Any chance to enforce safety statutes was for the common good.

Tonight, we had a different kind of informant. It was someone who had information about a bureaucrat who had violated safety statutes. Since it was political, Orwell wanted us to surveil this guy before we decided to use him. My presence was to make sure Wells didn't botch the job. Although, if he did botch the job, my presence didn't guarantee I would do anything about it.

"What's this guy's name?" I asked.

"I don't know. We just have a photo and a location."

"Where'd we get that?"

"Another informant."

I leaned the seat back and tilted the brim of my hat over my eyes. "Wake me up when we get there."

The gentle acceleration and slight sway of the van lulled me to sleep. I awoke when Wells tapped my shoulder and said, "It's time."

We were parked outside a restaurant. The informant was inside. Wells already had his binoculars up to his eyes. "He's at the third table from the right. The guy eating alone."

I stared at the front of the building and tried to imagine what he looked like. Wells was unwavering. He gripped his binoculars firmly, and he never once took his eyes off the target.

I leaned back in my seat again and said, "Wake me up when he does something interesting."

Wells woke me up again. We were moving, several car lengths behind a generic white car. This time, Wells was driving. The

Auto-Driver didn't have a "follow" function, so he had to take control.

"What happened?" I asked.

"He ate dinner and left. I have no idea where he's going."

"Home?"

"No, he's heading downtown," Wells said, agitated.

"What's wrong?"

"This guy was supposed to eat and go home. The job was only supposed to last two hours at most. But now he's headed who knows where. This could take all night."

"It's the night shift," I said. "The longer he takes, the less cases we have to work."

Wells snorted and turned the van right. "Maybe I wanted to knock off early."

"You got a date tonight?"

"No. Just going home to my wife, that's all."

"How long you been married?"

"Three weeks."

That explained his eagerness to get home, and his disheveled attire. "Why don't you let me take over? I'll drop you off at your house," I said.

"I appreciate the offer, but I can't. I'm lucky to have this job. I wouldn't want to upset Mr. Orwell by doing something I wasn't supposed to."

"Orwell likes it when his agents do what they aren't supposed to do."

"What do you mean?"

I decided it would be better not to tell him. Wells was a good kid, young, married, at the start of his career. I didn't want to put any ideas in his head and sabotage him. The last thing he needed was to end up like me.

"Forget it," I said.

For the next ten minutes, we drove in silence. The white car ahead of us parked on the street in front of a nondescript brick building. The target got out of his car and jogged inside. He was only out of sight for a few moments. He came back out holding a small package under his arm. He jumped into his car and drove away. We were back on the road, following him in silence for another twenty minutes.

The white car pulled up to a house and stopped. The target quickly left his car, and carried his package inside.

"Let's see what kind of goodies he has," Wells said.

He watched through his binoculars for several minutes before offering them to me. I looked. It was switched to X-ray mode. The target sat in the living room, a skeleton, with some kind of dense object in his hands. His phalanges moved in a flurry over the object. Occasionally, he picked up an object to his right and appeared to take a drink. It wasn't visible in the X-ray spectrum, so it could have been anything. I handed the binoculars back to Wells.

"What do you think?" he asked.

"Hard to say. He's alone. Seems to be having a good time."

"Anyone having that much fun is bound to be doing something illegal. Let's go."

I followed him to the front door of the house. I raised my hand to knock, but Wells caught me by the wrist.

"Don't. They always run. I can't deal with a runner tonight."

Wells spoke like a veteran. While I didn't disagree with him, his single-mindedness was starting to wear thin. I dropped my hand and stepped aside. Wells took out his multi-tool and opened the door.

The target stared at the TV. It flashed blinding colors at him. The sound was a cacophony of dings and booms. His fingers tapped furiously at the buttons on the object in his hands. A bag of junk food and a green drink in a plastic bottle stood on an end table. They were foreign to me, but most likely contraband. These were probably what had been in his package.

We walked into the living room. He was entranced and didn't notice us.

I thought I recognized what he was doing. He was playing an electronic pastime from centuries ago. They had long since been deemed unsafe due to causing irrevocable brain damage, epilepsy, and social inadequacy. He had the device jury-rigged from various spliced wires circling into the back of the TV.

After waiting several moments, Wells calmly said, "Safety Inspectors."

The man leaped to his feet, and tossed the object in his hands away. Wells already had his weapon trained on him. "Have a seat."

The man slowly returned to the couch. His eyes were wide and bloodshot. He breathed in quick bursts. His palms were shaking. "Wha-what's going on?"

"Shut that thing off," Wells said.

The man turned the TV off. The quiet that came after was welcome. The man started to blubber and said, "N-no, d-don't arrest me, please!"

"We're not here for that." With a sigh, Wells holstered his weapon and continued, "We're from Surveillance Detail. You have some documents for us?"

A flood of relief washed over him. "Yes, yes, of course. Let me get them for you."

He left the room.

"Who's he informing on?" I asked.

"You wouldn't believe it."

"Who?"

"Capek."

The name registered. I knew him from the old days, back when I used to run Prohibition Detail. The last I heard, he rose steadily through the government ranks. He was now the head bureaucrat in charge of finances, the CFO of the nation. He managed the flow of money into and out of everything the government touched.

The informant returned holding a thick folder. I flipped through it curiously. There must have been two years' worth of damning evidence in the file. Capek was involved in matters that would interest Healthcare, Prohibition, Sex, Traffic, and Entertainment Details. The file was a first class blackmail ticket. Capek controlled the money, and whoever controlled him would be the most powerful man in the country.

"So," the informant said, his demeanor starkly changing to one of overconfidence. "Am I going to get that promotion?"

"That's not for us to say," Wells replied.

"You tell your boss I risked a lot to get him this information. If he doesn't like it, I can let Capek know what he's up to."

Wells took out his multi-tool again, and took a picture of the informant and his contraband. "That wouldn't be a good idea, not with you in possession of all these illegal goods," he said.

A disconsolate look spread across the informant's face. "If it pans out, I'm sure you'll be rewarded," Wells said.

We returned to the van. I tossed the folder into the back seat. Documents spilled out in every direction. Wells didn't seem to mind. The Auto-Driver chauffeured us back to the Capitol Building. Wells checked his watch and huffed. We hadn't been gone too long. His wife would still be waiting for him when he got home.

"Wells," I started, "you seem like a nice guy. I think this detail might not be for you."

"What do you mean?"

"This department, it isn't for nice people. I'd hate to see you get mixed up in dirty deals. Have you ever thought about a different assignment?"

"This one pays the best."

"But what Orwell has you doing, it's not right."

"Maybe not."

"Can you honestly say you like being involved in this racket?"

"Like's got nothing to do with it."

"You should get out."

"You should mind your own business, Smith."

"Maybe I'll let Capek know what's going on. Sure, he's breaking laws, but blackmailing him isn't going to help."

Wells' eyes flashed crimson. He shoved his face within a centimeter of mine and spat, "You won't say a goddamn thing! Don't compromise this department! I won't go back to Sewage Detail! Stay out of it!"

He turned back to face the road. He remained silent for the rest of the drive. I had never worked Sewage Detail, but it couldn't be worse than Sex Detail, and I had worked there twice.

Both times I got demoted I had tried to do the right thing, to expose injustices. But doing the right thing only ever led to disaster. Maybe doing the wrong thing was better. It seemed to be the only way to get ahead.

The next few weeks went on like that. Orwell would send me along with a surveillance van or he would have me intimidate bureaucrats into doing his bidding. I felt disgusted. No matter how much I bathed, I couldn't scrub the slime off. I wasn't working Surveillance Detail any longer; I was now a member of the Blackmail Department.

24

Rays of light bombarded my face. The sun was rising and blasting through the window's UV filter. I squinted, but the strain gave me a headache. Orwell sat in front of me, his body cast in silhouette. It was a struggle just to look at him. He probably liked it that way.

"Inspector Smith," he started, "I've got something different for you today. I'm loaning you out to another department."

"I had no idea I was in demand."

"I owe a favor to Inspector Verne, head of Mortuary Department. He's down a man, and I need you to fill in."

"I didn't realize you did favors."

"My entire operation runs on favors."

"I guess that's true. All right, what am I doing once I get down there? You want to know what he's up to?"

"No. Just do whatever he asks. There isn't anything more to it."

Mortuary Detail was located in the deepest sub-basement of the building, in a bunker below the parking garage. The room was dismal. It had gray concrete walls, water dripped from cracks in the concrete ceiling, the concrete floor was stained brown by some unknown residue, and a pair of naked light bulbs flickered to illuminate the room.

Verne welcomed me in, and steered me into an ergonomic metal chair. He was about my age, with a bushy mustache, and a thick shock of gray hair atop his head. He looked at me earnestly with gray eyes behind his glasses. He tried to look upbeat, but the deep lines around his eyes betrayed his weariness.

"Welcome, welcome. I'm so glad to have you here."

"Thanks. You know, this is my first time in Mortuary Detail."

"Wonderful, wonderful. Where have you worked before?"

"Lots of places. A couple of them twice."

"How interesting. And how is it working for Mr. Orwell?"

I shrugged.

"I see, I see. In any case, we must get going. We have two very important inspections today. It should take quite some time. Here, let me give you this."

He pushed a clipboard into my hands. A thick stack of blank forms and a pen were attached. Verne held an identical clipboard in his hands.

I looked around the dark room, seeing only concrete. "Is this it? Is it just you down here?" I asked.

"I used to have a partner, but he was deemed insane a few weeks ago. Since then, Mr. Orwell has been kind enough to bring in replacements on a rotating basis. At least until we can find someone permanent. Well then, we must be going. We are already three minutes behind schedule. If you don't mind, after you, after you," Verne said as he directed me out of the room.

Inside the department car, Verne sat in the driver's seat. After the automatic seat belt buckled him in, he strapped on the Standard Driving Safety Helmet, adjusted the mirrors, and entered the destination coordinates into the Auto-Driver computer.

We didn't move. What was he waiting for? I looked at him, and he asked, "Excuse me, but aren't you going to wear your safety helmet?"

"No."

"No?!" He looked like I had just punched him in the gut. "But it's regulation. All passengers in a moving vehicle are required to wear a safety helmet. It's Safety Statute 52-14-81."

"Come on, Verne, who do you know that actually wears the helmet?"

"I do."

"Forget it. Let's just go."

He stared at me. He looked broken inside. I sighed and acquiesced. "Fine, just give me the damn thing," I said. It was going to be a long day.

Verne pulled a second helmet out of the storage compartment and gave it to me. Once I had it on, along with my seat belt, Verne put the vehicle in motion. As we drove out of the garage, he checked his watch and said, "Seven minutes behind schedule, oh dear, oh dear."

The first mortuary was located in a sleepy neighborhood. The sign above the door read, "City Mortuary 15." Once we parked, I stripped off the helmet and hopped out of the car.

Verne, however, was still inside. He remained seated, helmet and seat belt on, as the vehicle's engine whined down. Once it fell completely silent, he unstrapped himself and exited.

"Shall I explain the procedure to you?" he asked.

"No thanks, I'll follow your lead."

He looked like I had just kicked his dog in the head. I put my hand on his back and pushed him toward the building. Verne managed to compose himself by the time he reached the front door. He knocked politely and rang the doorbell. We waited. The only sound was that of a slow-moving car passing by on the street.

A man in a black suit opened the door. "Yes?" he answered in a deep tone.

"Hello, sir. Is this City Mortuary Fifteen?"

"Yes, it is."

"My name is Safety Inspector Verne. This is Safety Inspector Smith. We are from the Mortuary Department. City Mortuary Fifteen is scheduled for a routine safety inspection today. May we come in?"

"Of course," the man replied without emotion.

We stepped inside. Verne held up his clipboard and readied his pen. I had left mine in the car. Verne spoke to other man, "I would like to get started in the front office."

"Right this way."

The man in the suit led us there. It was nothing more than a desk, a terminal, and a few chairs. Verne immediately set himself to work. He scrutinized every detail of the room. He used the tape measure in his multi-tool to measure the dimensions of the furniture. He cataloged the amount of dust in the room: trace amounts. After each item was inspected, he jotted thorough notes on the paperwork. Meanwhile, the other man stood patiently, not saying a word. He had experienced this before. I grew tired with boredom.

"Well then, we're done in here, yes, done in here. Please show us to the reception room."

We moved into the room where a corpse would be put out for its family to gawk at it one last time. Currently, the room was empty. Verne went straight to work inspecting the curtains, the chairs, the wallpaper, and the riser that would hold a coffin, all while taking detailed notes.

Next, we moved into the preparation room. It was a stark contrast to the warm and comforting rooms we had seen before. This room was cold, with a tile floor, metal gurneys, and embalming equipment spread out. A corpse lay on one of the tables, covered by a thin white sheet.

"You've left a body out! A body out!" Verne exclaimed.

"I'm sorry, sir. My partner is away at the moment, and I was preparing this body when you came to the door," the man replied.

"This won't do," Verne said while furiously scribbling on the form. The man in the suit was taken aback. Apparently, this was something he hadn't experienced before. Once Verne finished writing, he looked at the man sternly.

"I'm afraid there are some serious safety violations here, sir," he began. "The guest chairs in the front office are two centimeters too close to the desk, which poses a great risk of a guest hitting their knees on the desk. The reception room's curtains were drawn one centimeter too close to the window which poses a fire hazard. The preparation room is by far the worst. Chemicals have been placed too close together, this hemostat has sharp edges, and, worst of all, a body was left unattended. What if this corpse had a disease? It could have killed us all!"

"This person died of natural causes. There is no danger—"

"That's not the point."

The man's jaw nearly hit the floor.

"Fortunately, you have barely come in under the mandatory minimum number of safety violations for an arrest. So, I will be able to let you off with a series of fines," Verne said.

"Sir, I won't be able to afford that. Is there anything I can do?"

"If you speak with the Appeals Department within thirty days, they might waive the fines if you qualify."

"How can I do that?"

"Just make an appointment."

"I'd like an appointment right away."

"I believe they are booked out nine hundred days for appointments at the moment."

"Is there anything else I can do?"

"You can make an appeal directly to me."

"Yes, let's do that. Can you please waive these fines?"

"I'm afraid you'll need to make an appointment with me within the next thirty days for that."

"Okay. When can I see you?"

"I have availability in sixty-two days."

"But if I can't see either of you in thirty days what can I do?"

"You'll have to pay the fines."

"Is there any way I can be seen earlier?"

"Yes, you can make an appeal for an earlier appointment with the Appeals Department. I believe they are booked out nine hundred days at the moment."

The man's head dropped. It swung between his shoulders like a pendulum.

Verne wrote something on a fresh sheet of paper and handed it to the man. When he saw the amount, he withered to the floor. The fines were exorbitant, and usually it was easier to be arrested than have to pay. Verne's assessment was going to leave him in financial ruin. I offered him a sympathetic look, but he was too shrouded in misery to notice.

"Good day to you, sir, good day," Verne said.

Back in the car, Verne was already strapped in with his helmet on. He was contemplating another checklist. "Very dangerous, very dangerous," he muttered. "He's lucky we got there before anything happened."

I reluctantly fastened my seat belt and safety helmet. I knew Verne wouldn't drive until I had done so, and I didn't want to waste any more time with this guy than I had to. He entered the coordinates of the next inspection site, and the Auto-Driver escorted us laconically.

The second inspection went much like the first. Verne sniffed out the tiniest details, much to the chagrin of the mortuary owner. The preparation room was the worst. The furnace used to cremate bodies had a small sliver of jagged metal twelve inches inside the aperture. This could potentially cut the skin of a corpse, which was a dangerous safety violation to the deceased. The mortuary owner was left with a crippling bill, and we left him in a blubbering heap on the floor.

When we returned to the car, the computer indicated a message awaited. Verne played it. There had been an accident at the city morgue. We were being called to conduct an emergency investigation and arrest whoever was responsible. Upon hearing the message, Verne's eyes widened with terror. With a tremulous voice, he said, "Oh dear, oh dear. This is going to ruin the schedule. Oh, oh, oh, oh, I hate it when this happens."

Inside, I was dying. This was only going to add length to an already excruciatingly long day. I now knew why Verne's last partner went insane. One day on the job with him, and I was ready to be committed.

The city morgue was a one-level building adjacent to a downtown hospital. Any person who was suspected of dying of something other than natural causes was sent here for an autopsy. But just to be certain that no dangerous safety violations were missed, every single body wound up here anyway.

Upon entering the building, we were met by the morgue supervisor. He welcomed us nervously and escorted us to the site of the accident. He took us back to a room that was stacked end to end with metal drawers stuffed full of bodies. I shivered. Several refrigeration units kept it quite cold in here.

In this room, we met a young doctor. He was rubbing his elbow tenderly, and he gave us a wan smile. Verne introduced us formally, and then asked what happened.

"One of the refrigeration units broke. There's a puddle of water on the floor. I didn't see it. I slipped and landed on my arm," the doctor said.

"Hmm, yes, quite a problem—" Verne began.

He was interrupted by a harsh bang. Everyone turned toward the sound. The room's door was flung open, and three safety agents sauntered in.

"Healthcare Detail," the lead agent announced. "What's going on here?"

The doctor and supervisor exchanged a confused look. Verne glanced at me. I could see anxiety boiling inside him. He timidly said, "Excuse me, Inspectors. We are from Mortuary Department. I'm Safety Inspector Verne. We have already started an investigation."

"Mortuary? What the hell are you doing here?" the lead Healthcare agent asked.

"We were called to inspect the accident."

"Why would they call you?"

"Well, this is a morgue."

"Yes, but a person has been injured. This is clearly a Healthcare case."

"The fact that this is a morgue supersedes the injury. My department has purview over all incidents occurring in locations dealing with storage or disposal of human remains."

"Give me a break!" the lead Healthcare agent said haughtily. "No one gives a shit about Mortuary Detail's purview."

The two agents continued to bicker. Verne held his ground. To my surprise, as he delved into a dizzying recital of facts and statutes, his confidence grew. The lead Healthcare agent replied with boasts about the importance of his department. His two agents stood like wax dummies on either side of him. The doctor and supervisor watched with growing alarm. With the argument getting heated, whatever the outcome, it was going to be bad for them.

Verne held an open, pocket-sized book in his hand. He thrust a finger at a line on the page. "It states here, that in this situation, Mortuary Department has complete authority."

"Don't you realize Mortuary Detail is just a subdivision of Healthcare? We own you!" The lead Healthcare agent shouted.

"We have complete autonomy."

"Go to hell, you slimy bastard!"

"I'm afraid I cannot. Besides, we were on the scene first, so that gives us control of the situation."

The lead Healthcare agent's face was bright red. He raised his fist and said, "If you don't leave right now, they're gonna have to put you in one of those body bags."

"Threats of violence are a violation of Safety Statute 00-00-04, an offense automatically punishable by Safety Re-Education. Not to mention that your shoelaces are dragging on the floor, a violation of Safety Statute 62-89-11, an expensive fine. Hit me if you must, but keep in mind there are five witnesses here," Verne replied matter-of-factly.

The lead Healthcare agent surveyed the room. All eyes were on him. He slowly lowered his trembling fist. He straightened his posture and adjusted his tie. "Well, Healthcare is a very busy detail. We've got plenty of other things to do. If Mortuary thinks they can handle such a complicated case, I would love to see them try."

He grumbled something to his agents. The three of them turned around in perfect synchronization and exited the room, slamming the door on the way out.

Verne looked at the doctor and supervisor. "My apologies, gentlemen. Please, tell me again what happened."

"There's a puddle on the floor next to the broken refrigeration unit. I slipped and landed on my arm," the doctor said.

"And the other units?"

"All in perfect working order," the supervisor said.

"When did the unit in question break?"

"I'm not sure. Sometime last night."

"Do you have any past history of accidents?"

"No. I've been supervisor here for eight years, and this is the first."

"I see, I see. And you, doctor, when did you report your fall?"

"I was just finishing an autopsy. I wanted to complete it. So, I don't know, maybe thirty minutes later."

Verne's eyes opened wide. "So long! Don't you know the maximum time for reporting an accident is five minutes?"

"No, I didn't know that," the doctor said.

"Ignorance of the law is not an excuse," Verne chided. "Have you called a repairman for the broken unit?"

"Not yet," the supervisor said. "I wanted to call you first so we could do everything by the book.

"That was very wise, very wise," Verne said. He looked at me and asked, "Do you have any questions for them, Inspector Smith?"

"None."

Verne took a few moments to write on one of his forms. When he finished, he said, "As you know, there are several egregious safety violations here." He looked at the supervisor and said, "I'm afraid I need to arrest you for failing to contact a repairman in a timely fashion." He turned to the doctor and said, "And I'm afraid I need to arrest you for failing to report an accident in a timely fashion."

"Wait! What? I thought you said it was 'very wise' for us to call you before the repairman," the supervisor protested.

"Yes, that was wise. Otherwise, we wouldn't have been able to arrest you."

"But I'm the injured one," the doctor pleaded. "Why are you arresting me?"

"In the time you didn't report the accident, several other people could have been injured. You placed this entire area in danger."

The room was empty save for us and the stacks of corpses.

I finally spoke up, "Hey, Verne, don't you think you're going a little too far? There's no one else here to get injured. Let's give these guys a break."

"A break? No, I'm sorry, I can't do that. That's inconceivable."

"Let's stop bothering them. They work hard enough as it is."

"I'm sorry, Inspector Smith, I can't overlook this. That would be a violation of Safety Statute 28-43-01, and I'm not about to break the law. I can't believe you would even ask me such a thing. Now, gentlemen, if you would please come with us."

Verne escorted the doctor and supervisor out of the building. They hung their heads in shame. I trailed behind them. I wondered how safe it was to leave the city morgue unattended, but I kept that question to myself.

We piled into the car, but didn't leave until everyone wore a seat belt and safety helmet. Thankfully, the ride to the Capitol Building was short. We deposited the prisoners in a couple of cells, and returned to the department's underground tomb.

Verne pulled out a pair of terminals from his desk. He divided a mountain of paperwork evenly and left one stack next to each terminal. "So much to do," he said. "Now, Inspector Smith, I'll have you take the stack on the right. If we both work without a break, we should be done by nine o'clock tonight."

I craned my neck around, taking in the full scope of the concrete bunker before settling my gaze back on Verne. "I don't think so."

His gray mustache twitched. "I'm sorry?"

"I won't be doing that."

"But you must, you must! Mr. Orwell has loaned you to me. For today, you must act as if you were a member of this department. And you must do the paperwork."

"Verne, the thing you don't realize is that I don't care."

His face turned the color of ash. He looked as if he had just walked in on me having sex with his wife. After a moment, he gasped, "But dereliction of duty is the most severe of all safety violations."

"Whatever you say. See you around," I said, walking toward the door.

"You are violating Safety Statute 99-99-99! This will have to go in my report!"

I rode the elevator back to the top floor. The farther I got from that dungeon, the easier it was to breathe. Surveillance Detail's subdued atmosphere was a welcome relief. I almost found myself relaxing.

I walked into Orwell's office to let him know I was done with his favor. Orwell's chair was empty. Nabokov stood beside the desk, tidying some papers. He cocked his head to the side and looked at me with cold eyes.

"I'm done with Mortuary Detail," I said.

"Very well. I shall let Mr. Orwell know."

"Can I ask you a question?"

"Yes."

"Verne. What's wrong with him?"

"I don't understand."

"Ah, forget it."

I turned to leave the room. Something nagged at the edge of my brain. I turned back and asked, "Verne is going to report me for a safety violation. Is this something I need to worry about?"

"Oh, no. No one reads his reports."

25

The party was in full swing. A woman staggered by, wine glass tilted in her hand, and the hem of her dress torn. People crowded together, sweating from the heat. The air was thick with jubilant shouts, like a summer night filled with trumpeting insects. All through the mansion, people carried on in various stages of chemically-assisted bliss, with all sense of inhibition locked away.

A man in a tuxedo, missing an entire sleeve, grabbed the staggering woman. He wheeled her around, forced his tongue into her mouth, and fondled her breast. She dropped her wine glass and oozed into his advance. The glass hit the marble floor and rolled away unbroken, leaving a trail of red wine behind in an arc.

A pianist banged away, sloppily striking several keys at once. He reeled back and forth on his bench, staring at the woman in front of him with glassy eyes. The woman, her brain already emptied, sat atop the piano, bouncing up and down in time with the rhythm, her top missing, and her flesh jiggling prominently.

A man to the right of the piano wore no pants. His glasses were askew on his face, and his hair was tousled. He passed from person to person, hugging them, and telling them how much he loved them.

Directly across the ballroom from where I stood, a crowd had gathered around a table where two men were facing off in a drinking competition. Lines of empty glasses stood in rows on either side of them. They simultaneously picked up a full glass of wine each, and guzzled them down without taking a breath. The spectators cheered them on, many of them sloshing their own wine onto the floor as they did.

People danced and shouted and laughed and sang. Some had collapsed unconscious onto furniture at the corners of the room. Others became sentimental and cried into their drinks. Somewhere in the crowd, a fight broke out. No one moved to stop it. It ended with one man's face a bloody pulp, and the other man screaming as he cradled a broken hand.

At long last, Orwell appeared. He had been sequestered in one of the upstairs bedrooms, meeting with an upper-level bureaucrat. He descended the half-moon staircase and approached me. He wore a finely tailored tuxedo, and stood out as one of the few sober individuals here. Nabokov, wearing his uniform, was close behind.

"Any sign of Capek?" Orwell asked.

"I saw him about half an hour ago. He took a couple of politicians into his office," I said.

"He's still back there?"

"He hasn't been out since."

"Very well. There's another bureaucrat I need to talk to. The next time you see Capek, I want you to leave your post and notify me right away."

"Okay."

Orwell murmured something to Nabokov. Then, the two of them ascended the half-moon staircase, melting into the throng of people.

Every year, Capek threw a huge party. All of the First Government's highest-ranking politicians and bureaucrats attended. The parties were legendary for their debauchery. The wine flowed freely, unencumbered by safety regulations. Nabokov and I, as well as three other agents, attended as Orwell's personal bodyguards. Assassination was unheard of in the history of the First Government, but considering the dirt Orwell had on Capek, he wanted to be prepared.

The party had started three hours ago. The three agents and I took up positions at each corner of the enormous ballroom so we could see everything. The sea of people was so confusing that we saw nothing. None of us had ever been a bodyguard, so we hoped that this was what bodyguards did. Nabokov kept himself by Orwell's side as a deterrent to assailants.

When the party started, guests filtered into the mansion, exchanged platitudes, navigated the room daintily, and sipped at their drinks. As the room became fuller, it became hotter. The guests drank more to quench their thirst. Their thirst turned to a desire to flood their brains with alcohol. By the second hour, the party raged at full-tilt with no signs of fatiguing.

Capek lived in a mansion on the northern outskirts of the city. No one questioned how he could afford such a home while everyone else had an identical one-level house. No one questioned this because everyone knew the answer. Still, no one seemed to mind. Ignoring this discrepancy was a small price to pay in exchange for one night of bliss each year.

The mansion was three levels high, and sat on a secluded plot of earth. The outside was designed with ornate columns and floor-to-ceiling windows. The inside was adorned with expensive paintings, white walls that seemed to stretch up forever, an ornately hand-carved ceiling with figures from First Government mythology, and gilding on every corner.

The ballroom was huge beyond belief. It was decorated like all the other rooms, but was dignified with a marble floor and a chandelier of hand-blown glass, each of its lights a sparkling prism.

The band had taken a break to lubricate their brains, leaving the pianist behind. Now, they stumbled back to their instruments. They played unmelodiously, and an altogether different song than what reverberated from the piano.

Being in a room filled with drunks is only fun for the drunks. I wanted Orwell and Capek to cross paths so they could sort out their business, and then I could go home.

I was no closer to sabotaging Orwell's plan, and I was no closer to avenging Lowry. I had settled into Surveillance Detail just like I had every other department. It had only taken a few days for me to become complacent.

The party dragged into its fourth hour. The wine poured and poured. New bottles materialized out of thin air. The band played worse, the guests became rowdier, and I grew more tired. My knees had locked and my legs ached. I didn't have the endurance to stand in one position all night.

At the far right of the room, Capek appeared. He was extremely tall, barrel-chested, with a face like a ham, and a thick beard to match the curls of red hair atop his head. He looked like a lumberjack that had been transplanted into a tuxedo. He flashed a toothy grin at his guests as he waded into the crush of party-goers.

Simultaneously, Orwell reappeared at the top of the stairs. He spotted Capek instantly. He said something to Nabokov, and they made a beeline toward the host. When they were face to face, each man glared at the other.

"Orwell, I'm so glad you could make it. Although, I don't recall inviting you," Capek said dryly.

"How could I miss out on the nation's most gala affair?"

"And did you have to bring your thugs?" he asked with a nod toward me.

"My entourage, nothing more."

"Enough pleasantries. What do you want?"

"To discuss my proposal."

"My answer is still the same. Now, if you'll excuse me, I have guests to attend to."

Capek tried to push himself past Orwell, but Orwell grabbed him, wrapping his hand only halfway around Capek's meaty bicep.

"Just a moment," Orwell said. "I believe I have something that will change your mind. And it can't wait."

Capek stared down at him, no doubt wondering if he could squash his adversary like an insect. He seemed to use all his energy to prevent his vehemence from spilling forth. He motioned toward the adjoining hallway and said, "Follow me."

The three men started toward Capek's office. Nabokov looked at me and jerked his head in the same direction. As I unlocked my knees and swung my legs, the stiffness melted away.

Capek's office was smaller than I had expected. It was a tiny square, with just enough room for a bookshelf, a desk, and a pair of chairs. The furnishings and carpet were as extravagant as the rest of the adornments that populated the mansion.

Capek stood behind his desk with his hands in his pockets. Two of his bodyguards flanked the room. Orwell stood opposite Capek, on the other side of the desk, with Nabokov beside him. The room was cramped. There was barely enough space for me to stand by the door.

Capek was less pleasant. "What is it now?"

Orwell maintained his composure. "Some new information I recently acquired. I think it might help persuade you to see things my way."

"You're insane. I'll never agree to it."

"Now, now, give it a chance. Why don't you peruse these documents before you make your final decision?"

Like magic, Orwell produced a folder from his tuxedo jacket. He slid it across the desk. Capek stared at it like it was a snake. Slowly, he reached down and opened the cover. He flipped through the first few pages. He didn't blink. His eyes drifted back up to Orwell.

"So, this is your game?" he asked.

"I assure you, it's not a game."

"Where did you get this?"

"I'm afraid I can't reveal my sources."

Capek furrowed his brow, and swept his eyes over me. "It was you, wasn't it?"

"That's right," I answered.

"Ah, yes," Orwell said. "You remember Inspector Smith."

"I should have buried you farther down than Sex Detail," Capek said. His hands clenched into fists. He motioned around the desk, but Orwell stopped him by simply raising his hand.

"You may not like Inspector Smith, but he's not your concern tonight," Orwell said.

"Where did you find that piece of shit?" Capek growled.

"He's one of my men now. That's all that matters."

"Fine," Capek said with a low grunt. "What do you want?"

"Control of your office, your finances, and your executive powers. You get to stay on as a figurehead. Otherwise, these documents get released, and you might find yourself working for Sex Detail. It's not a bad deal when you think about it."

Capek collapsed into his chair. The corrupt bureaucrat had finally been tamed by the only language he understood.

Nearly a decade ago, when I was head of Prohibition Detail, and Capek was the director of my local office, I brought criminal conduct reports about several top agents, his friends, to his attention. My hard work was rewarded with a demotion to Sex Detail. He flew up the ranks to his current position as puppet master of the Capitol.

I hated him for years while I toiled my way back to a decent department. History repeated itself when one of Capek's cronies busted me back to Sex Detail for a second time. Then, my anger thawed, melting into apathy. When I looked at Capek now, I felt nothing.

"All right, you win," Capek said feebly.

Orwell smiled and ran his hand over his smooth head. "Wonderful. I'm so glad we could come to an understanding."

"I need a drink," Capek said.

He reached into a drawer, and pulled out a bottle of whisky and a tumbler. He paused and looked at Orwell. He pulled out a second tumbler, and filled them both. He slid one glass across the desk, and lifted the other to his lips.

Orwell studied the brown liquid. Capek sipped the liquor and eyed his adversary. "You could at least take a drink with me," he said.

Orwell raised the tumbler up to the light. A glint from the lamp sparkled in the curvature of the glass. He gazed at it for a while, and then, satisfied with his inspection, he gulped down the drink.

He smacked the tumbler down on the desk. Silence fell upon the room. The two men stared at each other in state of suspended animation. An eternity passed.

"Oh," Orwell said casually. "You were expecting something? You thought the poison would have kicked in by now?"

"I don't know what you're talking about."

"You are trying to kill me," Orwell said matter-of-factly.

"Don't be ridiculous. I drank it, too."

Orwell went on, as if conversing with an old friend, "Of course you didn't poison the whisky. It would be a shame to waste your favorite vintage. Instead, you left a poisonous residue inside my glass."

"Don't be ridic–"

"I knew you would do it. Desperate men do desperate things."

"But why didn't it work?" Capek asked, exasperated.

"I discovered the type of poison. For the last three months, I've been dosing myself with it. In trace amounts at first, and then in larger quantities to make myself immune."

"How did you know?"

With his usual domineering smile, Orwell said, "I see everything."

He walked toward the door. I moved into the hallway to let him pass. As he exited, he said, "Now that this dirty business is concluded, I think I'll enjoy the rest of the party."

Nabokov followed Orwell. I peeked back into the office. Capek was stunned. Years ago, I would have taken pleasure at this sight, but now it didn't affect me. Capek looked like everyone else whose life had been ruined by safety agents.

I entered the ballroom. The party had reached fever-pitch. People danced and groped and swayed. Orwell jostled through the crowd like a pinball. Suddenly, a sharp noise rang out from above. Orwell clutched his shoulder and collapsed with a cry. A man stood at the second floor railing holding a rifle. Smoke curled from the barrel.

Shrieks of terror rose from the crowd. The people turned riotous as they streamed, panic-stricken, for the exit. Nabokov raced up the half-moon stairs like a man half his age. Several of Capek's bodyguards appeared and began to grapple with Orwell's other agents.

I started forward, but I didn't get far. A brawny arm wrapped around my neck and squeezed. My body snapped back. Air refused to enter my windpipe. I flailed, trying to escape, but the grip around my neck tightened. I flung both elbows back wildly, hoping to hit something. They landed in flesh. The arm around my neck loosened. Quickly, I shoved my right hand between the arm and my neck. Air rushed into my lungs. I kicked my legs out, using gravity to wrest myself down and free.

I rose and spun around. Capek snarled at me and lunged forward. I dodged and threw a fist at him. I connected with his jaw, but the attack didn't faze him. The beast lashed out.

The club he called a hand cracked against my skull. My vision exploded like a white hot star. My ears rang. The ceiling whirled by me, and the floor rotated into view. I reached out with both hands and caught it. I pushed back and righted myself, and swung out my elbow.

Bone hit bone. Capek recoiled, clutching his face, just beside his eye. I staggered toward him and jerked my knee into his groin. As he doubled over, he managed to fling his fist into my stomach.

I wobbled backward. Capek and I were at eye level. Hatred burned in his eyes, fear in mine. He started to rise. I stuffed my pain down and launched forward.

We collapsed to the floor together, me on top of the beast. I hit him again, but he didn't feel it. His hands shot up and wrapped around my neck. His thumbs pressed into my larynx.

I tried to choke out a breath, but released a wet gurgle instead. I flailed again, landing weak blows. Capek grinned and began to chuckle maniacally. The world grew dimmer. Purple blood pulsed in my eyes. My lungs were on fire. My fingers groped inside my jacket. They found hard molded plastic.

The weapon was in my hands. I pointed down and pulled the trigger. The electrodes didn't have far to travel. They buried themselves into the base of Capek's neck and lit him up like a bulb. Electricity coursed through him and into me. My body spasmed, and I was flung to the floor, banging my head against the hard marble. Every muscle in my body felt like it was about to pop. Air entered my lungs, but tasted like smoke.

Somehow, I didn't lose consciousness. I scrambled onto my knees, ready for another assault. Capek lay before me, eyes rolled into the back of his head, drool trickling from his mouth. His breath rattled in his chest.

The screams of the party-goers filtered back into my awareness. People were streaming out, but had formed a bottle-neck at the exit. They pushed into each other. Some fell to the floor. Some were trampled. Drunken confusion heightened their terror.

The gunman reappeared at the top of the stairs. He vaulted down them. Nabokov sprinted after him. "Smith!" he shouted. "Stop him!"

The gunman blew past me, racing down one of the hallways. I looked for my weapon. It had skittered away after I discharged it, and I couldn't see it through the whirlwind of legs. Racked with pain, I stumbled after him, blurting out some nonsense to make him stop.

I pursued him into the hallway. He had reached a dead-end, save for a window. He considered jumping through it, but whirled back around. I limped toward him. My mind felt like it was attached to someone else's body.

The gunman pressed the butt of his rifle to his shoulder. He trained the weapon on me. I was too exhausted to do anything other than let him shoot me.

Heavy footsteps pounded the floor behind me. Nabokov shouldered me out of the way, and I careened into the wall. He ripped something out from his jacket. It wasn't the standard issue weapon. It was a handgun. He raised it and fired four times.

The gunman arched his back and the rifle discharged into the ceiling. He fell against the window, but the glass didn't shatter. He slumped forward, his head hanging limply. The white shirt of his tuxedo slowly changed to red.

Nabokov barked something at me, but his words were garbled. He moved toward the gunman, his firearm still aimed. I wandered into the ballroom.

The room was almost completely cleared out. All that remained was smashed furniture, shattered glass, and bodies. Capek's bodyguards smoldered on the floor. Two of Orwell's agents were transformed into bloody heaps. Several dead party-goers lay twisted and broken. Capek dozed with a peaceful expression on his face.

Orwell sat up with one of his agents at his side. His right hand squeezed the opposite shoulder, which seeped with blood. He groaned.

"Don't worry, sir, the ambulance will be here any minute," the agent said.

Orwell gave me a sardonic smile. "Glad to see you're still alive, Inspector Smith," he said between grunts.

"I'm like a bad penny," I replied, equally exhausted.

Nabokov returned to the ballroom and said, "The shooter is dead, sir."

Orwell nodded.

"Orders?" the old man asked.

"I want Capek in Safety Re-Education. Make sure he signs over full control to me within the hour, whether he's conscious or not."

Paramedics burst into the room. They surrounded Orwell and immediately began to work. The dead bodies were inconsequential. They rushed Orwell out of the mansion and into a waiting ambulance. Nabokov and the remaining agent took Capek away in handcuffs.

My weapon was underneath the piano. I picked it up and admired several new scratches in the plastic. It had seen a lot of abuse.

I ambled up the half-moon staircase, and wandered into one of the bedrooms. It was decorated luxuriously. I peeled back the covers of the bed and slipped inside. Sleep overtook my wrecked body. I didn't awaken for an entire day.

26

Orwell almost had complete control. All he needed was the bill James was working on. Once he had that, he would be the de facto dictator of the First Government. He had no plans to become president of a Second Government. My plot to impede him never materialized. If I didn't do something now, no one would be able to stop him.

James was the key. I had to plead to her, get her to believe that I wasn't one of Orwell's yes-men. Together, we might draft a bill that would secretly strip Orwell of his newfound powers.

I rode the elevator to the forty-seventh floor of the Capitol Building. James' office door was closed. I knocked, but there was no answer. I opened the lock with my multi-tool and went inside. The place had a foul stench. The desk was in disarray. The waste basket overflowed onto the floor.

By this time of day, James should have been here. I checked with the front desk. She hadn't shown up for work yesterday, either. No one had heard from her. I flashed my credentials and they gave me her home address. It was time to take a drive.

She lived in an apartment on the east side of the city. She was set to live here for another year before being assigned a husband, lucky guy. Her apartment also happened to be on the forty-seventh floor.

The same wet dog odor wafted from beneath her apartment door. I knocked but received no answer. I unlocked the door and entered.

Stacks of miscellaneous items were piled from floor to ceiling. A narrow path snaked through the apartment. Huge mounds of objects, chairs, clothes, empty food containers, plastic bags, and more, rolled through the place. It was a garbage dump. Strangely, the one thing it didn't have was a dog. I struggled forward despite the obstacles and odor.

"James?" I said to no reply.

It was a small apartment, so my search wouldn't take long. I checked the kitchen. It was similarly decorated with the sink bubbling full of random objects. Flies buzzed around a stack of dirty dishes. James had quite a collection of stuff. The side hallway and bedroom contained more of the same.

I found her in the bathroom.

Somehow, she had cracked open the ceiling and tied a thick rope around the plumbing for the apartment above. She hanged over the bathtub, her toes dangling just above the porcelain. Her eyes were turned up and to the right. Her skin was pallid, and her mouth lolled open. She wore the same outfit she had on when I last saw her. The air was putrefied, far worse than the rest of the apartment. She must have been like this for days.

I couldn't easily approach because the room was stuffed with as many items as the rest of the apartment. I didn't bother searching for her telephone. I went across the hall and asked to use the neighbor's. I called Healthcare Detail to report the body. I asked the neighbor the last time he saw James alive. He didn't know. He said she kept to herself and never spoke with anyone in the building.

I returned to the apartment. I tried to sift through the mountain of garbage to see if anything was suspicious or out of place. A large pile of debris inched toward me, slowly at first, and then turned into an avalanche. Junk swarmed around my legs and settled at waist height. If I was shorter, I would have drowned.

I waded out of the mess and went back to the building's hallway. Outside the door, two men were waiting: Wells and Verne.

"I don't remember calling Mortuary Detail," I said to Verne. I turned to Wells and said, "Or Surveillance Detail."

"Mortuary Department has full authority over any case dealing with human remains," Verne said.

Ignoring him, I said to Wells, "I guess it's your turn to fill in, huh?"

Wells' face looked ready to detonate. "Just tell us what's going on," he said.

"I came to visit James. When she didn't answer the door, I became very concerned. I went in and found her dead, hanging in the bathroom."

"Oh dear, oh dear," Verne said. He wrung his hands together and walked into the apartment. He shrieked in dismay when he saw what waited for him inside.

"What business did you have with James?" Wells asked.

"No business," I said. "She was a close, personal friend of mine."

Wells contemplated whether or not I was lying. Verne whooped again. Wells sighed and entered the apartment.

"Have fun," I said.

I slapped at my suit and knocked away the dirt in little plumes. After enough time had passed, I decided to go back inside. Verne and Wells had freed James' neck from the noose, and were gingerly lowering her body into the bathtub.

"Who was she?" Verne asked.

"A mid-level bureaucrat," I said.

"Is that how you talk about all your close, personal friends?" Wells asked suspiciously.

"You should hear what I say about people I don't like."

The two men hefted the corpse again, and carefully walked single-file toward the bathroom door. They had to move cautiously. One wrong move could topple over the stacks of objects and trap us all inside. I backed away and navigated the bedroom's mounds of garbage so they could pass. They continued on through the living room.

I re-entered the bathroom. I examined the noose that was coiled on the porcelain tub. It was coarse and thick. The knot had been loosened in taking her down, but I could tell it had been well tied. I took a cursory look around the room. If there had been a struggle, it would be impossible to tell.

When I stepped out of the apartment, James was being zipped into a black vinyl bag. Wells looked bitter. Verne looked bewildered as usual.

"Verne, will you let me know when the results of the autopsy are ready?" I asked.

"There won't be an autopsy. It's obviously a suicide," Wells said.

"Oh, I see. That's how Mortuary Detail pays back Orwell for use of his agents."

Verne's body shook, and his bushy gray eyebrows sprang high into the air. "I know it's highly irregular. It makes me sick, sick not to follow protocol. But I must do this."

"Anything else, Smith?" Wells asked intensely.

"No. Have a good day, fellas."

Verne and Wells carried the body away. They slid into the elevator and disappeared. I faced the open door of James' apartment. Should I call someone to clear this stuff out? It would probably be faster to take a match to the apartment. I pulled the door shut. It wasn't my problem.

At midnight, I returned to Surveillance Detail. Nabokov's office was near the entrance. I half-expected to see him sitting there, motionless, silently awaiting instructions. But his office door was closed and the lights were off.

The rest of the department appeared empty, but the night crew was here somewhere. I had to be sure to avoid them. I crept through the interior halls. The lights were turned down and the rooms were quiet, save for the hum of terminals running in the background.

I followed the signs to a room marked, "Data Storage." It was locked. I looked up, I swung my head around in either direction, and I checked the hall behind me. There were no cameras nearby.

My pulse quickened as I slid my multi-tool into the lock. A sense of dread pulled me back. Doing this could land me someplace far worse than Sex Detail. Then again, I didn't get here by playing it safe.

I unlocked the door.

The room was cramped. One wall was lined with terminals. The rest of the wall space was lined with filing cabinets that went up to the ceiling.

From what I knew about the department, they stored this month's surveillance footage hard copies in the filing cabinets, and after a month, they would be transferred to a storage facility someplace else in the Capital.

The files were organized by date. Unfortunately, there were thousands of them. After two hours of searching, I was able to pull up the surveillance footage around James' apartment.

I basked in the cool, green glow of the terminal's screen as I watched the video feed. From multiple angles, I watched as she gloomily entered the apartment building, rode the elevator, and entered her apartment. She looked just as unpleasant as the day I had met her. Nothing seemed amiss.

There were no cameras inside the apartment, so I would have to check the external infrared feed. I pulled up the footage. The apartment building was a giant red and orange blob. There were far too many heat signatures to make out anything. My last chance was an X-ray feed. X-ray feeds only came from surveillance vans, which were common but not ubiquitous. I checked. There it was, an X-ray feed.

James was a skeleton, treading carefully through her apartment. She opened the front door. She stood there, her mandible moving up and down, but no one was in the doorway. It looked like she was talking to a ghost.

The skeleton was forced back, pushed by nothing, and the front door closed on its own. James turned and dipped, bent and pirouetted. With skeletal legs kicking, she was dragged by the wind into the bathroom. Her head snapped back as if hit by something. She collapsed to the floor. Over the bathtub, the ceiling plaster crumbled, broken by a phantom. James was then hoisted above the bathtub. Her bones thrashed violently as her life faded away.

Unless she really had been attacked by a ghost, the image of her murderer had been erased.

Next, I found a video feed of Orwell's office from earlier in the day. There was no audio, but he was barking at Nabokov. Was he ordering James' death? Although it proved nothing, it could be useful.

I snapped my multi-tool into the terminal and copied the videos. Quickly, I returned everything to where I found it. I stood in the small room, unsure what to do. The next move wasn't obvious. I decided to go home and get some rest. I hoped the next morning would bring an answer.

Six hours later, I returned to Surveillance Detail. Nabokov sat at his desk. His hands were folded together, and his eyes stared ahead like a doll's. I shook away the creeping feeling that rippled over my skin. I walked to Orwell's office. He dismissed a few other agents and bade me to sit. His arm was in a sling.

"How's the pain?" I asked.

"Improving."

"Got anything for me today?"

"Yes, I have a message for you."

"A message?"

"From Inspector Verne. He wanted you to know that they did an autopsy on Ms. James, after all. She died from, let's see," he diverted his eyes to a piece of paper on his desk and read from it. "Asphyxiation. Strangled herself with a rope. No evidence of foul play."

"Is that right?" I said coldly.

Orwell looked back up and said, "A true tragedy."

"What about the bill she was working on?"

"I've assigned it to someone else."

"Good thing."

"Yes, indeed. Well, I appreciate your hard work at the party. If it wasn't for you, we might not be having this conversation. Why don't you take the day off and relax?"

"Thanks."

My feet carried me out of the building and to my car as fast as possible. I fired up the engine and sped away. When Wells and I had tailed the informant, he picked up a bag of contraband. The little brick building shone like a red beacon in my mind. I drove there, keeping my foot pressed hard against the accelerator.

The building appeared dark inside. I pounded on the front door with a fist. There was no answer. I opened the lock and entered.

Light streamed in behind me, a rectangular shaft cutting through the darkness. To my right was a long, moldy wooden bar. Huge boxes stood where the liquor bottles would have been. Chairs and booths were stripped out and replaced by more boxes.

A man stood behind the bar, dazed, not believing that someone had just walked in. "Hey! Who are — what the — get out of here!"

His eyes darted side to side. He looked for an escape.

I held up both hands and said, "It's okay. I'm not here to cause trouble. I'm actually working for your boss, Mr. X. I need to get a hold of him."

The man hesitated. His head dripped with sweat. His hands shook. He continued to look around the room.

I tried to calm him. "Have you ever seen a safety agent in here? Of course not. The truth is nobody cares about the contraband. It's just a job to pay the bills."

The man's brain snapped back to coherence. He reached under the bar and grabbed something. He was trying to pull it out, but it appeared to be stuck. I leveled my weapon at him. He froze.

Calmly, I said, "Mr. X and I worked out a deal. I need to talk to him. I'm here because this is one of his way stations, and, honestly, I don't know how to get a hold of him. Once I'm done, I'll leave and forget all about this place."

The man nodded. He moved slowly, bringing his hands into view. He held a telephone. He placed it on the bar. With my weapon trained on him, I pulled the receiver to my ear and stepped backward, stretching the cord as far as it would go.

"Dial," I said.

He dialed the number. As it rang, I kept my weapon locked on him.

"Yeah?" a gruff voice answered.

"Mr. X, please," I said.

"Think ya got the wrong number, pal."

"Tell Mr. X it's Inspector Smith."

"Don't know what yer talkin' about."

"Tell him it's about Orwell, and it's urgent."

There was a pause. After a moment, the gruff voice said, "Hold on a minute."

The minute stretched into five. At length, a new voice came on the line. It was a female voice, soothing and arousing at the same time. I recognized it instantly. She was the woman I had spoken to in the church.

"Mr. Smith, I thought you had forgotten about me."

"I've been busy."

"And what can I do for you?"

"I've got what you want, a way to take down Orwell, but you may have your work cut out for you."

"What is it?"

"A video feed from Surveillance Detail. It shows a bureaucrat being murdered. It's not exactly iron clad, but it should be enough to make Orwell play ball with you."

"Good work, Mr. Smith."

"I didn't do this out of the kindness of my heart."

"Yes, you'll be rewarded. I'll have a representative of mine—"

"No, I want you."

"Pardon?"

"I'm heading back to the city immediately. Once I'm there, I want an audience with you. It's the least you could do."

The other end of the line clicked. I dropped the receiver. It swung back and banged against the side of the bar. I reached into my jacket with my free hand and removed the multi-tool. I tossed it onto the bar where it landed with a clatter.

"Make sure that gets to Mr. X right away."

The man behind the bar grunted an affirmative. With my weapon still aimed, I backed out of the room. I pulled the door shut and holstered my weapon. Now all I had to do was get out of town.

I turned around. Nabokov stood on the sidewalk. His arms were crossed over his chest. His bowler hat was cocked at an odd angel. He narrowed his eyes at me.

My heart stopped beating. My lungs froze. The way station's door had been open the entire time. He had overheard everything.

"Smith," he started.

I didn't let him finish. I bolted to the right. I kicked my legs as hard as I could. Nabokov was fast. I hoped I was faster.

My car was parked at the end of the block, about twenty yards away. My legs pistoned up and down, and my arms wheeled at my sides. Behind me, Nabokov's footsteps pounded the concrete, getting closer. I pumped my legs harder. Adrenaline surged through my veins. I suddenly felt lighter. My feet were like feathers, and I glided over the sidewalk. My hat popped off and fluttered backward. Fear propelled me faster. I gained distance on the spry old man.

The car was in sight. I turned my feet on their sides and skidded to a stop. I flung the door open. I dove inside. I uprighted myself and revved the engine.

I grabbed at the door handle and pulled. It was pulled back. Nabokov was next to me, yanking the door open so I couldn't get away. I pulled harder, but was met was greater resistance. Nabokov gripped the door with a single hand. With the other, he reached for his weapon.

I dropped the car into gear and floored the accelerator. The door was ripped free from Nabokov's iron fist. Force slammed the door shut. I shot into traffic with the engine roaring.

I glanced at the rear-view mirror. Nabokov stood motionless as he watched me drive away. His face was a blank. He wasn't even out of breath. He was a machine.

Winding through traffic, I settled into my seat. The adrenaline drained away, and I started to shake. Somehow, I felt like I hadn't escaped.

A black government car pulled out behind me. I sped up. At an intersection, a second car barreled toward me. I swerved hard to the right, and headed down a new street. Both cars were behind me, very close. I weaved around the slow-moving traffic.

At the next intersection, a third black car attacked me. I swung right again, and was diverted once more. These guys were funneling me someplace. Wherever we ended up, they'd have the upper hand. I couldn't allow that.

My rear-view mirror was filled with black cars. The regular traffic had turned into nothing but roadblocks. I couldn't drive around them fast enough to put any distance between me and my pursuers.

Another intersection was upon me. I gripped the steering wheel hard. A fourth black car appeared, thundering toward me. Instead of veering right, I turned toward him. He spun away. The sides of our vehicles scraped, and my side-view mirror snapped off. My body jostled from the impact.

I looked ahead. The Capitol Building stood before me now. There weren't any side streets to turn down. I had no escape route.

Two of the cars sped up and crushed themselves against either side of the Challenger. I jerked the wheel, but couldn't make them budge. I was boxed in. The three of us sped forward at breakneck speed. I slammed the accelerator down as far as it would go.

We burst out of the shadows of the skyscrapers and bounced onto the front steps of the Capitol Building. Pedestrians screamed and scattered. There wasn't enough room to stop. I drew the seat belt over my chest and buckled in.

We crashed through the tall glass front doors. The world turned into a dizzying eruption of shattering glass, screeching steel, and flashing lights. A heavy concrete column inside the building flew up before me. There was a heavy thud. The engine instantly became silent. My body flew forward but stopped abruptly. My chest crunched and burned simultaneously. I felt like a tomato thrown against a brick wall.

The two cars that flanked me were both overturned and smoking. The hood of my car was a crumpled mess of red and white metal parts. The windshield was gone. My body was covered in tiny chips of glass. Warm blood trickled down my forehead.

I popped off the seat belt and crawled out of the wreckage. Outside, more government vehicles converged. Before I limped into the bowels of the building, I stopped to take one last look at the Challenger. I smiled wistfully at it.

I hobbled toward the Senate Hall. The guards had cleared out. I didn't know what to do, but I hoped to hide here long enough to formulate a plan. I opened the heavy wooden doors, and was greeted by the clamorous shouts of the Senate in full session. They were still here, oblivious to what was happening outside.

Blood dripped into my eyes. I wiped at it, smearing my hands, as I tottered down the steps toward the front of the room. The shouts around me were deafening. The politicians seethed with unintelligible rage. Items flew in every direction. I focused my vision and continued until I reached the foreman. He was still feebly trying to curb the lack of decorum.

I mounted the stage, and shoved the foreman out of the way. I faced the crowd. Men in suits and bowler hats were streaming into the room. I raised my arms and shouted at the rolling sea of people.

"Everyone! Please! Listen! You need to vote down Orwell's next bill! He's taken over the government under your noses! You have to stop him before it's too late! For once, please, work together!"

The men and women in the crowd bickered and rabbled incessantly. They didn't stop even when the room was filled with safety agents.

Fifty of them surrounded the podium. Each held a weapon at the ready. The combined electric charge would kill me. The people that filled the center aisle parted ways, making room for someone.

Nabokov approached, walking slowly, staring at me with cold blue eyes. Soon, we stood face to face. When he spoke, it was like I was paperwork waiting to be filed.

"Are you finished, Smith?"

"Yeah, looks like I am."

27

The judge's stand towered over me, three times my height. I craned my neck back so I could glimpse the inquisitor looming above. He was a sallow, waxy man with dark eyes and a gloomy countenance. His black robes matched the atmosphere of the room. He glowered at me with the same contempt he held for every delinquent who graced his court.

Trials were rare events. Typically, safety agents handed down sentences to perpetrators immediately after their arrest. That was safer for the public because in a trial a guilty person might go free by mistake. Trials were reserved for those who flagrantly violated safety statutes. They reminded the populace what could happen if they did not follow the rules.

The courtroom was a perfect circle. I stood in the center. Around me was a small wooden railing, coming up to my waist, intended to pen me in. A fat spotlight illuminated me from above. Encircling the room was a gallery filled with spectators. It was elevated too, but not as high as the judge's stand. The gallery was dark. It was the first dark public place I had ever seen. I squinted to discern who was watching, but I couldn't make out any of the shadowy faces.

The judge banged his gavel. The sharp crack of wood upon wood echoed across the room. The gibbering spectators hushed. The judge's gravelly voice rumbled, "Order! The court will come to order! Mr. Prosecutor, who do you bring before this court?"

The prosecutor, who stood to my right, cleared his throat and said, "Smith, a Safety Inspector with Surveillance Department. He stands accused of insanity."

"Insanity, hmm," the judge said. "How do you plead, Inspector Smith?"

"Not guilty," I said.

"Very well. Let the trial commence. Call your first witness."

"Yes, your honor. The prosecution calls Safety Inspector Wyndham."

My back stiffened. I thought I hallucinated the name, but I hadn't. The fat man waddled into the room, snorting and wiping sweat from his forehead. He took up the traditional position for witnesses, standing opposite the prosecutor. He was already out of breath and looking for a chair. Unfortunately, the courtroom had none.

"Mr. Wyndham, is it true that Mr. Smith used to work under your supervision?"

"Yes."

"And how was his performance?"

"Awful, just awful."

"How so?"

"He shirked his duties. He was caught sleeping on the job. He let depraved sex criminals go free. And he blackmailed me."

The audience gasped in unison. Wyndham was still wiping sweat from his chubby face. I couldn't believe they got him out here so quickly. Who else did they have waiting for me, ready to get even?

"Blackmail?" the prosecutor asked, stunned. "What did he do?"

"Well," Wyndham said, twiddling his thumbs, "he had his partner, a female partner, make sexual advances toward me. Then he told me that if I didn't promote both of them, they'd use it against me."

"Are you certain these were unwanted sexual advances?"

"Of course!"

"Do you have anything else you would like to add?"

"Only that I was glad to get rid of him. I was afraid for my life every day."

"That's ridiculous," I said.

The judge banged his gavel and shouted, "The defendant will remain silent!"

I shut my mouth and waited my turn. Wyndham was a sniveling idiot. I would be able to pick him apart with ease. He'd lose all credibility as a witness.

"Thank you, Mr. Wyndham," the prosecutor said. "No further questions, your honor."

"The witness is excused," the judge said.

"Hey, wait a minute," I interjected.

The prosecutor looked at me with disbelief. Another collective gasp radiated from the gallery. The judge glared at me and said, "Inspector Smith, you are not allowed to interrupt legal proceedings while they are underway."

"But don't I get a chance to question the witness?"

"We can't have an insane person asking questions to perfectly sane people."

"But I'm not insane."

"Then why are you here, Inspector Smith?"

"I thought the point of this trial was to determine my sanity. If you already think I'm insane, then what's the point?"

"That sounds like something an insane person would say," the judge snapped back. He looked at the prosecutor and barked, "Call the next witness!"

"Safety Inspector Atwood."

She blew into the room like a whirlwind. She looked like she had swallowed a stick of dynamite. Her hands were clenched so tightly her knuckles had turned white. Her chest heaved up and down. Her forehead vein bulged more prominently than ever. When she spoke, it was through clenched teeth.

"Ms. Atwood, you were Mr. Smith's direct supervisor while he was with Healthcare Department, correct?"

"Yeah, that's right. And that son of a bitch deserves the harshest punishment you have," she said. The words spilled out like diarrhea. The prosecutor stood back, inching himself farther away from her ferocity. "He was always a good for nothing layabout. He put in the least amount of work possible. His paperwork was absolute shit. I would have to work with him for hours until he got it right. Once, we were raiding a hospital, and he was drinking coffee instead of arresting doctors. He has the worst attitude I've ever seen. It's like he doesn't even care about his job. He doesn't care about arresting criminals. He doesn't care about doing things by the book. He would rather throw everything into disarray than just do his damn job. What's worse, there was an investigation at a winery. He kept pushing me to sample wine until I got drunk. After that I was demoted. I know Smith was behind it. He planned it all out from the beginning, just to get rid of me. Well, I want you all to get rid of him. Lock him up in the deepest, darkest cell you've got! And one more thing—"

Wood cracked loudly. Atwood's rant sputtered to a stop. She looked up at the judge. He rubbed his temples. Wearily, he said, "Thank you, Inspector Atwood, that will be all."

With burning eyes, she said, "Your honor, there's so much more I have to say. Smith is a pathetic, lowlife, disgusting—"

"You are excused," the judge interrupted.

Atwood retreated into herself. Her breaths slowed and the vein in her forehead shrank. She unclenched her fists, the knuckles cracking with relief. She pivoted stiffly on her feet and walked out of the room with the all the grace of a machine.

"Call the next witness."

"The prosecution calls Safety Inspector Bradbury."

Bradbury appeared. He was as perplexed as ever. He stood in the witness position, and looked around the room, uncertain where he was or how he got there.

"Mr. Bradbury," the prosecutor began, "is it true that you were Mr. Smith's direct supervisor while he worked for Prohibition Department?"

Bradbury furrowed his brow. His eyes were glassy. The gears in his brain slowly grinded to a halt. "Smith? I don't recall any Inspector Smith."

"You don't recollect this man working for you?"

"No, he doesn't look familiar."

"Are you certain? Didn't he commit several egregious safety violations while he was working for your department?"

"I don't think so. Yes, that's right. I can positively say that I've never seen this man before in my life."

I smirked. He honestly didn't remember me. At least there was one witness who wouldn't incriminate me.

Verne appeared next. He spoke about my dereliction of duty. After that, it was Wells. He detailed my lack of participation in an important surveillance operation. Next, a shivering man named Lewis told the tale of how I confiscated his illegal Dodge Challenger for my personal use. Then, there was a man I had never seen before. He was the quartermaster from my home city. He listed all the equipment I had failed to return. After that, the curator of the Archives spoke about the book I had stolen.

The parade of witnesses seemed to go on endlessly, and I found my body getting heavy. Listening to my sins was exhausting.

"Call your final witness," the judge said.

"The prosecution calls Safety Inspector Orwell."

His footsteps resonated through the courtroom. He wanted his presence to be felt by everyone. He sauntered into the witness position. He no longer wore his arm in a sling. He seemed taller somehow; perhaps the darkness of the room amplified his stature. He pulled at his shirt sleeves, so his attire would be meticulous. He smiled smugly at me. That smarmy bastard was the ringleader of this entire circus.

"Mr. Orwell, you are Mr. Smith's current supervisor at Surveillance Department, is that correct?"

"Yes."

"Since he has worked for you, have you seen him engage in any unsafe activities?"

"Yes, several."

"Go on."

"There are so many, I may not be able to remember them all."

"Please, try your best."

"I have detailed records of Inspector Smith's activities before and after he started working for me. Before he came on-board, he made a deal with a known criminal, a Mr. Karp, who put him in contact with Mr. X, a notorious black market dealer. It is my understanding that Mr. X employed Inspector Smith to infiltrate the First Government. The purpose, it seems, was to completely overthrow our way of life."

"That sounds very unsafe."

"I'm afraid that's only the beginning. While he was a member of my department, he immediately went rogue. He planted false evidence on a bureaucrat who was working on a bill for me. After that, he used his underworld connections to bring contraband dairy and sugar products into the Capital. I can only assume it was to be sold on the black market."

"You lying bastard!" I shouted.

The gallery went up in a tizzy. Orwell ignored me and continued, "At a party recently, Inspector Smith brutally assaulted a fine, upstanding former member of our government, Mr. Capek. He is currently in an undisclosed location, but I believe he is not long for this world."

"That was all your doing! You're twisting everything against me!"

No one heard me. All eyes were fixed on Orwell. The people were enthralled. The prosecutor salivated at the deluge of damning information. Orwell went on, "As you all know, Inspector Smith engaged in reckless driving, a dangerous spree of wanton destruction across the Capital. He put the lives of every citizen in danger that day. The reason why is unclear. Maybe that was when the last vestiges of his sanity finally slipped away."

The audience groused excitedly. The car chase was big news. There hadn't been such a wild incident in a lifetime. Even if all these other charges didn't hold, I wouldn't be able to escape that one. My mind spun wildly, trying to think of a way to defend myself against Orwell's barbs.

"Finally," Orwell said with a gleam in his eye, "I have it on good authority that Inspector Smith murdered his wi–"

The judge cracked his gavel. He pounded it again and again until the courtroom fell silent. The judge dropped his gavel with a clatter. He dug his fists deep into his temples. He grumbled, "I think that's quite enough. I have a headache. The witness is excused."

Orwell looked surprised, but quickly regained his composure. He gave me a friendly nod as he walked by. The judge cradled his head in his hands. Slowly, he raised his eyes and glared at me.

"In all my years, I have never had such a deranged lunatic in my courtroom. Your reckless disregard for the public safety knows no bounds. What do you have to say for yourself?"

I had a lot of ground to make up. I spit the words out rapidly, "Your honor, these people all have grudges against me. They were specifically chosen, not to tell the truth, but to—"

"*Quiet!*" the judge shouted. "I'll not entertain the incoherent ramblings of a madman. Now, settle down. Tell me, what is your defense, hmm?"

I took a deep breath and exhaled slowly. I measured my words carefully, trying not to sound excited like before. "Orwell is plotting a takeover of the First Government. He's nearly succeeded. He ordered me to—"

"*Quiet!*" the judge bellowed. "Stop interrupting me. How someone as crazy as you got so far as a government Inspector is a mystery. The recklessness, the danger, the violence, the . . . unsafeness of it all. How do you live with yourself?"

I decided to wait for him to prompt me to speak. His features contorted with confusion. He groaned, "Why don't you answer when I ask you a question?"

"Your hon—"

"That's enough! This court has been presented with enough evidence. And seeing how the defendant cannot compose a rational argument to defend himself, I have no choice but to find him guilty as charged. He will be sentenced to a lifetime of Safety Re-Education in an asylum. Court is adjourned."

A clamor rose through the audience. Cheers of excitement and jeers of derision circled round me. A few small items were tossed toward me, but fell limply short. The judge rose from his stand and slithered into the shadows beyond. The courtroom door banged open and two safety agents traipsed in, handcuffs at the ready.

The prosecutor wore a satisfied grin. He started toward the exit. I shot forward. My waist rammed into the wooden railing. I grabbed a fistful of his suit and yanked him toward me. Fear electrified his face. Desperately, I said, "That's it? How can that be it? Don't I get to defend myself?"

"You just did," he said, trying to pull away.

"He wouldn't let me talk."

"He doesn't listen to the ravings of a madman," he said, trying to shake out of my grip.

"But don't I get a lawyer?"

"Defense attorneys were banned last week. Too unsafe," he said, pulling harder.

"But, but—"

He wrested himself free and stumbled backward. Once he steadied himself, he caught his breath. The frightened look in his eyes dissipated. Now, he looked at me with disdain. "You really are crazy," he said.

The two safety agents stepped into my holding pen. I weakly raised my hands, and let them manacle my wrists. As I was escorted out, I looked back. The round courtroom was empty, the life sucked out of it.

Maybe they were right after all. Maybe I was insane.

28

My roommate was snoring. He sounded like the engine of the Challenger. Ever since I arrived, I hadn't been able to sleep. He slept like a baby. Sleeping was the only thing he ever did. Any time, day or night, he was in bed, snoring. I hadn't slept in three days.

I propped myself up on my thin pillow, and let my eyes wander over the details of the ceiling. In three long nights, I had memorized every crack and blemish. A spider hung in the corner, sleepily awaiting its prey. The fat fluorescent lights in the ceiling were off. Bedtime was the only part of the day the lights in patient rooms went off. The lights everywhere else stayed on around the clock.

A soft hum emanated from two screens in the room, one above each bed. They displayed our vital signs. Monitors had been sewn into our clothes so staff would know our pulse, heart rhythm, respirations, etc. at all times.

My roommate's breath caught in his throat. For one moment, two, three, he was silent. And then a gagging sound, followed by a gurgle, preceded the resumption of his snoring. He did this several times a night. I wished that just once, the breaths wouldn't restart. Maybe then I would get some sleep.

Thoughts drifted to me and floated away. Ideas, memories, and dreams were one and the same. Eventually, my mind wandered to a project. I was building a log cabin in a deep, secluded forest. The cabin was stout, and made of thick oak. I designed it room by room. I turned the layout around, altered the dimensions, and moved the entire house from place to place. It stood in the forest, on the beach, at the crest of a waterfall. I dug a wine cellar, and crafted an observatory for gazing at the stars. The house's well-furnished library was stocked with my favorite books from the Archives. I slept in a big, soft bed. Each morning, I drank coffee from a steaming mug on the balcony. Each evening, I drank a glass of dry red wine, and basked in the sunset. Wildlife chirped around me. I lounged on every type of chair and couch. And when I tired of that, I tore the house to pieces and rebuilt it. Always different, but always the same.

Beside me, my fat roommate choked again. What did he dream about? I couldn't imagine it was anything other than dinner.

After letting my mind slip to and fro for several hours, my eyes caught a glint of light. The moon was fading, and the blackness of night lightened to a shade of purple. It turned silvery, and was soon cast in red and orange hues. The top of the sun peaked over the horizon.

I had greeted my first day here with morbid curiosity. I knew of people being sent to the asylum, but I knew nothing about it. Would it be more akin to a hospital or a prison?

A high speed rail line connected the continent's two major cities. It sped through the Wasteland. I wondered briefly about the strange man in the bunker, the starving people from the encampment, and the cheery commune as I traveled. My head rested against the cool glass window. The terrain whizzed by as a brown blur. It only took a single day to reach my destination.

I stepped off the train, and was ushered into a waiting car at the station. The car ride to the asylum took about two hours. The asylum was located on the northern outskirts of the city. The area was slowly becoming forested. The region around the city had seen greater reclamation of natural habitats than the rest of the world. Environmental safety statutes had allowed regrowth after centuries of abuse at the hands of our ancestors.

When the car stopped, I was led through a Sally Port and into the asylum grounds. They were overly cautious about making sure I didn't escape. The truth was they didn't need to bother. There was no point in resisting. I resigned myself to the fact that this would be my new home for life.

I entered the main building. The lights above were searing. The bulbs were triple the usual number. There was no place for a shadow to hide.

"It's bright," I croaked.

"You'll get used to it," one of my escorts replied.

They walked me to the front desk. A sleepy guy sat behind a pane of bullet-proof glass. He yawned and said, "Name and serial number."

"Smith. Number 1872124482."

He clattered at his terminal. He yawned again. The two escorts shifted languidly beside me. The terminal clicked and whirred. Eventually, the sleepy guy got the information he needed. "All right. Head through."

A pair of thick, metal, windowless doors to the right opened. A pair of burly men wearing hospital uniforms greeted me. The safety agents passed me to them without a word. Each man grabbed me by an arm, their heavy hands wrapping completely around each bicep. They lifted me and carried me down the hall. My toes lightly scraped across the vinyl tile floor.

My new escorts carried me to a small square room which contained only a folding chair and a set of clothes. My new outfit was a simple gray shirt and pants, very loose fitting. I pulled at the shirt, trying to get it to rest on my shoulders, but it kept drooping one way or the other. The pant legs trailed all the way to the floor and swallowed my bare feet. It felt strange to wear something different after decades in my uniform. I didn't feel like myself.

My escorts lifted me again, and carried me down the hall once more. It was nice to be carried. I didn't have to tire my legs with needless walking.

We passed through another set of metal doors. The other side contained a hallway with several offices. They took me to one near the end. The plaque on the door read, "Dr. Collins." They dropped me to my feet as one of the men knocked on the door.

A moment later, a female voice said, "Enter."

I was pushed into the office. It looked like any other standard government office. The doctor stood up from behind her desk and said, "Please, have a seat."

I slumped into the single wooden chair that stood opposite the desk. The doctor sat down, as well. She had a face like a squirrel. The door behind me remained open. The two men stood outside, as a safety precaution, no doubt.

"Name and serial number," she said.

"Smith, 1872124482."

Collins typed the information into her terminal. She perused whatever data appeared on the screen. I could see the green reflection in the lenses of her square glasses, but it was too small to read. She frowned, then she smirked, then she grimaced. After nearly ten minutes of reading, she turned to me, slightly horrified, and said, "Welcome to Safety Re-Education, Mr. Smith."

"Thanks."

"How are you feeling today?"

"Fine."

"Depressed?"

"No."

"Anxious?"

"No."

"Angry?"

"No."

"Any suicidal or homicidal thoughts?"

"No."

"Are you having any hallucinations?"

"No."

"Are you certain?"

"Positive."

"Oh, my," she said. She quickly typed something on her keyboard.

"What?"

"I'm afraid you're so insane you don't even realize it. Most people with psychosis are aware of their hallucinations. With such limited insight, your prognosis is quite grim."

"I'm not hallucinating."

"You must be. Only a psychotic person would do all the things you did."

"I did them because I could."

"Oh, my, my, my, my, my. And a personality disorder, too. It's even worse than I imagined. In your condition, I'm surprised you can even function. Tell me, which medications do you take?"

"I don't take any."

"You don't? Well, you should."

"Why?"

"So you can get better, of course."

"Why should I care about that?"

"Anyone deemed sane is discharged."

I leaned forward, taking interest in the conversation. I didn't know it was possible to leave the asylum. If I played by the rules, I might be able to get out of here. "Which medications?" I asked.

Collins looked up, thoughtfully stroking her chin, and said, "You'll need a mood stabilizer, a sedative, and several antipsychotics. But that will make you quite sedated. You'll also need a stimulant, perhaps two, to stay awake."

"And if I take all those, I'll get to leave?" I asked, trying not to act too excited.

"Only if you recover."

"Of course. In that case, I'm ready to start right away."

"Unfortunately, I won't be able to prescribe you any medications. The side effects of all those would be too unsafe. So, you'll have to make do without."

"But isn't it more unsafe for a lunatic like me to be unmedicated?"

"Yes, you're quite right. I'll prescribe you the medications. You absolutely need them to get better. But under no circumstances are you to take them."

I sank back in the chair. I was never getting out of here.

She looked beyond me and into the hall. "Gentlemen," she called, "please take Mr. Smith to his room."

They didn't wait for me to stand. Their hands slipped beneath my armpits, and they hoisted me up. Collins wrinkled her nose and said, "Good day, Mr. Smith."

We made a right turn at the end of the hall and went through another set of metal doors. We entered the Day Room. Every inch of ceiling space was covered with fluorescent lights. Security cameras hung at each corner, housed within tamper-proof glass. The walls and floor were the same color beige. It produced an illusion that the room was one continuous surface.

Populating the room were couches and chairs, small tables, and a surprisingly large TV. People played cards and board games at the tables. Some lounged on the couches reading authorized books. A few others were involved in art projects. A lone person stared blankly at the TV. Its volume was turned off. The images on the screen were the usual First Government propaganda.

As I floated through the room, hardly anyone noticed me. A few gave me quick glances. One looked up from her book and gave me a half-hearted nod as I passed by. The rest were mesmerized by their activities.

Soon, I was out of the Day Room. I was carried to a seemingly infinite hallway lined with patient rooms. I was dropped to my feet in front of the eighteenth room on the right. Without a word, my escorts vanished.

The room before me burned almost as brightly as the hallway. A strange growling emitted from within. It was a cramped room, more like a cubicle. There were two narrow beds, side by side, with a small margin between them. The floor, walls, and ceiling were the same color. A small window on the far side overlooked what appeared to be a garden. There was no light switch. The lights were automated.

On the closer of the two beds lay a huge bulk of flesh, covered by blankets. The growling was his slumbering breath. I looked up at the bright lights again. It was going to be impossible to sleep in here. Even so, I was exhausted. I slipped under the sheets of the bed closer to the window and closed my eyes. I spent the first night like that, waiting for sleep that never came. Even after the lights shut off, slumber eluded me.

Now, the sun was higher on the horizon. The fourth day had begun. I kicked off the bed sheets and wandered to the Day Room. I headed for the one thing that sustained me despite my insomnia.

Dismay rocked me. The space that held the coffee pot was empty. I looked around. It was nowhere in sight. Another patient, Burgess, walked over to me.

"Where's the coffee?" I asked.

In his serene voice, Burgess answered, "A new safety regulation. Coffee was just declared unsafe for insane people."

They had done it. They had finally gotten to me.

29

I wilted onto the couch, and sank between two cushions. Burgess sat beside me, his face incredulous. "Smith," he said. "It's just coffee. Don't be so dramatic."

I flicked my eyes toward him, too tired to turn my head. "You don't understand. They did this to antagonize me. It was Orwell."

"Who?"

"The head of Surveillance Detail. He chewed me up and spat me out. Now, he's adding insult to injury."

"I doubt this is related."

"I bet he's having a good laugh about it."

Burgess sighed, and then became lost in thought. At length, he said, "I know it's hard to be here, it's a big change. Believe me, it's for the best."

I choked out a single laugh.

"It's true," he said. "I used to be like you. I was overworked, completely stressed, seeing conspiracies everywhere. One day at work, I had a nervous breakdown. Then they put me in here. Now I have time to relax, to think things through. Everything is much clearer."

"You like being in here?"

"I've never been so healthy in my life."

"Don't you want to get out?"

"Hardly," Burgess scoffed. "Go back to that rat race? For what? My wife's been reassigned, and I have no kids. And I certainly wouldn't go back for the job. That was the thing that put me in here in the first place."

"I don't know. It's just — to let him win — it doesn't seem right."

Burgess nodded knowingly. He folded his hands over his lap and leaned forward. With a silky voice he said, "Things are confusing right now. You're at the beginning."

"The entire last year of my life doesn't make any sense."

"It will. Give it time. You've got to let all that negativity from the past go. Once you do, things will make sense again."

"What if that doesn't happen? What if I'm too crazy to get better?"

"At least you're in good company."

I groaned.

Burgess' attention was caught by something across the room. He rose and said, "We'll talk later. Feel better soon."

I was alone on the couch, staring into the blinking void of the TV. It was set to the news channel, and the sound was off. A man and a woman on the screen spoke very animatedly. I tried to push myself up, to escape the snare of the flashing monster, but my strength failed me.

A man appeared at the far end of the couch. He scratched his thick mustache and curly brown hair simultaneously. After considering me for a minute, he quickly approached. He sat close and leaned in to speak in hushed tones.

"Are you Smith?" he asked.

"Yeah."

"It was Orwell, wasn't it?"

"Huh?"

"Who banned the coffee. Orwell, right?"

"How did you know?"

"Any time one of his enemies gets sent here, he has something banned. Usually something they love. I'm guessing you love coffee."

Blood pumped more quickly through my veins. My muscles began to creak back to life.

"I think that's what happened," I said.

"That's what he always does, the bastard."

"You know him?"

"I can't talk about it now."

"Did you work for him?"

"Until things went sideways and he put me in here."

The man suddenly looked spooked. He jumped off the couch and looked around. I turned my head and saw the expanse of the Day Room. Patients were filtering in from the hallway. A lone staff member stood on the far side, chatting with a patient. I turned back to the man.

"I gotta go," he said.

"Wait, what's your name?"

"Vonnegut."

He zoomed away.

The encounter left me feeling more energized. I stood and walked over to one of the small square tables. Three other patients had just started a game of cards. I joined them.

I was never much of a card player. I lost almost every hand. My fellow players loved me, an easy mark. If we had any money to bet, they would have quickly cleaned me out. Gambling was illegal, anyway. Without money, we played to stave off boredom.

After an hour, the usual burly staff members reappeared. They grunted my name like simians and told me to come with them. I put my cards on the table, a winning hand. "It's been fun," I said. My fellow players nodded to me.

Hands slipped beneath my armpits, and I was hoisted off the ground. Levitating my way through the building wasn't bad. At least my feet didn't have to touch the cold floor. I was eventually deposited in Collins' office.

I adjusted myself, trying to get comfortable in the hard wooden chair. Collins typed at her terminal, not acknowledging my presence. Her hair was frizzier than last time. She had attempted to wrangle it into a ponytail, but the hair tie barely held it together. When she finished typing, she turned her attention to me.

"How are you feeling this morning?" she asked.

"Tired."

"How did you sleep?"

"Terribly."

"Is the bed not comfortable?"

"It's not the softest mattress I've ever slept on."

"Oh, my. We can't have that. It isn't safe for your back. I'll see that it's switched out straight away."

"Thanks, but it's my roommate's snoring that's keeping me awake."

"I'm sorry to hear that. Well, let's move on. How is your mood?"

"Fine, I guess."

"Any suicidal or homicidal thoughts?"

"Not yet."

"Any hallucinations?"

"No."

"Are you certain?"

"Yes."

"That's wonderful!" she said, beaming. "The treatment is working!"

Since I entered the asylum, all I had done was play cards, have conversations, and stay awake all night. I wasn't sure what treatment she referred to. Then again, I was the crazy one, so who was I to argue with a doctor?

"Does that mean I'll get to leave soon?"

Collins chuckled, her squirrel-nose crinkling. "Oh, my, no. You're much too insane for that. I'll continue to see you weekly from now on. Over time, perhaps, your insanity will improve enough for us to have an actual conversation. Now, do you have any questions?"

"Can I have some coffee?"

She gave me a pitying look. "I'm afraid not. It's far too stimulating for you. We do have a nice selection of juice and milk and water."

"Thanks. Can I go?"

"You're dismissed."

On cue, the two burly men hefted me once more. As they brought me into the Day Room, I said, "Take me over to the couch, boys. Gently now, lay me down so I can take a nap."

I found myself airborne. I tumbled through the air until gravity grabbed me and flung me to the floor. My body sang with pain. When I righted myself, the two men were gone.

I wandered down the hallway and into my room. The fluorescent lights blazed above, but my roommate continued to snore. To my surprise, I saw Vonnegut sitting on my bed.

I sat next to him. He scratched his hair and mustache. Looking at me with electric eyes, he said, "Your roommate snores so loudly, the listening devices will never hear us."

The fat man's poor health paid off, after all.

"Okay," I said. "So, who are you?"

"I used to work Surveillance Detail. I was in deep. Orwell had me working undercover in a black market ring."

"Mr. X's organization?"

"That's right," he said with a quick nod. "Mr. X and I were close. So close, I got their real name. It's Rand."

"Rand, huh?" I turned the bitter name over with my tongue.

"Orwell wanted to stage a military coup. He needed high-powered explosives."

"Explosives? Where would he get those?"

"Rand has access to an old stockpile from the last world war, before the First Government. But Rand wouldn't sell them to Orwell. So, he sent me to get close, to get them. I worked there for three years."

"What happened?"

"I came to my senses. The First Government has a lot of problems, but the last thing it needs is a dictator. So, I hid the explosives someplace Orwell would never find them. When he learned I betrayed him, he sent me here."

"How long have you been here?"

"Over two years."

"And what did he ban when you got here?"

"Slippers."

"Slippers?"

"I never told him I loved slippers, but somehow he knew. He is the head of Surveillance Detail, I suppose."

"Vonnegut, why are you telling me all this?"

His lips trembled. He wiped his mouth with the back of his hand. "I read the newspapers. I put the pieces together. He wasn't able to stage a coup, so now he's taking control insidiously. Pretty soon, he'll dissolve the Senate. I want you to help me escape so we can stop him."

"Where did you hide the explosives?"

Vonnegut held his index finger over his lips. He was starting to perspire. Conspiring with me these past few minutes was probably the most excitement he'd seen in two years. I tried to regulate my own breaths, to avoid getting caught up in his agitation.

Whispering, I asked, "Do you have a plan for getting out of here?"

"We'll talk later," he said. He shot off the bed, and then darted out of the room.

Meanwhile, my roommate slumbered. I stared at him for several minutes. The rhythm of his rotund chest moving up and down was hypnotic. My vision grew blurry. His snores turned to white noise in my mind. I fell onto my side. When my head hit the pillow, I was asleep.

My eyes opened. A hand gripped my ankle and hauled me off the bed. My face hit the floor, and I saw stars. One of the burly staff members had done it. He pulled the mattress off the bed frame, and replaced it with a new one. A moment later, he was gone.

I was too tired to think about revenge. I clambered onto the new mattress. It was exactly the same as the old one. I closed my eyes, but sleep didn't return. After lying in bed for a while, I returned to the Day Room.

The clock revealed that only two hours had elapsed. In a daze, I wandered to the back corner of the room, by the bookshelf. I dropped into a vacant chair. I pulled the most boring-looking tome off the shelf and started to read. My eyelids became heavy. My chest tingled with warmth as I welcomed sleep once more.

Chair legs scraped across the floor, and a hand shook my shoulder. I awoke with a start, and leaped out of my chair. Burgess was sitting beside me. For an instant, I saw myself strangling the life out of him. Luckily, I was too drained for that.

"I saw you talking to Vonnegut earlier," he said.

"That's right," I said, sitting down.

"You should keep your distance from him."

"Why?"

"He's insane. In fact, he's probably the most insane person here."

"He seems all right."

Burgess shook his head and replied solemnly, "That's the thing about him. He's so insane that what he says sounds reasonable."

"He seems harmless."

"Physically? Sure. But not mentally. He sees conspiracies everywhere. Did he tell you how he used to work for some bigwig who wanted to stage a coup?"

"Yeah, he did."

"He tells that story to everyone. Every single person in here has heard it. None of it is true. He's insane."

"So what's the harm in talking to him?"

"The more you talk to him, the more convincing he'll become. You might start incorporating his wild ideas into your own memories. It happened to another patient. You're already insane enough. You don't want to go down his rabbit hole and get worse."

I thought about Orwell for a moment. I suddenly had trouble recalling what he looked like. I yawned. I was so tired. How long had I been in here, anyway? Was it really only four days? It felt longer than that.

"Hey, Burgess, let me ask you something."

"What?"

"Where did you get that gun? The day you went crazy and shot the equipment box."

"The black market. I don't even know why I bought it. I guess that's what insanity will do to you," he said sheepishly.

"Did you ever meet someone named Mr. X?"

"No. Who's that?"

"Their real name is Rand. They run a big black market organization. Funny thing is, I was head of Prohibition Detail for years, and I just assumed they were a myth. It seems like everyone else knew they were real. How did I miss it? Am I crazy, after all?"

Burgess nodded. "Yes. We all are. That's why I'm trying to help you. If you don't stay away from the likes of Vonnegut, you'll never get better."

"If you say so."

"Trust me. Don't worry about all that nonsense, either in here or in the outside world. You're here to rest and recover. Focus on that."

"Thanks, Burgess. Right now I'm going to focus on resting."

Without waiting for a response, I laid the open book over my eyes, and leaned back in the chair as far as I could. I dozed intermittently until night came. Then, I shuffled back to my room and stared at the ceiling while the great beast drowsed nearby.

30

A week passed. Then a second. Then a third. By the fourth, I looked like a different person. My eyes had sunken into my skull. My complexion had drained to a deathly pallor. Thick hair covered the lower half of my face. Food had lost its flavor, and I'd become emaciated. The paunch around my waistline had dripped away. I had begun my transformation into the walking dead.

Sleep remained elusive. I caught a few hours here and there, but never had a full night's rest. I tried to sleep on the couch in the Day Room, but the burly staff members hurled me back to my room. Patients couldn't be left unattended in the Day Room, it wasn't safe.

Day and night were one and the same. There were no longer any cycles. Everything melted together. As the lights burned tirelessly above, it was like the sun never set. With no end in sight, it was clear there would be no reprieve. I would go on like a zombie until I died or something lodged me free.

I met with Vonnegut on several occasions to discuss an escape plan. Unfortunately, there was no way out. Digging was impossible because of the reinforced walls and floor. Windows were made of shatter-proof glass and couldn't be broken. Inciting a riot couldn't be done because the patients were happy and comfortable. Electrical circuits couldn't be shorted to force the security doors open because there were no electrical outlets. We racked our brains desperately to formulate a plan, but nothing came to fruition. The safety of the asylum was inescapable.

And so we stayed, conspiring to escape, but never finding a way out. Every plan ended in failure before it could begin. I began to feel as if I was repeating my actions over and over again. I was stuck in an endless circle of hell. This place mocked me.

The only reason I knew four weeks had passed was by marking each visit to the doctor. Collins' interviews were always the same. She would ask about my symptoms, and I would deny having any. She would cluck approvingly and send me away. She was in her own repeating circle of hell, but completely unaware of it.

I was in the Day Room, playing a game of chess. Burgess sat opposite me. He moved a white piece diagonally across the board. I grumbled. My next move was not apparent.

"You look terrible," he said.

"Thanks for the compliment."

"I'm worried about you, Smith, that's all. You clearly haven't adjusted. I see you going around with Vonnegut, scheming. It's wearing you down."

"My roommate's the one wearing me down."

"It's your refusal to accept what's happened. If you would just admit that you're insane, and stop obsessing about escaping, you'd start to feel better."

"How can you be sure?"

"It happened to me. I wouldn't accept that I was the problem. I blamed all my issues on the world, on external forces. Once I started taking responsibility for my actions, I was able to move forward with my life."

I scratched my head. Several strands of hair pulled away from my scalp, stuck beneath my fingernails. I goggled at the sight.

"You see? The stress is causing your hair to fall out. You need to start relaxing."

I moved a random piece to a random location on the chessboard. "And how do I do that?" I shot back. "I can't even sleep."

My opponent studied the board carefully. He moved a piece up and to the right, taking away one of mine in the process. Still looking at the board, he replied, "First, stop talking to Vonnegut. He can't help you. Second, accept what happened, and stop blaming others. Third, take Doctor Collins' treatment to heart. Trust the process. Someday, you'll think clearly again."

I supposed he was right about Vonnegut. The guy really was crazy. When he and I weren't conspiring, he was going up to the other patients and soliciting them for help. Everyone knew we wanted to escape. The staff didn't care. They knew, just like us, there was no way out. If I gave up the desire to escape, Vonnegut would go on as usual. He had already accosted the new patient that had arrived after me. Eventually, he would find someone else to work with. He would be fine.

Something flashed. Burgess saw it, too. We both looked at the TV. The screen was different. The blathering celebrities and First Government shills were gone. They were replaced by X-ray footage. I watched as a familiar scene played out.

A skeleton danced through its apartment, and strung itself up in the bathroom. The footage blinked away. It was replaced by nearly the same footage, only with the outline of a man moving the victim around. The surveillance footage had been reconstructed to prove James had been murdered.

I rose slowly and walked toward the TV. Both video feeds, original and reconstructed, looped several times. It was followed by the footage of Orwell and Nabokov. A crowd of patients joined me, encircling the TV, transfixed. In the back of the room there was a loud bang. Several staff members ran out.

A live feed from an aerial surveillance drone was displayed. On the street, a mob of people was yelling. A surveillance van pulled up. Several agents emerged and attempted to quell the crowd. Someone threw an object at the van. It smashed onto the hood, and the entire vehicle erupted in an orange ball of fire. People scattered in every direction. Several patients gasped. The image abruptly cut out.

After a brief interlude of static, the image changed to a brightly-colored TV studio. It was the set used for the First Government's morning news show. The talking heads were gone.

They were replaced by an unfamiliar man who spoke sternly into the camera. A line of people, equally stern, stood in solidarity behind him. The volume was off, so we couldn't hear what he was saying. He was energetic, and with actions alone, he conveyed that he was fed up with the First Government.

I scanned the faces behind him. I recognized the person on the far right. A woman, short and slightly plump, with thick red hair stood with her arms crossed over her chest. She wore the black suit of a safety agent, but had lost her tie. Her face bore a defiant look. I cried out in surprise. She had survived.

But she had joined these guys. With the riot on the street, she was in more danger now than ever before. A crawling sensation worked its way through my legs and stomach. I had to find Lowry. I had to protect her. I had to get out of here.

The heavy security doors banged open. Ten burly staff members, cardboard cutouts of one another, barged in, followed by Collins. Collins' hair stood out in every direction, a nearly perfect sphere of frizz. Her hair tie must have finally given up. She adjusted her square glasses, wrinkled her squirrel nose in disgust, and asked, "What is this?"

"The news. Something's happening in the city," a patient replied.

"Oh my, this won't do. Not at all," she said. "Take it away."

Two of the burly men pushed through the semi-circle of patients. They grabbed the TV on either side and snapped it off the wall. The screen instantly went black. A chunk of plaster crashed to the floor.

"We need that!" someone called out.

"How will we know what's going on?" another asked.

The group began to speak at once, desperate to have the TV returned. The noise in the room quickly grew raucous. Dozens of voices clamored for the same thing. This was it. A riot. My chance to escape.

Collins raised both hands and shouted, *"Quiet!"*

When the room settled down, she said, "I will return the TV when it is safe to do so. For now, you will have to do without it.

I'm sure whatever's happening will be over soon, and we can all return to normal. Furthermore, there has been enough excitement for one day. I am going to start lights out early. Good day."

She turned around sharply and strode out of the room. Her men remained. The crowd of patients broke up, muttering reservedly. People returned to reading and playing games, soon forgetting about what had just transpired. My hopes of escape were dashed.

My fluttering agitation did not abate. It continued to worm its way through my arms and legs. I flexed and extended my fingers in rapid succession. Everyone else was so complacent. What was wrong with them? Couldn't they see something was happening? Didn't they care?

The metal doors banged open for a third time. I turned around while everyone else ignored the sound. Vonnegut flew through the air, tossed out of his weekly meeting with Collins. I raced over and helped him up.

"You missed it," I said breathlessly.

"Missed what?" he asked, wincing and rubbing his knee.

"Something's happening in the city. A riot. Or a revolution. There was an explosion, and some people took over the news station. It was on the TV before they took it away."

Vonnegut looked at the hole in the wall. Flabbergasted, he merely shook his head.

"I saw my friend," I said. "She was with them, whoever they are. We've got to get out of here. I need to make sure she's all right."

"Yes, you're right," he said, his pupils becoming huge. "Perhaps we could try tunneling again. I know a spot where the integrity of the structure may be weak. Tonight, I'll try to dig . . ."

He rambled on, and as he did, dismay fell over me. He didn't have any new ideas. He was doomed to repeat the old ones over and over again. His circle of hell was living under the delusion that there was a way out of here. We were both wrong. There was no escape. I was destined to die in here, decades from now, while

Rand and Orwell would get to live out the rest of their lives in freedom.

A chime sounded three times. That was the cue for lights out. The other patients meandered down the long hallway toward their rooms. Not knowing what else to do, I joined them. Burgess came up beside me. He already knew what was on my mind.

"Whatever's going on out there, there's nothing we can do about it," he said.

"What if I could do something?"

He clapped my shoulder and said, "Focus on your recovery, okay?"

"Yeah, sure," I replied glumly before entering my room.

I scooted past the slumbering beast, and then fell face-first onto my pillow. The three chimes sounded again, and the lights snapped off. I didn't expect to sleep. My mind was swirling. Thoughts of Lowry's safety, of Orwell, of escape all plagued me. Knowing that I was stuck in here filled me with impotent rage.

I suddenly felt hot. I pushed myself off the pillow. My face was slick with sweat. My eyes were dry. I was groggy. I peered through the window and saw the moon was high. I had fallen asleep, after all. How many hours had it been? As I pondered this, I felt a creeping notion that something was wrong. Oddly, it was quiet.

My eyes panned to my roommate. His chest no longer moved up and down. His rattling breath no longer filled the room. Sometime in the night, he had snored and choked and never recovered. The silence had allowed me to doze.

The vitals monitor above his bed showed a series of flat lines. The one above my bed showed all the usual signs of life. I had an idea, but I would have to move quickly.

I stole out of the room, and hustled down the brightly lit hallway. I hoped that whoever was in charge of security wasn't watching the surveillance monitors at that moment.

I ducked into Vonnegut's room. He was in the first bed. I crouched beside him, and gently shook his arm. He blinked his sleepy eyes and murmured, "Smith, what's wrong?"

"I don't have a lot of time. I have a way to escape. But it's for one person only, and I've got to do it right now. You've got to help me," I whispered.

"Wha? What is it?"

"The explosives. Where did you hide them?"

"Smith, I can't tell—"

"This is my only chance. Please, you've got to tell me."

Whether it was sleepiness that lowered his defenses, or the urgency in my voice, he relented. "The western fault line," he said. He told me the coordinates. "I buried them."

"Buried? Why?"

"When they go off, the fault line will collapse. A huge chunk of land will break off the continent. I thought Rand and I could have our own private island. Romantic, huh?"

"You're a regular Don Juan. Where's the detonator?"

"Rand has it."

"Okay, thanks. Don't worry, once all this settles down, I'll come back for you."

"Good luck, Smith."

His eyelids sank, and he began to breathe deeply. I was jealous of how easily sleep came to some people.

I hurried back to my room. My roommate was still dead. I leaped into bed and threw the sheet over my face. I waited. In the distance I heard the metal doors open. Footsteps approached.

Two men entered the room. "Check the machine," one said.

A few moments passed, accompanied by a ratcheting sound. "It's working," the other replied.

"Okay, let's look at him."

"Oh yeah, he's dead all right."

The two men chuckled, and one of them said, "Get the bag."

An object plopped onto the floor. An unzipping sound followed. The two men grunted as they hefted the corpse off the bed. The springs of his mattress creaked with relief as the weight upon them lifted. The body hit the floor with a thud. The zipper moved again, enclosing the corpse in the bag.

"He's too heavy."

"Let's get the cart."

Their footsteps fell away. I slowly brought the sheet down so I could peek out. The room was dark and empty. I cautiously got out of bed and crept over to the body bag. It bulged, hardly able to contain the monster within. I unzipped it and saw my roommate's face for the first time. It was mangled by death. It was a face I don't care to remember.

The next part would be the hardest, especially considering his weight. But I would have to do it. If I couldn't, there would be no way out.

I gripped the corpse beneath the armpits and lugged it up. My back muscles wrenched closed while my vertebrae split in half. He must have weighed a thousand pounds. An anchor seemed attached to him, drawing him back toward the floor.

My legs and arms began to shake. Every sinew attaching muscle to bone was about to snap. I held my breath and summoned an unforeseen strength. I mustered enough might to pull him fully upright, drag him over to my bed, and fling him down. There was a heavy crack, and the bed frame splintered. There was no time to fix it. I hoped the men were incompetent enough not to notice.

I pulled the bed sheets over his head. I gathered up the two pillows and bed sheets from his bed. Cradling them in my arms, I laid down in the body bag. I arranged my props to form the contours of a fat man. Then, I reached down and grabbed the zipper. As I drew it closer, I heard the metal doors of the Day Room open. I pulled faster, with my heart beating wildly. The footsteps were approaching, accompanied by the sound of squeaking wheels. I had the zipper up to my face now. I brought my hand back inside the bag, pressed a finger against the back of the zipper, and pushed it past my forehead. I was entombed in complete darkness.

The men gossiped casually as they entered the room. A pair of hands grabbed my legs, and another grabbed my shoulders. I held my breath as they picked me up. I thought the pounding of my heart would betray me. Undoubtedly, they would hear it. They dropped me hard onto the cart.

"Seems lighter."

"That's because I didn't really help pick him up last time."

They shared a hearty laugh, and suddenly we were underway. I took the shallowest of breaths, and prayed they wouldn't see the bag move. I stiffened my body the best I could, to better play the part of a dead man.

The temperature around me changed as we went through the Day Room, the corridors beyond, and further into the asylum. My surroundings soon grew cold. They wheeled me around a bit longer, conversing about trivialities, oblivious to the life within the black bag.

Finally, the cart halted.

"Now what do we do with him?"

"Leave him. The doctor will do the autopsy in the morning."

"Damn, it's cold in here."

"Yeah, but the dead don't mind," one man said, followed by a burst of laughter.

I listened intently as a set of metal doors opened and closed. Silence followed. No light penetrated my shroud. I waited, rigid as a board, still breathing shallowly. I waited an eternity. Every time I thought it was safe to move, I anticipated one of the men returning, having left something behind. Fear made me want to leap out of the bag, but a different kind of fear kept me immobilized.

I lost track of time. An hour, perhaps two, passed in the frigid room. At last, I could wait no longer. I pressed my finger against the back of the zipper and pushed it down. Once the hole was large enough to fit my hand through, I ripped the bag open. I tore myself out like a diver desperately surfacing for air.

I was in the morgue. Stacked refrigeration units lined the wall to my right. At the far end of the room was a set of lockers. Above me was a kind of spotlight, shut off, although ambient lighting around the rest of the room was still on. I sat up and looked at the refrigeration units. How many of them were empty, and how many had corpses nestled inside? I shivered. The thin clothes I wore afforded little protection against the cold.

I hopped off the cart and padded toward the lockers. They were all unlocked. The first three contained nothing. The fourth had a long white coat and green surgical scrubs. When I opened the fifth, I found a spare safety agent's uniform. Photographs of the agent's family were stuck to the inside of the locker door. I pulled the rumpled clothes on over my gray shirt and pants. I needed to keep the shirt on so my vital signs would continue to register on the computer system. I didn't know what the range was, but it certainly would extend throughout the building.

Once I was completely dressed, I inspected myself in the small locker mirror. The clothes may have fit me before I lost weight, but now I looked like a skeleton in a black sack. I slid the bowler hat off the locker shelf and adjusted it on my head. The disguise was complete, but whether it got me anywhere remained to be seen.

Fully dressed, and with the brim of my hat low over my brow, I walked out of the morgue. The hallway was empty. I began to navigate the asylum's maze, using signs to guide me. I passed several familiar staff members, but they didn't recognize me. My scruffy appearance was obvious, but nobody seemed to think I looked out of place.

I reached the final barrier to my freedom. A pair of metal doors stood just beyond an unmanned security desk. Perhaps it was the late hour or perhaps the agent was in the bathroom. In either case, luck was on my side. I walked briskly to the doors and pulled.

They didn't budge.

I hurried to the security desk, but I did not see an override button. I had no security badge, no key, and no way out. I didn't have much time, and the longer I stood here, the more likely I would be caught. Rather than let panic set in, I steeled myself as I gauged the doors. There had to be something I could do. I looked down at the desk again. There was a terminal and a hand scanner, just like the ones in the Archives.

A thought came to me. It was a rash, perhaps even stupid, plan, but it was the only thing I could think of. If it didn't work, I was going to be caught anyway, so I might as well try it.

I pressed a button on the terminal. It booted up. A familiar female robotic voice spoke to me, "Please state your name and serial number."

"Smith. Number 1872124482."

"Processing . . ."

The hand scanner illuminated. I pressed my right palm against the glass, and the machine whirred and blinked. I held my breath. My skin felt hot, and I began to sweat. The machine chimed and the light on top turned green. A metal clack announced that the security doors had unlocked. "Approved," the voice said.

I couldn't believe it. The geniuses in charge hadn't canceled my security clearance when I was demoted to Sex Detail, and they still hadn't canceled it when I was sentenced to the asylum.

I pulled the handles and raced out of the hallway. I dashed through the Sally Port, going past a pair of unobservant staff members. I exited through the other side, and raced into the cool night air. I quickly walked around the compound until I was facing south.

With the asylum at my back, an expanse of two miles lay before me, ending in the foreboding city. The city lights sparkled against the black sky. A deep orange color throbbed within the heart of the city.

The events of the night were almost too convenient. The dead roommate, the perfect timing, the spare clothes, the security clearance, all of them had to be a combination of poor planning and incompetence. Whether it was dumb luck or the mechanics of fate, I couldn't be sure. But I planned to take full advantage of my situation.

I walked toward the city. I had no plan. Like always, I would figure out the next part as I went along.

31

The city pulsed with a heretofore unseen energy. Men and women marched in lines holding hand-made signs aloft. Their chants boomed up and down the streets. Youths chased each other, delighting in the chaos. Delinquents had smashed glass storefronts and looted valuables. Several fires raged with great curls of smoke billowing into the black sky.

Fire trucks and government vans whizzed by, sirens blaring. One of the vans pulled up alongside me. An agent stuck his head out and implored me to hop in, because they needed some extra help. I shook my head and told them my shift was over. As the van sped away, I took off the bowler hat and flung it down the street. It landed on its brim, and rolled into a puddle.

In the Central Corridor, the peaceful demonstrations had become a frenzy of violence. People ran about, screaming, fighting, destroying, and seething with anger. A First Government monument in the square had been toppled. It lay on its side, being graffitied and urinated on all at once. Standing at the perimeter of the square, watching, were a half-dozen safety agents.

I walked over and asked, "What's happening?"

"Where've you been?" an agent asked, rolling his eyes. "What does it look like?"

"I've been in the Capital on special assignment. I just got back."

The agent leaned against his van. The other agents talked among themselves. "Some concerned citizens took over the news station. They have evidence that the First Government is corrupt, and has been lying to us," he said.

"That's not exactly a revelation."

"Yeah, no shit," he replied. "They broadcast a call to arms. Ever since then, the people have been going ballistic."

"And you're not going to stop them?"

An explosion rippled through the far side of the square. People screamed and scurried away. The agent didn't flinch. His comrades continued talking as if nothing had happened. He put his hands in his pockets and said, "They don't pay us enough."

"I saw other agents who looked like they were getting involved."

"Probably Surveillance Detail. They're the only ones interested in stopping this."

I thanked the agent and continued around the square. I pushed hard to make my way through the throngs of people. Greater numbers streamed down the streets to join the fray. Centuries of unreleased frustrations were being expelled tonight.

The television building loomed before me. The glass front had been blown in. The fluorescent lights of the lobby were dark. Rubble littered the floor inside. The building seemed hollowed out.

My shoes crunched over shards of glass. I walked past the vacant security desk and toward the back wall with its bank of elevators. Along the way, I passed a string of agents lying on the floor, their suits stained with blood. When I got to the elevators, two men greeted me with automatic weapons.

"Whaddaya want?" the first guard asked.

"My friend is in the studio. I saw her on TV. I want to check on her, make sure she's all right," I said.

"Nice try, Inspector. Move along."

"I'm not an Inspector. I was, but not anymore. I just want to see my friend. Then I'll go."

"I don't care if you is or ain't an Inspector. You ain't gettin' inside."

"Her name is Lowry. I'm Smith. Please, let me talk to her. The radio would be fine."

The first guard grumbled while he chewed over the idea. He kept his eyes and gun locked on me while he told the second guard to call upstairs. The second guard produced an ancient radio, and conversed unintelligibly with whoever was on the other side. After some deliberation, the second guard grunted to the first.

Grudgingly, the first guard said, "You can go up. Twenty-fourth floor."

I entered the elevator. The LCD screen above the panel of buttons flipped through the floors as the elevator ascended. The tightness in my chest was slowly relieved as I drew farther away from the crosshairs of those guns.

The elevator dinged, and the doors slid open. Several hands darted inside and dragged me out. Two men pinned me against the wall, a third frisked me, while a fourth pressed a handgun to my forehead. This violation of my personal space wasn't anything I hadn't already experienced at the hands of the First Government.

"He's clean," the man frisking me said.

The three of them backed off, leaving the man with the gun. He, too, put some distance between us, but he kept his gun aimed at my head. I recognized him from the TV broadcast. He was the guy who had been doing all the talking.

"You're here to see Lowry?" he asked.

"Yes."

"Why?"

"I want to make sure she's okay."

"You're an Inspector."

"Not anymore."

"There's a war going on out there. You expect me to believe you risked your life just to check on your friend?"

"You can believe it or not, but it's the truth."

"And once you see her, then what? Are you going to run back to your boss? Tell him what we're up to?"

"Honestly, I don't care."

His face contorted into one of confusion. He angled the gun up slightly.

"I don't care about them or you or your little war. I just want to talk to Lowry. After that, you'll never see me again," I said.

He considered this at length, and then said, "Fine. This way."

He escorted me, gun to my back, into the TV studio. Papers were strewn across the floor, desks were overturned, and several monitors had been smashed. All of the people I had seen on TV were here. They bustled about in a flurry of activity. They jabbered on telephones and radios, coordinating activities in the city. They looked exhausted. Adrenaline kept them going.

We marched across the studio floor to the news anchor desk. Lowry sat there, speaking into a telephone. When she saw me, her face brightened. She dropped the phone and jumped out of her chair. She threw her arms around my neck, and I sank into her body.

Lowry pulled back and looked at me with alarm. "Smith, what the hell happened to you?"

"Orwell had me in an asylum."

She pulled out a chair, and beckoned me to sit down. While I did, the man with the gun lowered his weapon. "Lowry, do you know this guy?" he asked.

"Yes," she said, sitting down beside me. "He's a friend. Put that thing away."

He looked at her guiltily before holstering the gun. "That's Butler. He doesn't trust anyone from the government," Lowry explained.

"Lowry, are you okay?" I asked.

"Yes, yes, I'm fine."

"I was worried about you. I thought you were going to die in the hospital. But then I saw you on TV, and I escaped the asylum to see you."

She passed me a lilting smile. "That's sweet."

"Are they treating you well?"

"Oh, yes, just fine. It's dangerous, but better than being a Safety Inspector."

"What happened? How did you get mixed up in all this?"

"A month ago, I was tracking Butler on a contraband charge. When I caught him, he was in the process of restoring the killer to the surveillance feed. As soon as I saw that, I knew I was done with the First Government. He was doing it for Mr. X. They were going to blackmail Orwell into resigning. But Orwell refused, so we formed this group, and released the video to the public. After that, it was easy to recruit people to help us."

"The public is easily persuaded."

"They don't want to live under a government that executes its own citizens."

"They were probably looking for any excuse to revolt."

"Yes, well, we decided tonight was the night we would fight back."

She looked at Butler and smiled affectionately. He returned a knowing glance. For an instant, they forgot that anyone else was in the room.

"Lowry, you're the leader of this outfit?"

"We're egalitarian. But, yes, Butler and I were the founders."

"What are you trying to do?"

"We want every citizen of the First Government to protest, to rise up. We want an end to the surveillance, the police state, the loss of decency, the intrusion. We're going to stop the corruption. Continents Two and Three have already joined us. The movement is catching fire."

"This is dangerous. You should walk away."

"Walk away!" she exclaimed, pushing back in her chair. She swept her arms in broad gestures, her face became animated, and her hair whirled behind her like flames. "If we do that, then nothing will change! Someone has to draw a line in the sand! We have to stand up for freedom! We're going to keep fighting!"

I had never seen Lowry so passionate about anything. Her comments were only pieced-together rhetoric, but her soul was behind her words. I looked around the room again. They were all just kids. None of them were older than thirty. Rashness, brazenness, desire, they had all the qualities of youth that could sustain such a quest. Fires burned within them that had been extinguished from me long ago.

Lowry sat down again, and she placed her hand over mine. Her's was warm, plump, and had a healthy pink glow. Mine was skeletal and pale.

"Smith, I'm so glad you're here. We could use your help."

"With a revolution? Lowry, I think you know me better than that."

"I knew you'd say that. It's okay. I'm just glad you're all right. I can do all the fighting for both of us."

"Lowry, I know you think you can handle this, but Orwell hasn't shown up yet. He'll do whatever it takes to win, including killing all of you. What are you going to do about him?"

"We have weapons."

I looked at Butler, and then back at Lowry. "I don't think you have enough."

"Don't worry. We have a supply coming soon. Mr. X is working with us."

"And what does Mr. X want in return for supplying your glorious revolution?" I sneered.

She smiled, and the dark circles beneath her eyes momentarily faded. "I know it's odd that I'd work with Mr. X, especially after what happened. But we have a common goal, and I can forgive the past," she said.

Lowry was sincere but naïve. She and Butler and their friends were earnest, but none of them knew what Orwell was capable of. He wouldn't let some kids stand between him and total control. I wanted no part of their revolution, but I still had to protect Lowry.

"I want to help."

"Wonderful!" Lowry beamed. "There's so much to do. Your knowledge will be invaluable. Do you want to coordinate our movements from here? Or do you want to hit the streets?"

I shook my head and answered, "I need to talk to Mr. X."

"No way. Forget it," Butler said.

"You know that famous security tape you have? I was the one who got it. I was the one who sent it to Mr. X."

"That's amazing!" Lowry said with surprise. "None of this would have been possible without you! We owe everything to you, Smith. You're the reason we're fighting."

My stomach became queasy at those words. I waved away her sentiments and said, "In that case, you owe me."

"Lowry, forget it. What if he's still working for Orwell? We can't put him in contact with the one person we need the most," Butler said.

"Smith wouldn't do that," Lowry snapped. She turned back to me and asked, "Can you tell us what you have in mind? That might put Butler at ease."

"I can't," I said. I couldn't let her know about my plans for revenge. "I just need you to set up a meeting. Tonight. Have I ever steered you wrong before?"

"It would be better if we killed him. He can rot in the lobby with his friends," Butler said.

Lowry stood up again and, with blazing eyes, fired back, "I trust Smith more than I trust anyone else. If he says he can help us, then he can. Make the call."

Butler reluctantly picked up a telephone. He spoke only a few short moments. When he returned, he glowered at me and said, "Mr. X will meet with you in one hour. Get to the parking garage west of here, and someone will pick you up."

I stood up, feeling weary. The escape and walk through the city had sapped me. I didn't have any reserves, at least not like these kids. "I'll need a pair of radios," I said.

Offering no further resistance, he fetched them quickly, and I stuffed them into my jacket's pockets. I gave Lowry a weak smile.

"Good luck with your revolution. You're a bright girl. Please be careful."

Tears welled up in her eyes. "You are coming back, aren't you?" she asked.

I shrugged.

32

The fabric bag was flung off my head. Blackness gave way to a steepled building before me. It was rickety, with much of its wood peeled and cracked. The stained-glass window above the front door was smeared with dust and grime.

Beyond the structure, the horizon had turned silvery. Stars twinkled in the sky, but they would soon be washed out when it changed to blue. A cold gust of wind howled, rustling the leaves of the trees that encircled the area.

A pair of undexterous hands fumbled behind me. My wrists felt a sharp pinch, and I heard a metal ratcheting sound. I pulled my hands around in front of me, and rubbed my wrists where the handcuffs had left red indentations.

"Go on in," a gruff voice said.

I walked toward the building. The standard-issue weapon and multi-tool weighed lightly against my ribs, concealed beneath the suit jacket. I had taken them from one of the dead Surveillance Detail agents before I exited the television building. When Rand's goon picked me up, he hadn't bothered to search me. Rand was slipping.

The interior smelled of mold. Rows of pews flanking a center aisle stretched toward a dais near the back. Two people stood there, their faces indistinguishable in the murky lighting. I approached, stopping about twenty feet away when the man commanded me to halt. The other I recognized immediately, the alluring woman I had spoken to the last time I was here.

"Welcome back, Mr. Smith. I didn't expect to see you again," she said. "You're here for your reward? Mr. X offered you a great deal of money, after all."

"Drop the act, Rand. I know you're Mr. X."

Her eyes widened with disbelief. Not for my deduction that she was Mr. X, but upon my declaration of her true name. Dealing with her, it was only a matter of time before clients determined she was in charge of the organization. But it was doubtful any had learned her real name. They didn't have access to her former lover like I had.

Her shock slowly transformed into a knowing smile. She stepped to the edge of the dais. Her head appeared centered in the circle of stained-glass behind her, illuminating her head in a grimy halo.

"Tell me," she said. "How did you find out?"

"Your old pal, Vonnegut. He didn't say it outright, but I put two and two together."

She measured her expressions carefully, so they would not betray her emotions again. "I see. And how is he these days?"

"Wasting away in the asylum."

"Too bad."

"He told me something interesting. A cache of explosives somewhere in the Wasteland. You might be able to help me with the detonator."

She thrust her hands on her hips and said, "I don't know what you're talking about."

My eyes flicked down to the floor. Dust and slivers of wood were scattered about. A dark, brownish-red stain was smeared beneath my feet. Everyone who had an audience with Rand must have stood here. Some didn't walk away.

When my eyes tracked up again, they settled on the man. A gun was in his hand, but the barrel was pointed at the floor. He appeared at ease.

"I did what you asked. I got into Orwell's organization. You're a businesswoman. It's time to pay up," I said.

"You're right. Things have gone exceedingly well. And I always pay my debts. How does a million—"

"Keep your money. I don't need it. All I want is the detonator."

"Why?"

"When I started down this path, I made a decision to protect someone. This will, I think, ensure their safety. Besides, it won't cost you a dime."

She considered this for a while. Her capitalistic brain probably couldn't comprehend what I had just told her. Concepts like friendship, compassion, humanity, anything that couldn't have a monetary value affixed to them were foreign to her. She shifted her weight back and forth between each foot. Finally, she said, "One moment."

She disappeared into a back room. I waited, looking at the guard who looked back but didn't see me. His eyes were glassy, his mind was somewhere else. Like me, he appeared starved for sleep.

Rand returned holding a small black box in her right hand. It had an antenna, a switch, and fat round button in the center. She tossed it to me. I caught it and deposited it in my pocket.

"Very well, Mr. Smith, I'd say our business is concluded."

"Can I ask you one thing?"

"Go ahead."

"You're supplying the revolution, but what do you get out of it?"

"Nothing at all."

"I doubt you're doing it out of the kindness of your heart."

"When the war is over, all I ask is that I be considered a legitimate business owner."

"Is that where the rest of your men are? Helping the war effort?"

"They need all the help they can get."

My eyes shifted back to the guard. His mind was still on another planet. My hand snaked into my jacket and emerged holding my weapon. I aimed and fired, leaving him on the floor.

Rand cried out. She reached for the gun that lay on the dais. I leaped forward, and kicked her hard, sending her reeling back. She struck at me with both hands, but I was stronger. I forced her onto her back, and I sat on her, with all my weight on her chest.

My hands wrapped around her throat. She struggled. She bucked her torso, kicked her legs, and rained fists into the sides of my head. The punches were strong, and more than once I found my head ringing. But they didn't hurt. I felt no pain. I felt nothing at all.

I squeezed harder. Rand's attacks turned to desperate motions. She clawed at my hands. She choked out unintelligible noises. Her eyes bulged out of their sockets. Her beauty was replaced by ugliness. I continued to hold fast. I thought of Lowry, and of everyone that Rand had ever harmed. I would avenge them all.

Rand's body slackened. She slapped at me weakly. The life was nearly gone from her. As her last moments passed, I saw a final vision. Orwell had come to the city, razed it, and left the dead visages of his enemies in public view for all to see.

I let go.

Rand inhaled sharply, the air drawing in with a high pitch. She rolled to her side, and coughed uncontrollably. I stared at her with my mouth agape.

I stumbled to my feet. My clothes were torn and dirty. A terrible aching in my head began to pound its way forward. I walked off the dais, and staggered out of the building.

Outside, I stunned the guard who had driven me here. He was unaware of what had transpired inside. I grabbed his car keys, and drove toward the city.

The first rays of dawn pierced the sky. The city appeared to be in far worse condition in the daylight. Buildings were obliterated. Glass was smashed. Streets were scorched. Debris littered the ground. Black smoke filled the air. People ran and screamed. Safety agents stood by and watched, but a few joined the protesters. This place where I had lived my entire life in safety had, in the course of a single night, become danger incarnate.

The deeper I drove into the city, the thicker the hordes of protesters grew. I took several detours, but every avenue was flooded with people. I wouldn't be able to drive through the city to reach my destination. I would have to take the long route around it.

I clicked the car radio on. A First Government newscaster was speaking agitatedly. "We have a special bulletin. The national director of the Surveillance Department, Inspector Orwell, is with us by remote to discuss the emerging crisis. Welcome, Mr. Orwell."

"Thank you."

"Tell us, what is the latest? What is the government doing to stop this terrible turn of events?"

"As we speak, I am in the city where these terrorist activities began. We are working very hard to bring these unsafe events to an end."

"What about our law abiding citizens who want no part of this?"

"Stay indoors. We should have everything under control soon."

"How can you be certain?"

"Well," he said with a sinister chuckle, "I was just informed that my men have captured one of the leaders of this little rebellion. She has already given us information on how to track down the others. The rest of them will be captured soon. I promise to restore safety to our great nation."

"What a harrowing ordeal, Mr. Orwell. I wish you and your Inspectors the best of–"

I turned the radio off.

He must have captured Lowry. I knew this was going to happen. I should have taken her with me. It was only a matter of time until Orwell captured them all, and tightened his iron grip on the rest of the country.

I parked the car and got out. A black van rattled by with an agent leaning out of the window, holding a megaphone. He shouted, *"Disperse! Martial Law has been declared! Disperse!"*

The furious crowds ignored him. The vehicle continued down the street repeating the message for no one to hear.

At the end of the block, the van stopped. Four agents jumped out, and immediately started zapping and beating protesters. When the larger crowd took notice, they raced to the aid of the others. The agents were quickly overwhelmed. They disappeared, like a stone thrown into a lake.

To my right was one of many vandalized properties. I walked through the smashed front door and found the telephone. Miraculously, there was still a dial tone. I dialed the radio station. A hoarse voice answered, "How can I help you?"

"I need you to get a message to Orwell."

"Who?"

"The guest that was just on the air."

"Listen, buddy, we've got more important—"

"*Tell Orwell Smith has his explosives, and if he wants them, he can meet me at the following coordinates!*"

The hoarse voice quieted while I recited the exact location. I slammed the telephone down without waiting for a reply. It didn't matter if he gave Orwell the message or not. Someone from Surveillance Detail would be listening.

When I got back in my car, the street had become a war zone. I managed to slowly maneuver my way through the surge of people, going back the direction I had come. I passed the black van, which was now on fire.

I eventually reached the freeway that looped around the city. There was virtually no traffic. I drove west, keeping the city on my right. The fires continued to burn. When I cleared the city's outskirts, I raced through the Wasteland, headed for the fault line. The journey took less than an hour. When I reached my destination, I exited the car slowly.

I could smell salt in the air. I was close to the ocean, but the land around me was flat and arid. I double-checked my location. I was in the right spot, but there was nothing here. I thought there might have been a plaque or something. There was no indication anything had ever been here.

I thumbed the detonator in my pocket. What if there were no explosives? What if Vonnegut was completely insane? I would find out soon, and it would spell out Orwell's undoing or my own.

I removed the pair of radios Butler had given me. I set them to the same channel, and my ears were greeted by a squelch of static. I put one radio down on the hood of the car, while the other went into my pocket.

To the north was a series of low dirt mounds, half a mile away. I trudged toward them, the wind howling around me, kicking up dust as I walked.

I reached the mounds and sat down. I removed my new multi-tool and turned on the binoculars function. My car, now distant, came into focus. The upper half was blue, and the lower half had turned brown from dust.

I caught a glint in the distance and trained my gaze on it. Approaching, amid a huge pluming trail of dust, was a motorcade. My stomach tightened into a firm knot. As the three vehicles drew closer, I began to make out figures inside. Although their features were obscured, I could tell they were safety agents. The wind howled again, blowing a curtain of dust across my field of vision. When the wind died and dust settled, the motorcade had surrounded my car.

A dozen men piled out of the vehicles. Two of them caught my interest. One was tall and aged. The younger one had an average build and stature. The latter picked up the radio from the hood of my car.

"Mr. Smith, I'm here, where are you?" Orwell asked through a warble of static.

"I'm glad you made it," I replied. "Looks like you brought the old man with you."

"I don't have time for games. As I'm sure you're aware, I've got my hands full at the moment."

"Then I won't waste any more of your time. I've got your explosives, and I know you could use them now more than ever."

"What do you want in exchange?"

"The resistance leader you captured. Who was it?"

"Your former partner."

Even at this distance, I could see a smile on his face. A tiny part of me had hoped they hadn't captured Lowry. Now that hope was dashed. My stomach tightened more.

As we spoke, Orwell continued to look around, scanning the terrain, trying to find me. Nabokov gave an order to the other agents. With their weapons drawn, they fanned out, forming a larger circle around the motorcade. I slithered onto my belly and hugged the ground.

"I want you to let her go," I said.

"You'll give me my explosives back so I can use them against my enemies, but only if I let one of their key players go? Mr. Smith, I thought you were smarter than that."

"Orwell, you know me pretty well by now. Well enough to know I don't care about governments or rebellions. All I want is to live someplace far away from all this."

"Then go."

"I will, as soon as Lowry is safe."

"Fine, fine. Whatever you want. I'll send Lowry back into your waiting arms. In fact, I won't even go after you. Just as long as I never see you again."

"Deal."

Orwell lowered his radio, and said something to Nabokov. The old man, in turn, spoke into a separate radio, communicating with an unknown party. Meanwhile, the other agents continued their advance into the surrounding areas. So far, I remained invisible.

The wind howled again. Grains of sand whipped across the landscape. Orwell shielded his face. The current of dust blew directly toward me, and burrowed into my eyes. I dropped the multi-tool. I rubbed my burning eyes. The wind and sand whirled around me, invading my lungs. I began to cough in fits. When the wind faded, I heard Orwell saying something through the radio.

I loosed a final cough, and choked out a reply, "What's that?"

"I said it's done. She's free. Now, give me the explosives."

I blinked rapidly. I scraped the multi-tool off the ground and held it up. I saw Nabokov looking directly at me, pointing and shouting orders to his men. The agents broke into a run. There was no point in hiding any longer. I put the multi-tool away and rose. I dropped one hand into my pocket and wrapped my fingers around the detonator.

"I have to say, Orwell, your plan wasn't very good. You're so meticulous. I thought you would have accounted for me."

"I did account for you. I knew you would be determined enough to find the explosives just so you could stop me. Why else would I put you in the same asylum as Vonnegut?"

He was clever, after all.

"One last question," I said as the agents sprinted toward me. "Who killed James? Was it the old man?"

"Mr. Smith, I don't know what you're talking about."

"That's what I figured."

"By the look of things, my men will reach you soon. Hand the explosives over to them. I don't have any more time to waste on you."

"The explosives? You can have them now."

I pushed the button.

An enormous column of earth heaved upward. Orwell and Nabokov turned around to look at it with baffled dismay. Then, another column of earth jetted upward, directly beneath them. Their figures vanished in a cloud of dust. Several more explosions occurred in quick succession, each one moving north, toward me. They thumped and roared and sent massive chunks of earth rocketing into the sky. Beneath the wall of dirt, which now clung to the air, the ground had been split apart, leaving a canyon in the wake of each explosion. The screams of the other agents were drowned out by the booming maelstrom. The final blast was so close, I could almost touch it.

The column, a colossus, thundered upward, and blew me into the ether. I was airborne, sailing backward into infinity. I never felt the landing.

33

I thought I had died. I was disoriented at first. I struggled to move and breathe for a long time. Days passed. Consciousness slowly drifted back to me. When I was strong enough to stand, I did, and surveyed the wake of my destruction.

A rift had formed where the explosives had detonated. To my right, across glittering water, was a new land mass. It was a small island, jettisoned away by the blasts, just as Vonnegut had said. There were no signs of the vehicles or men. Everything had been vaporized.

I began the long walk back to the city. A kind soul picked me up on the outskirts and drove me to a hospital. There, I was bandaged and rehydrated, and told there was no permanent damage.

I caught up on the revolution. The revolutionaries quickly took the city and the Capital. People on all continents rejoiced. The revolutionaries had to fight a few opportunistic politicians, but without Orwell's resources or infrastructure, they were little match for the revolutionaries and Rand's supply of weapons. Within a month, the conflict was over.

The day I was set to discharge from the hospital, Lowry found me. We hugged briefly before fatigue directed her into a chair. The revolution must have caused her many sleepless nights. I was glad to see her.

"So, you got out," I said.

"Got out from where?"

"From Orwell. I wasn't entirely sure he'd let you go."

"Orwell never captured me. We heard his radio broadcast. It was a lie."

Lowry's false kidnapping was yet another ploy. Orwell had manipulated me like one of his many pawns. He knew Lowry was my weakness, and he exploited it effortlessly. Although, none of his cleverness helped him in the end.

"We're still looking for Orwell and his lieutenants. So far, we haven't found them. Some say he left the continent. I know we'd all feel better once we have him in custody."

"You don't have to worry about Orwell."

A satisfied expression crept across Lowry's face. "What did you do?"

"I gave him what he wanted."

"Where is he?"

"You know that new beach-front property west of the city? He's there. Scattered into a million pieces."

"The Second Government will be pleased to hear it."

"Second Government?"

"That's what we're calling it."

"You don't win any points for originality."

"The Senate has been dissolved, and so have the safety statutes. We're starting from scratch," she said. "Smith, we could use your help. You've been in this game longer than anyone. You could help make a just, lawful nation that really works. Will you help me?"

"Easy on the rhetoric."

"What do you say?"

"I'll do it for you, and only for a little while. But first I need a favor."

She granted my request, and told me to meet her in the Capital as soon as possible. When I discharged, I put on a fresh suit of clothes and drove to the asylum.

When I arrived, I was greeted like a visiting dignitary. The staff members groveled at my feet. I represented the new government, and they wanted my visit to go smoothly. Soon, I was face to face with Collins. She wrinkled her squirrel nose, trying to remember where she had seen me before, but not recollecting.

"It's wonderful to have you here. What can I do for you?" she asked.

"You have a patient named Vonnegut."

"Yes."

"He's to be released immediately."

Collins was taken aback. "You can't be serious."

"Oh, yes, I am."

"He's a very insane individual. He can't be released to the public. It wouldn't be safe."

"The only thing making him insane is being locked up in here. Now, will you release him, or do I need my friends in the Second Government to persuade you?"

Her teeth chattered. "Oh, my, my, my. There's no need for that. Please, follow me."

Collins escorted me to the Day Room. Two burly staff members opened the metal doors for us. She called Vonnegut over. When he saw me, his face brightened.

"Smith! I thought you were dead!"

"Not quite."

"It's great to see you! Are you coming back?"

"On the contrary, you're leaving."

"Leaving?"

"You're free."

His mustache twitched, and his eyes became saucers. He dropped to his knees and started to cry. I knelt beside him, clapping one hand on his shoulder. He tried to suck back the tears, but they burst forth violently.

"I-I never though this day would come. Thank you."

As Vonnegut slowly wobbled back to his feet, I made eye contact with Burgess. He cautiously ventured over and asked, "What's going on?"

"I came to free Vonnegut. I wasn't dead if that's what you were thinking."

"No," he said meekly.

"Burgess, if you want, you can come with us."

He nervously looked around the Day Room. His self-assurance had been shattered. He had been so certain of our insanity, it had given him strength. Now, that inner strength was gone.

"No, I'd better not," he said.

"It's all right. You can leave and do whatever you want. Live wherever you want."

"I want to live here."

"Really?"

"I need to stay here. I'm quite insane, you know," Burgess mumbled sullenly.

"Tell them if you change your mind," I said.

Burgess remained silent, hanging his head. Vonnegut looked better now. He wiped away the last few tears with his hand. Collins' initial bewilderment had left her. Now, she looked annoyed that I was here and interrupting her routine.

"Are there any other insane patients you would like to set free?" she asked.

"Not today."

I escorted Vonnegut back to the city. Before we parted, he asked me what I was going to do next. I told him about my plans for returning to the Capital. When he left me, I didn't know where he was headed. I hadn't asked. I felt comfortable not knowing.

When I reached the Capital, I was welcomed like a hero. I refused to attend any of the celebrations. Butler and Lowry told me countless times that none of this would have been possible if not for me. Each time they told me, I felt embarrassed. I preferred that people didn't recognize me as their savior.

I spent six months in the Capital. Lowry, Butler, and their cabinet worked day and night to craft new legislation for the Second Government. I could hardly keep up. I was ancient and ready for bed by the time they hit their daily stride.

My biggest contribution was crafting my own bill. I hoped it would set a good precedent for the Second Government.

Lowry and I stood on the observation balcony, looking over the Senate Hall below. The new foreman called the new Senate to order. The weeks had been arduous. Bickering and infighting had made the legislative process nearly grind to a halt. It seemed that even with new politicians, nothing had changed. Nevertheless, today was the day for my bill. It was crucial.

"Your bill is next," she said.

"I hope it works."

"A bill that forces politicians to debate? We'll make sure it passes."

The bill didn't explicitly force the politicians to debate. It did, however, remove the policy that all bills passed automatically in the cases of ties or no votes tallied. Without a debate, no laws would pass. The politicians would finally have to do something worthwhile.

The foreman called my bill up for a vote. The first second ticked off the clock. As always, the Senate worked itself into a frenzy. Politicians screamed, cursed, and threw objects across the room. When time ran out, the horn blared. The politicians quieted and took their seats. The electronic board registered no votes for either side. The bill had passed.

Lowry and I hugged.

"We did it!" she said, ecstatic.

The foreman announced the next bill. Still holding Lowry, I turned my head to look down at the Senate floor. The digital clock rest itself. Lowry and I exchanged a nervous look. This was it. If they didn't vote, the next bill wouldn't pass. They would have to vote.

The clock started.

In a flash, the politicians were back on their feet. The chaos continued. Even though the politicians were new, they were still more interested in squabbling than legislating. When the clock ran out, no votes were cast for either side. For the first time, a law didn't pass.

In the brief interlude that followed, Lowry shouted down to the foreman, "Make the announcement!"

He nodded and spoke to the politicians, "May I remind you all of the details of the last bill passed into law. From this point forth, for any future bills to pass, there must be at least one vote cast for either side. Without any votes, no bills can become laws."

Lowry looked at me and said, "That should do it."

The foreman called the next bill to a vote. The politicians picked up on feuds where they had left them moments ago. As they battled each other, the clock ran out, and the bill failed to pass. The same thing happened with the next bill and the next.

I shrank from the balcony. I woozily lurched toward the exit. Lowry grabbed my arm and said, "Wait! Don't go!"

"It's pointless," I said, jerking my arm free.

I slipped into the dark corridor with no desire to turn back. That night I gathered my belongings, and got in my car.

I drove for days upon days. I drove endlessly across the continent. I drove as far northwest as I could until I reached the ocean. There, amid the cold frothing water, rocky shores, and pine trees, I decided to remain.

Lowry tracked me down a few months later. By then, I had already erected the skeleton of my log cabin. I built everything by hand. I lived in complete solitude, sleeping in the car at night, and working on the house during the day.

She implored me to return to the Capital with her, "Please, Smith, we need you."

"That place is beyond saving."

"No, it isn't. We've made progress since you left. We've been making the politicians work together. Things are moving in the right direction. It is absolutely worth saving."

"I've seen enough of that place, Lowry. I won't ever go back."

34

A bird twittered nearby. I slowly opened my eyes. The bright disc of the sun was directly above me, surrounded on all sides by a cloudless blue sky. Stretching upward, reaching like fingers from the earth, were great green pine trees. The bird twittered again.

I picked myself up and looked across the lake. Its water was like a mirror, disturbed only by a duck that suddenly took flight. The sun, the sky, and the trees all reflected back at me. I stretched, and my muscles tightened in a pleasant way. Yawning, I made my way back to the house.

The boards of the dock clunked beneath my feet. My rowboat was moored to one side, sitting on the placid lake as if it were frozen. Tired from a few laps around the lake, I had rested on the dock and closed my eyes, taking in the warm rays of the sun.

My feet reached dry land. I disappeared through the wall of great trees. The scent of fresh pine was an odor I never tired of. Shed pine needles blanketed the forest floor. I walked at a gentle incline. The farther into the forest I went, the shadier it became. The warmth on my face gave way to coolness.

I emerged in a small clearing. A two-level structure stood before me. It was a simple rectangle built from the very timber provided by this forest. The house was a tiny island within an ocean of trees. Large windows afforded views of the trees and lake. A deck, still under construction, lay with tools and lumber left haphazardly from this morning's work.

Parked beside the house was a black government car. I knew she'd be back, but I hadn't realized it would take so long. She must have been very busy.

The house had no locks, there was no need. No one else lived for thousands of miles in any direction. I went inside and entered into the living room.

From one of the chairs, a woman smiled at me. She wore a blue skirt, white shirt, and no tie. Her hair was much shorter, and the frizz had finally been tamed. She moved to stand up, but I motioned for her to remain seated. I dropped into the chair opposite hers.

"Welcome back," I said.

"I like what you've done with the place."

"A man can get a lot done in two years when he doesn't have any distractions."

"I can see that."

"And how are you?"

"Busy."

"I can imagine."

"It's good, though. Things are coming along nicely."

"So, what brings you all the way out here? You're not here just to say hello."

"We could still use your expertise. We're struggling with aspects of the Second Government."

"It's like I told you last time, Lowry, I'm done with all that."

Lowry sat with her back straight and her hands folded neatly in her lap. There was something different about her. She had a calm and assuring aura, a matriarchal look.

"I'm sorry, where are my manners? Would you like a cup of coffee?" I asked.

"I'd love one," she said with a smile.

In the kitchen, I set two mugs down on the counter and fired up the coffee maker. I heard the sound of something sliding toward me. Lowry had pushed a small box across the counter.

"What's this?"

"A present. Go ahead."

It was a plain cardboard box, unwrapped. I folded the flaps back and pulled out the contents. It contained packages of sugars of differing varieties. I looked at Lowry, unsure what to say.

"It's legal now. Why don't we try it?" she said.

I tore into the products. We moved onto the incomplete deck with our steaming mugs. Lowry tasted hers first. She puckered her lips and said, "It's a little sweet."

I remembered the first time I had sugar in my coffee, and had been sure to use less. I took a drink and savored the flavor. I smiled involuntarily and said, "Mine's perfect. Thanks, Lowry."

We sat side by side, in a pair of hand-carved wooden chairs, and gazed through the pine trees toward the lake.

Lowry noisily slurped her coffee until it was finished. She set the empty mug down on one of the unvarnished wooden slats. I rocked back in my chair, and purposely avoided her gaze. At length, she said, "It's hard to believe you did all this yourself."

"I've always wanted to build something."

"How did you manage?"

"I took my time. I've got nothing but time out here."

"Seems nice," she said non-commitally.

"It's no Fallingwater, but it's good enough for me."

"What's Fallingwater?"

"Never mind."

A cool wind blew across the lake. The water rippled over itself in thin folds. The air played through the branches of the pine trees. When it reached the deck, my hair and Lowry's skirt ruffled. It carried on behind us. A wind chime tinkled in the distance.

"How is Butler these days?" I asked.

"Good. He asked me to marry him."

"And?"

"I did."

"I'm sorry I missed the wedding, Lowry. I'm happy for you."

"Sometimes I think this is all too much. How could we do something so selfish when the country is still in shambles? Shouldn't we have built a solid foundation first?"

"Don't put your life on hold. The world's problems will never be fixed. If you wait until they are, well, you'll be waiting a long time."

Lowry laughed suddenly.

"What?" I asked.

"I never thought I'd hear you say something like that," she said. After a moment, she composed herself and said, "You're right, though. Thank you."

"Can I get you another cup?"

"Sure."

I left her on the half-finished deck while I brewed two more helpings. It was nice having her here, being able to talk to someone. Sometimes my thoughts were loud, and it was nice to ignore them for a while. I honestly didn't miss the company of others, but I did miss her. I had exhausted myself trying to make sure she would be safe. And now, I never saw her. That was exhausting, too.

Lowry and I sat in silence while we drank from our mugs a second time. I looked into my half-empty coffee mug. My weathered features reflected back at me. I took countless sips until all the coffee was gone.

When we finished, she put her mug down in the same place as before. She smoothed over the wrinkles of her skirt with her hands. "Do you really like it here?" she asked.

"It's beautiful. Why wouldn't I?"

"I mean, don't you get lonely?"

I didn't respond.

"You can't enjoy being alone all the time," she said.

"I suppose you're right. Sometimes I get lonely. But being around other people means being around rules and regulations and safety statutes. It gives me a headache just thinking about all that. This is better."

"We're going in a different direction now. No more overbearing regulations. People will have freedom again."

"Even so, I can't go back."

Lowry stood up. I rose clumsily and followed her back into the kitchen. The aroma of fresh coffee filled the room. It reminded me of the first time we had gone to the diner. She traced a finger around the countertop, her mind calculating what to say next.

"Is there any way I can convince you to come back?"

"Not today."

She looked through the large open patio door. Outside, the wind had settled and the water had calmed. She took a deep breath and said, "It is beautiful. I'm glad the Wasteland doesn't exist here."

"So am I."

"Too bad there aren't any cities nearby so people can enjoy this."

"The last thing we need is another city."

Lowry nodded. I accompanied her to her car. She started the engine and rolled the window down. It looked like she wanted to say something else to me. Perhaps I was projecting onto her.

She put the car in gear and said, "Any time you want to come back, you're always welcome."

"Thanks, Lowry."

"Thank you, Smith."

The black car drove back through the forest, dematerializing amidst the trees. A bird chirped close by. It darted from one branch to another. I started toward the lake, still sparkling under the mid-day sun.

Suddenly, I stopped. An unknown force pulled me toward the house.

The master bedroom closet didn't have a lot of clothes. Mostly, it held jeans, work shirts, and sweaters on hangers. I slid them all aside and looked at the back.

The black suit was there, the shoulders sprinkled with a fine layer of dust. I had worn it almost every day of my adult life. It still felt strange to wear anything else. It beckoned me. Maybe I could put it on one more time? Maybe I could go back and things would be different?

I slid the other clothes back, burying the suit.

I shut the closet door, and I made my way outside. I hiked back down to the lake. I sprawled lazily on the dock and closed my eyes. The sounds of the forest enveloped me once more. I took in the air, the sun, and the tranquility.

ACKNOWLEDGMENTS

I am eternally grateful to several people, without whom this book would not have been possible. Cathy Ulrich for her solutions to random writing quandaries. Chaz Scriven for his wit and moral support. David Huxtable-Reid for creating such beautiful cover artwork. My wife for supporting all my endeavors. And my parents for always encouraging me to write. Thank you.

www.ingramcontent.com/pod-product-compliance
Lightning Source LLC
Chambersburg PA
CBHW020236180626
46810CB00006B/2223